READY FOR A FIGHT

The drover faced Link, quirt in hand.

"That'll cost you, cowboy," he said. "Now you get the beatin' first, then the kid."

"That right?" Link said.

Wild horse herd forgotten, some of the cowboys crowded the top rail next to the gate while others made a wide circle around Link and the drover. This was better than any bunch of broncos could be.

Link took out the heavy, leather gloves folded over the belt of his chaps and drew them on. The drover merely stood there with his legs well spaced, quirt at the ready, and studied his opponent. It was becoming clear to the drover, and everyone watching, that the tall, bearded stranger was a man who never backed down from any other man. Ever.

THE DEAD RIDE ALONE

James C. Work

LEISURE BOOKS   NEW YORK CITY

A LEISURE BOOK®

January 2006

Published by special arrangement with Golden West Literary Agency.

Dorchester Publishing Co., Inc.
200 Madison Avenue
New York, NY 10016

ISBN 0-8439-5651-8

The name "Leisure Books" and the stylized "L" with design are trademarks of Dorchester Publishing Co., Inc.

Printed in the United States of America.

Visit us on the web at www.dorchesterpub.com.

THE DEAD
RIDE ALONE

Prologue

It had been drizzling rain since suppertime, leaving the Larimer County Fairgrounds shining wet in the floodlights. I found a little bit of shelter under a small roof sticking out over a wooden door. A sign on the door said **Rodeo Office**. I was waiting for the evening rodeo to begin, loitering around the contestants' entrance hoping to pick up some images or ideas for my next Western. I was also hoping to sneak into the covered part of the grandstand next to the chutes, since my general admission ticket was for the open bleacher section.

As the night became darker, the rain eased off into a steady mist whipped by the breezes coming around the corner of the grandstand. I looked across the wet roofs of the animal barns where the colored neon tubes on the stalled Ferris wheel glowed dimly in the mist like a washed-out electric rainbow. All of the carnival rides were stopped. The crooked arms of the Whirligig and Tumblebug stuck out, frozen in space like insect legs decorated with yellow and red and blue lights.

The rain smelled good to me after two weeks of dry, dusty weather. It gave a fresh edge to the smells of dissolving cow-manure piles, wet straw, and stale popcorn.

Rodeo cowboys stood talking in clumps at the holding area. In full-length yellow slickers and dripping cowboy hats they could have been placed there as models for Charlie Russell. Or maybe Norman Rockwell. All-American boys, these, with that distinctive certain posture which comes from having backbones made steel-strong from years in the saddle and from that forehead-forward attitude which probably comes from too much walking in high-heeled boots.

Some of the cowboys walked over toward the rodeo office carrying their long duffel bags and undersize bucking saddles, crowding into the shelter of the meager overhang. One by one, or sometimes in pairs, they went into the tiny office and stood, dripping water on the floor, to ask the manager's assistant whether he thought the rain would cancel their ride. For many of them a month's wages might depend on that one ride. I smiled, watching them as they stood at the arena manager's desk. These are muscled, clean-shaven athletes who can "cowboy up" on anything with four legs under it, be it a man-eating mustang or a hell-bending Brahma, yet there they stand, bow-necked and with hat in hand, to ask if they're going to get their ride or if the rain will stop the show. They reminded me of schoolboys asking if they were going to be able to go out and play.

Back and forth in the rain-soaked alleys between the animal barns the paying public came and went. I watched adults with soaked feet trying hard to avoid puddles while the kids whose hands they were holding stretched their arms to the limit in order to walk through the deep part.

They carried blankets, folding seats, umbrellas; programs, seat cushions, plastic ponchos; oversize tubs of popcorn and super-size cups of soda pop and ice, mostly ice. A gaggle of four giggling teenage girls went past me and up the concrete steps to the reserved seating area where a sheriff's volunteer stood guard. He had gray eyes and a thick salt-and-pepper mustache and he wore a plastic cover over his cowboy hat. The girls went up to him and shivered and cringed and giggled and begged him to let them sit under

8

the roofed part of the grandstand even though they had general admission tickets.

He smiled. Maybe they reminded him of his granddaughters. Maybe he just liked kids. He told them they could stand there under shelter at least until the show started. If some of the reserved seat holders don't show up . . . well, why not?

The rodeo announcer's loudspeaker came on, and suddenly everything around me shifted into the present tense, the immediate NOW. The first event is bareback bronc' riding, but first there are announcements to make and sponsors to thank and officials to recognize.

Six or eight bronc' riders in slickers and dripping hats are gathered in a yellow clot at the rear of one of the livestock company's horse trailers. Three have managed to squeeze inside the trailer out of the rain. All of them are busy checking straps, refastening chaps they've fastened and refastened a dozen times already.

The clowns walk past me. I recognize one of them from his picture in the program; he was voted Best Clown of the National Rodeo Association last year. The other two are his assistants, carrying props for him. The bareback riders by the stock trailer also watch him go by. He's in a cheap, transparent-plastic raincoat and plain black hat and he wears stockyard boots under his Levi's. Except for the white paint on his face and the black circles he drew around his eyes to give them a look of frozen surprise, and the painted red mouth covering the whole lower half of his face, he looks like most of the other fairground workers.

But he is different. The difference doesn't come from clown make-up. It's a difference that makes him the most respected man in the arena, period.

The arena out there looks to be inches deep in mud. The

backs of the bucking bronc's are slick from rain. The leather rigging is soaked to where it can't be properly tightened. When the rider says — "Let 'im out!" — and that gate springs open, when the bronc' makes a jump as high as the floodlights and then dives for the steel railings, when the rider feels that never-expected jarring that runs from his teeth clear down to his butt, that clown needs to be there. That clown needs to have the reflexes of a gymnast and the footwork of an acrobat. He has to be as quick as a kick boxer, with the endurance of a long-distance runner.

Upon that clown much depends.

The cowboys greet him with nods and half smiles. I'm too far away to hear, but it looks like there is some pretty serious kidding going on between him and them. They eye him, size him up, give him a professional going over. He gives them a nonchalant shrug. All in a day's work, right? A job to get done, whether it's in the rain or the sunshine, whether it's an afternoon show or at night when there's more tension and tiredness in the air. He stops and says something to a bronc' rider and a rise of laughter reaches me. Followed by two apprentices, also in clown make-up, he enters the arena. With his hands thrust deeply in the pockets of his baggy pants, he solemnly scuffs at the mud and finds dry dirt an inch down.

He waves to the announcer, who has been watching him uneasily.

The footing in the wet arena seems safe enough to him. It's cowboy up time.

"Ladies and gentlemen," the tinny loudspeaker shrills, "it's a go. There's a show. Let's rodeo!!!"

It's the signal for three beautiful riders to gallop full speed into the arena. They're wearing silky blouses and plastic-shrouded Stetsons and they ride straight in the saddle, leaning forward behind the arched necks of their palominos, each girl gripping a long flagpole anchored in her stirrup. One of them carries the American flag, one carries the Colorado flag, and the third one flies the banner of the rodeo livestock company.

People close their umbrellas and rise to their feet. Men hold their hats over their hearts as the flag passes by. A pure soprano voice comes over the loudspeaker, singing "The Star Spangled Banner".

When the posting of the colors is done and the girls ride out the gate, the mustached deputy gives me a come-along signal. "Thanks," I say. "I appreciate it." And I walk past him, dripping wet, into the covered section. He saw me making notes earlier and I told him I was writing a book. He said he'd get me into the covered stands if people didn't show up to claim their reserved seats. I told him I noticed he was letting some pretty girls do the same thing, and he grinned.

I sit down near the giggling teens and try to write some notes but drips of water falling from my hat brim make little blue puddles on the notebook page. I put it away and take a slug from my contraband pocket flask — **No Alcoholic Beverages or Flash Cameras or Animals Beyond This Point** — and just watch.

I think back to the beginnings, the 1800s in Cheyenne and North Platte when cowboys first began to change. Where once they had just been a bunch of working stiffs in saddles, they became bronc' riders and bull busters, calf ropers and steer wrestlers. I remember reading about the events leading up to the birth of the first "Wild West Show", a sequence of mostly obscure local week-end rodeos that paralleled and nourished the cowboy metamorphosis from laborer to legend, from hired man to myth.

There was the 4th of July celebration in Deer Trail, Colorado when Emil Gardenshire got himself the title of "Champion Bronc' Buster of the Plains", and there was a whoop-up in Cheyenne, Wyoming in 1872 when some cowboys demonstrated courage if not good sense in attempting to ride wild steers. But the year that intrigues me more is 1882, the 4th of July. North Platte, Nebraska. Back when no event was considered too big or too elaborate for the celebration of the United States' birthday, a thirty-six year old frontiersman named Cody wanted to round up wild buffalo and get some cowboys to ride them as a show for the folks. A big show. And he would promote some good roping, too, and racing and bucking contests. And shooting exhibitions.

Spring roundup was just about over and by July 4th there would be livestock and cowboys aplenty, just outside of town in the shipping yards. Get 'em together, rain or shine, do the 4th of July up right, by God! And word spread that the Honorable W. F. Cody was chairman of this show and it would be worth seeing. So, cowboys from far corners of the short grass prairie began to drift toward North Platte. Others came from Wichita and Abilene, from Denver and Greeley, from Cheyenne and Laramie.

Some came from a big cattle ranch that I imagine sprawling across eastern Wyoming's high plains. I call it the Keystone.

Chapter One

Trouble on Four Legs

The man sitting on the saddle blanket selected another dry branch from the pile of sage beside him and tossed it onto the fire. The man on the opposite side of the fire, lying on his side and supporting himself on one elbow, nodded approval. Both men kept their Stetsons pulled down low and kept their neckerchiefs pulled up against the fierce mosquitoes and biting flies. The insects were the reason for having a fire on that hot summer evening out there on the high rolling plains. The fire also kept the coffee pot simmering; no matter how blistering the day has been, a cowboy wants his evening coffee as hot as he can get it.

The younger man, Garth Cochran, known around the Keystone Ranch as "the new kid", poked at the fire with another stick of sage, then pointed it in the direction of the dozen horses grazing below them.

"Might want to hobble that dun mare tonight?" he asked, hoping the answer would be no.

The other man, the one with the luxurious black mustache, turned his head to examine the horses they had been driving before them all day. He frowned and studied the bunch with curiosity, as if he hadn't been looking at their equine backsides ever since breakfast.

"I guess so," he finally said. "Hobble 'er, and that snaky little chestnut gelding. I'm gonna put that damn' stud on a picket rope, too. Rest of 'em will stay around. Better picket our saddle mounts up here by the fire somewhere."

"They like the smudge," Garth said. "Both of 'em like to just stand in it so the bugs leave 'em alone."

"Yeah. Well," Link said, heaving himself to his feet, "best get 'er done while we got the light."

The two cowboys mounted up, shook out their lariats, and rode quietly and softly toward the grazing horses, keeping the ropes down at their sides and well out of sight. Drawing closer, Link jerked his chin at the troublesome mare to indicate they would start with her. Garth nodded. With a light touch of the rein and even lighter pressure of his knees he put his saddle horse into an easy trot past the mare, looking totally unconcerned with her as if he was just trotting off to visit another part of the territory. The mare suspected he was holding a rope down against the other side where she couldn't see it, but she didn't let it spook her. She brought her head up just to see where he was going.

The other man roped her. Just for an instant she had looked around to see where one of them was off to, and in that instant a loop of hard, stiff rope dropped over her head. She turned to fight it, and felt the second rope descend. Caught.

Both saddle horses were veterans of this sort of open-range work. Link stepped down, the hobbles already in his hand, while his horse kept the rope tight. Garth kept his tight, too. Now all that remained was for Link to slip the hobbles over the mare's forelegs and tighten them.

"Whoa, lady," he said softly, sliding his hand up the rope to her neck and along her neck to her shoulder, patting the solid muscle as he went, soothing her with his voice, letting her have time to get used to his smell and his touch next to her. "Whoa, there. Easy does it, now. Easy does it."

She seemed to calm down as though she liked the attention he was showing her, the stroking and the talking, and soon she was standing stockstill, watching him over her shoulder. Link went on patting her and stroking her gently, making his soft "whoa there" sound.

"I think she'll be all right," he said to Garth. But the instant he said it, the mare felt a slight relaxing in the ropes and took advantage of it to dart her head back like a snake, baring her teeth to bite her assailant. She got herself a little taste of Mr. Levi's denim, including a hunk of cowboy thigh and heard him yelp as he jumped back.

The fight was on. While it was true it would have been less trouble for the two men simply to throw the mare and hobble her, it was also true that Link did not like to change his idea of how something was going to be done once he had gotten it set in his mind. While the mare plunged and tried to bite him again, he grabbed a foreleg and twisted it up as if he were going to shoe her, and got half the hobble in place. The other leg was more trouble, and she got her teeth into his denim again, but finally he had the hobbles fastened.

He went to pick up his hat before tossing the lariat loops off her neck.

"Now let's get that stud on a picket," he said.

Later, back at the fire, sipping scalding coffee and taking turns feeding green brush into the flames to keep the smudge going, the two men watched the last color of sunset fade over the western horizon. Against the brightness they could see the outline of a bluff far in the distance and a solitary finger of rock beside it sticking up into the sky.

"That it?" the kid asked.

"Yep," Link replied. "Chimney Rock. Looks close, doesn't it? I'll bet it's thirty miles away, though. People comin' up the Platte with their covered wagons used to see it from farther away than that, and thought they'd get to it by nightfall. Some saw it for day after day and never thought they'd get there."

"So, one more day after that and we'll be back on Keystone range," Garth said. "Funny, but that Chimney Rock just now made me think of a tower I saw once. Somebody made it, I guess."

"Oh, yeah?" Link said. "And where's this?"

"South of here a long ways, and down along one of those rivers. There's a old hermit there they say is feeble-minded an' he keeps workin' on a stone tower all the time. People call it a castle, but it ain't. Strange place. The ol' man's always digging up the ground and stackin' up stones. Nobody else around there for miles, so he doesn't bother anybody. That Chimney Rock reminded me of it, is all. So, you figure tomorrow we'll be there, and maybe home by the next night?"

"Not if it's thirty miles, not with this bunch. Maybe, if we keep movin' right along, yeah. If the Platte isn't in a flood. If we don't break a leg or run into a prairie fire. If those Army bastards don't get loose and come after us. Figure three, four days. Much more than that an' I might have to shoot me that damn' horse."

Garth chuckled. "You see the way she looked back at y', just before she took a bite of your britches? God, that was funny."

"Your idea of what's funny doesn't exactly match up with mine. Y'know, that mare put me in mind of somethin' when she did that. Or somebody."

" 'Cause she bit you?"

"Nah. It was that look she gave me first, but never mind."

"Why 'never mind', Link?"

" 'Cause I don't believe in talkin' about ladies, and you

shouldn't neither. I'll just say I know one who has a way of givin' you that quick look over the shoulder."

"You mean that look that kinda stirs up a man?" Garth asked.

"Sometimes, yeah."

"Hey," Garth said, "speaking of those Army guys, you sure were handy with your six-gun back there. I sure wouldn't have tried that shot when you hit that mean one's lariat."

"Ah, a coiled up rope is a big target," Link said.

"How'd you know he was gonna draw, while he was wavin' that rope around, I mean?"

" 'Cause he looked mean, that's why."

"Yeah, but how'd you know?"

"I'll tell you something for free. When a man quits the Army without tellin' the Army he's doin' it, he's generally sullen about it. And when a whole bunch turns deserters, they're likely to turn into a damn' gang of cut-throats."

"All of 'em?" Garth asked. "Must be some of 'em that are OK. Maybe they just don't rub along so good with Army life."

"Kid, when y' see a bunch like that, with a couple of 'em riding Army saddles or carrying Army holsters or canteens, any sign at all that they've been Army, you stay clear. Get clear as quick as scat, and stay clear."

"Did Art know they were deserters when he sent us to get the horses back?"

Art Pendragon, owner of the Keystone Ranch, had earlier received word of a dozen horses carrying the Keystone brand being herded north by a half dozen ruffian-looking characters and had sent his best man, Link, to look into it. He had sent the "new kid" along, too, mostly because he sensed that this newest member of the Keystone crew had a good deal of intelligence and capability, in spite of the numerous accidents he had caused during his first few months of work.

"Doubt it," Link replied. "I think Art figured them for range bums. Or they could 'a' been reps from another ranch, looking for stray stock and mistakin' the brand. It happens. Might have turned out to be an honest mistake. The thing is, with the Indians pretty much settled down, we got too many fort soldiers in the territory and not enough for 'em to do. Take Fort Tyler, now. Nobody wants to live anywhere near it. Steal livestock, get drunk, just walk away and turn into bums. Some might be honest, but. . . ."

"Nothin' honest about the ones we met," Garth said. "Except that one, now. You made an honest rustler out of him, for sure."

"I guess he won't steal any more horses."

"I never saw a shot like that, neither," Garth said. "He up an' levered off three shots your way from that Thirty-Thirty and missed every one of 'em. What was that, a hundred yards?"

"I reckon. Less than that, probably."

"Hell, I *heard* one of his shots go past me. An' you pulled down on him with your Colt, just as cool as that . . ." — Garth raised his hand and extended a finger to show how Link had drawn a bead — "and *pow!* One shot and he dropped right out of the saddle."

"Yeah. But don't make too much out of it, when we get back. They've all seen me shoot an' they don't think much about it any more."

The kid stirred the embers and piled on more green sage. With the sun down, the high plains were darkening into blue and purple shadows and soon the circle of firelight was the only thing to be seen in the whole empty land.

"So, about women," Garth began, lying back on his saddle blanket with his Stetson over his face against the bugs. "You suppose when a woman gets a man hog-tied, he can still get out on his own like this? That why married men on cattle drives never talk about it? You suppose they get to spend much time in the open like this? Sometimes, y'know, I see a gal in some saloon or at a dance and she gives me that look . . . you know the look, sort of like she's tellin' me to get away closer? . . . and, Link, I get a shiver. Yes, sir. It just gives me a shiver. My pa told me never to take up with saloon girls or whores, but sometimes it sure is a temptation. And, of course, a man's always wonderin' what the girl's thinkin' of him. . . ."

"Kid?" Link mumbled from beneath his hat. He, too, was stretched out with his boots off and his head on his saddle.

"Yeah, Link?"

"Remember you tellin' me about a crazy hermit that spends his time pilin' up rocks for no particular reason?"

"Sure."

"You start tryin' to figure women out and you'll end up just like him. Go to sleep."

After breakfast Link took time to heat a little more water so he could shave and wash up. Garth, who didn't need to shave every day, saddled up and rode out to collect the remuda. Link was just about finished packing his shaving gear into his saddlebag when he heard a god-awful war whoop and turned to see a cloud of dirt twirling like a dust devil over where the horses had been.

He got into the saddle just in time to see the dirt storm coming straight into camp. It was Garth being "the new kid" once again. He was astride that big ornery stud horse, bareback and using a makeshift rope halter, hanging on and whooping like an Indian every time the big horse made a plunge.

And plunge he did. One minute the bronc' was arching his spine toward the sun, the next minute he came down with his hoofs in a bunch; one minute he was twisting his neck down and sideways, the next minute kicking both forehoofs skyward in a fury to dislodge the young cowboy sitting on his back. He spun, he screamed as only a stallion can, he made sidewise jumps and lashed out with his hind hoofs.

Link had seen hundreds, maybe thousands of bucking horses. Especially during roundup when each man had a remuda of six or maybe eight horses and half of those had to be "broke" every time they were used. Some were just green and rough and seemed to go to sleep tamed and wake up in the morning wild again. Others were just frisky on cold mornings. But he'd never seen one ridden like this one was being ridden.

The kid made it look easy. With his neck bent down to keep from getting his head whipped off, he would reach forward with his spurs and touch the stallion's shoulders, setting off another round of jumping and whirling. When the horse's hindquarters were kicking holes in the sky, the kid seemed to lie back like he was in an armchair, a big smile on his face. The horse tried spinning himself around like a toy top, and there sat the kid, grinning away and sitting straight up in the center of it all.

The stallion finally took it into his head to run away, and away the two of them went through the brush, the horse plunging over bushes and up and down shallow draws while Garth rode him with one hand on the halter rope and the other hand at his side, more like a trooper on parade than a kid on a crazy bronco. Link watched the dust cloud as it went out of sight, and after a while the stallion came back again, tired out and walking along like an old plow horse, the kid still on his back.

"I went to undo his picket rope," the kid explained, "and he started rollin' his eyes at me and showin' his teeth. So I figured we'd better start the day by figurin' out which one of us the boss was. He'll be fine now."

"Nice riding," Link said.

"Yeah," Garth replied. "I've always been pretty good with bucking broncos. Ever since I can remember. I won't say I've never been throwed, but I've got back on and rode every one that throwed me. I guess it's one of those natural things, like you being able to shoot so good."

"Maybe you could give me some pointers," Link said. "I've had to ride the green off my share of ponies, too, but I never enjoyed it much. Not like you seem to."

"Well, I'll tell you what!" Garth said. "Let's catch up that snaky gelding for you and I'll see if I can give y' a lesson or two. We'll catch him and you can ride him right now."

"Done," Link said. He took off his gun belt and rolled it up and put it in his saddlebag.

In no time at all the gelding was standing there, close-hitched with a neck rope to Garth's saddle horse, while Link put the halter on him. Grabbing a handful of mane and the lead rope, Link jumped onto the animal's back and squirmed around until he found a good seat.

"I guess you can let 'im go," he said.

The kid slipped the noose off from around the gelding's neck and backed his horse away to see what would happen. The horse hadn't been ridden in months and had acted up on them the whole day before, so neither of the two cowboys believed it would just stand there and do nothing.

And they were right.

He looked around like he was making sure he was free of the rope, and then reared, pawing skyward with his forehoofs and dancing on his hind hoofs. Link nearly slid down and off, had he not grabbed a handful of mane. Feeling that tug, the gelding whirled to the right and lashed out with his hind hoofs, then pounded to a stiff-legged halt before doing it again.

"Now keep your head kind of hunkered down in your neck!" Garth yelled to Link. "Don't let it flop around! Next time he rears up on you, throw your spurs forward on him. That's the way! Get a hold with 'em! Watch him, now! He's gonna whirl on y'! Don't lean into it or he'll get y' off balance! Glue your butt down now, glue it down!!"

Link tried to listen and he tried to follow the kid's suggestions, but the plunging and pounding were turning his brain to pudding. He did try that trick of throwing his heels up toward the horse's shoulders, and it actually made it easier for him to keep his hind end in place. The gelding whirled on him, but he kept his weight centered, instead of trying to lean into the turn, and that seemed to help as well. The bronc' had a few more bucks left in him, but Link could tell he was nearly through. It was about time, too, because Link felt like his eyeballs were coming loose. One jump drove his Levi's rivets right through his underdrawers and he thought he saw far-off Chimney Rock swimming in a lake.

The stud might have been nearly through, but the game wasn't over quite yet.

The bronc's kicking and plunging brought them close to where Garth had picketed the remuda. Seeing the action, the snaky mare, still in hobbles, decided to get in on it.

22

Raising up her forehoofs together and chopping them down viciously, she came toward the gelding with teeth bared, making a hissing sort of nickering that sounded like an enraged sidewinder. The gelding tried to avoid the mare by twisting; the mare tried to get her teeth into Link's leg. Link tried to whip her between the eyes with the knotted end of the halter rope, and, as he raised his free hand, he had another quick glimpse of Chimney Rock standing up like a castle tower on the far horizon. Then he brought the knotted end down on the mare's face and felt the gelding fall beneath him and that was the last he knew.

Before Garth could make a move to help, Link and the horses went down in a heap of flying dirt. He thought maybe the mare had jerked her head up and hit Link in the jaw, but, before he could think much more about it, he saw only the hoofs and legs in the air, the gelding on its back on top of the mare, then both horses on their sides struggling to get up, and he knew that Link was underneath.

Chapter Two

Dreams have two gates
Book XIX, line 562
The Odyssey
HOMER

Garth dropped to his knees beside Link's motionless body, not knowing what to do. He didn't know if the legs were drawn up like that out of pain or if they were broken and bent into that position. He knew he should take his bandanna and wrap the bloody place on Link's leg where the pant leg was torn, but he saw a jagged end of broken bone sticking out crookedly below the knee and he didn't know if there was any point in wrapping it. It was bleeding, but not too much. He couldn't see any way he could stop it by wrapping it up.

Link's left arm was twisted into an impossible angle with his shoulder. When Garth touched it, Link jerked and moaned. Garth thought he might go get the canteen from his saddle and wash the dirt and blood off Link's face and bring him around, but then he thought Link would be in less agony if he stayed unconscious. Maybe he should get him turned on his back and straightened out, but that didn't seem the right thing to do, either. Finally all he could find it in himself to do was to kneel there gingerly touching his friend's scraped forehead and repeating: "Link? Link? Link, you all right? Can you hear me?"

Stupid thing to say. Of course, he wasn't all right. He was badly, badly hurt, maybe dying.

As he knelt there and the shock began to wear off, Garth felt the cold numbness going away and the world came back into focus again. The first thing he heard was the sound of horse hoofs, and he figured it was the saddle mounts and remuda milling around. Some of the horses were grazing cautiously, keeping their ears pricked toward the men. A couple of them stared with wide eyes and with their legs braced, ready to bolt and run if they smelled any more blood or heard any more cries.

A large, dark shadow fell over Garth. A prickling chill began a cold itch inside his hatband as a tremor ran around his scalp. It was the shadow of a man; the man was standing behind him.

Garth turned his head. Looming above him was the largest man he had ever seen in all his young life, a giant, bearded brute in battered broad-brimmed hat and patched dungarees. The man's coat was open, showing a leather vest and thick belt, but no gun. He leaned over Garth's shoulder and looked at Link's still form.

"Better leave him to me, son," the voice rumbled. "Go tell the boy to bring the wagon on over here. You two go ahead and get the tailboard off of it."

Something was there in the tone of the big man's voice that didn't leave room for discussion or reply. Garth had no idea where he came from or why he hadn't heard the man walking up, much less the two teams and wagon he now saw less than fifty yards away. He got to his feet with his legs shaking under him and stumbled off in that direction. The driver was a boy no more than twelve or thirteen.

The boy stopped his teams, set the brake, and jumped to the ground. Garth saw that he might be more than thirteen, but not by much. He hadn't shaved yet, and his clothes were those of a rapidly growing kid — the pants several inches too short, the shirt a couple of sizes too big. The boy looked at Link, then at the big man bending over him who gave him a signal with his hand, and without more than a nod to Garth he stepped to the back of the wagon and lowered the tailboard. He climbed in and arranged trunks, boxes, and bedrolls to make a place for the injured cowboy.

It took only a minute for the boy and Garth to unhook the chains, slide the hinges apart, and carry the tailboard to where Link was. The giant had Link lying on his back with his legs straight and had just finished putting the shoulder bone back in its socket with a sharp, sickening, popping sound. He told the boy to get into one of the boxes in the wagon and bring some cloth to tear into bandages; meanwhile he lifted the limp body as easily as a man might lift a newborn calf and placed it on the makeshift stretcher. The bandages served two purposes: with one he bound up the leg after pulling the bone out of the wound and maneuvering it back into position, and with others he wrapped Link to the tailboard so he wouldn't roll over and dislocate the shoulder again, or hit his broken arm against something.

Garth studied the stranger. His thick leather vest was spotted with burns, as were his leather wrist protectors. His beard, too, showed that it had often been in the way of showers of sparks. The hands were muscled and still agile and dexterous. There was only one thing he could be, and it was a blacksmith.

The man stood up to inspect his handiwork. The cowboy wasn't bleeding anywhere he could see. The wrapping around his chest covered the broken arm and kept it immobile. The shin bone was lined up where the break was, he figured, and tightly wrapped. It was all he could do.

"Better get him some place," he said. "I'm thinking of Fort Laramie. Might be able to get there by dark. There's a pretty good surgeon there, a sober one. Two, sometimes three of them, in fact. If we can get him to Captain Paulding . . . he's the post surgeon . . . I think we can save that leg. They've got a civilian surgeon there, too, a vet named Doctor Bock. Solomon Bock. You know Fort Laramie?"

Garth nodded. "I know he wouldn't want to go to Fort Tyler."

"Fort Tyler is a longer drive. Let's get him in the wagon and we'll give him a little pain-killer."

Garth saw another wagon coming toward them. This one was drawn by four heavy horses and driven by a woman about the same age as the big man. The blacksmith unrolled a sougan and doubled it to cushion the wagon bed, then he and Garth and the boy picked up the tailboard with Link on it and slid it feet first onto the sougan.

The woman wrapped her lines around the brake handle and climbed over the seat for the medicine chest. The boy went to help her down. Meanwhile the giant held out his hand to Garth, a hand so large it completely hid Garth's when he gripped him. The hand was heavily callused with years of coal dust and soot worked into the creases.

"Evan Thompson," he said. "Blacksmith."

Garth was "the new kid" on the Keystone range, but he had already heard the campfire and bunkhouse stories about the legendary Evan Thompson, the mysterious figure who seemed never to stop anywhere for very long and who seemed to show up out of nowhere. He was always on the move, they said, together with the two wagons and the woman and the boy. Some stories told of the blacksmith's chain, a chain with links some men said were the size of barrel hoops. Other men said the links were smaller, no more than the length of a man's forearm. But all agreed that

27

Evan Thompson was always seen hammering at his forge, drawing bars of iron into links for this chain he never seemed to finish. Several men had witnessed the forging of the links; not one of them, however, could say he had ever seen the whole chain itself. Once Garth heard a strange story about a cowboy named Pasque who supposedly saw it.

The woman came to the wagon with a small flask. It looked very old and had intricate Oriental designs on it. She opened it and held it to Link's lips, making him take it drop by drop.

"Blanket," she said, her voice low and sweet. The boy climbed up into the wagon and found a blanket to put over Link. Link groaned and moved his head from side to side, the woman still getting him to swallow the thick liquid.

"All my fault," Garth suddenly began. Having begun, he seemed unable to stop the torrent of words pouring out of him. "I was showin' off how I ride bronc's, see, and Link had to try it. I was tryin' to give him some tips about stayin' on and how to keep movin' with the horse and it just rolled on him . . . that damn' jughead mare done it. But it's my fault, dammit, I did it all. If I hadn't been showin' off and pissin' around like that . . . 'scuse me, ma'am, I shouldn't be usin' cusswords in front of y' . . . now Link's all smashed up and I gotta go back to the Keystone and tell Art about it and he oughta sack me right then and there. Serve me right, by God!"

Garth babbled on. Numbly, automatically, he stumbled over to where Link's hat lay smashed into the dirt. He picked it up and dusted it off and tried to restore the shape to the crown, mumbling about being responsible and not knowing what Art was going to do or if Link would even live.

"An' what if he gets the gangrene and they cut his leg

off? What am I gonna say to him then, huh? Dammit, every time I get given a job to do, it seems like I just make a hash of things. Mister Thompson, that horse just fell over that other one, he just couldn't do nothin' . . . I couldn't help any at all."

The blacksmith's hand descended to lie on Garth's shoulder where it seemed so heavy it might force him down into the ground like a fence post in quicksand. He stopped his chatter to look up into Thompson's face.

"He won't die, he won't lose the leg," Evan Thompson said, "and it won't be held to be your fault. Put it out of your mind, all of it."

The blacksmith made a signal to the woman, who went to the side of the wagon and opened the grub box. Directly she brought Garth a tin cup of sweet wine. The blacksmith walked the young cowboy away from the wagons, encouraging him to drink it and clear his mind.

For several minutes neither man spoke while the quiet of the high prairie came rushing back to fill the morning. Garth again could hear the animals grazing and snorting, wagon chains clanking. Again he smelled the dust and the grass damp from dew.

"Tell me," Thompson said at last, "which way were you and Link headed?"

Garth pointed toward the distant stone landmark.

"That way. Toward Chimney Rock. We figured to maybe get pretty close to it tonight, and be back at the Keystone tomorrow night, maybe."

"Your direction is south, then."

"Yeah. South. Like we been comin'. We'd planned to turn west at Chimney Rock."

"You know Cheyenne ways?" Thompson smiled.

"Been there lots of times," Garth said.

"I don't mean the town. I mean the tribe."

And while the woman made Link comfortable with pillows and blankets and her elixir, the blacksmith told young Garth the story he had told so many other riders, the story of the medicine circle. He told how the Cheyennes believe each person is born with a particular kind of behavior already in them, a way of looking at things and a way of doing things that is natural and right. It shows where they are supposed to start their lessons in life.

Some, he said, seem born with a lot of wisdom already in them. Some are moody, quiet people from the start, little shavers who like to be alone and seem to look inside themselves a lot. Others look around more. They see how things tie into other things all the time. One sees a prairie dog, for instance, carrying dirt out of its burrow in its mouth and blowing it onto the mound around the hole and that one is a "north" person, wise to things, and sees how the prairie dog accepts the way things are, accepts the fact that he needs to dig deep holes and tunnels to get away from his enemies. This person knows about death as well as life, knows how serious things can get.

"I guess I never think like that," Garth admitted.

"Someday you'll make a journey in that direction, and learn that way of looking," Thompson said.

Now, Thompson went on, take a youngster who seems to be always contemplating things deep inside himself. You know the kind. He's got the power of bear dreaming, they say. Like bears, he spends lots of time alone and in dark places. He's the kid who is happy playing alone in a woodshed or under the house or up in a tree. He sees that same prairie dog and to him it's more of a reminder of how a person goes into his mind and thinks and thinks and comes up with something. He's likely to take that thought he's had and surround himself with it like a wall. Like that prairie dog's mound.

That first one, the wise one, he's what they call a dreamer of the north, the age and wisdom direction. The second one, he's a "west" person, where the sun goes down and where you see the dark come from. Could be a she, too. Anyway, Thompson went on, that prairie dog might be seen by a third kind of person, born as a dreamer of the east, the kind of person who sees like an eagle, sees everything connected like a big old world 'way down underneath their wings. Everything's bright and clear to such a person, like sunrise. This one sees the prairie dog making a tiny burrow among hundreds of other burrows, sees maybe the big herds of buffalo coming along and trampling it. Sees that the prairie dog is just like any other prairie dog out there, like all the ones that have been before.

"I guess I don't have the hang of that, neither," Garth said.

"No, probably not," the blacksmith replied. "Otherwise, you'd see that this accident here is just one part of a big old pattern. You'd worry, but it wouldn't rile you up and get you shaky and confused, 'cause you'd take it as one more thing that happens when men work with horses. Happens all the time, all over all the ranges.

"So," the blacksmith went on, his heavy hand still anchoring Garth to the earth as they walked back toward the wagons again, "there's different kinds of people, just like there's different directions on a compass. I see you as one of the 'south' people. The direction of looking at things innocent-like. You don't see consequences, you don't see how anything could turn out. Sometimes you don't see how you connect to anything. Usually you don't even ask yourself why you do some of the things you do. Am I right?"

"Hit it right on the head. That's the way I am, all right."

"Your friend Link, he started out much the same way. A lot like you when I first met him. When he came West some years ago, came to the Keystone, he was starting to get moody, trying to look inside himself more and more. Starting to wonder why he did certain things. He was a wild one, though, before that.

"Now he needs to move east again, and a little south. When he gets well, he'll need all the innocence he can muster just to keep from going crazy. He's going to need to see the whole world and his place in all of it, too. He's had enough of looking inside himself. He keeps that up and he'll end up close-hitched to a whiskey bottle, or else a hermit somewhere talking to himself all day long.

"No shame, no guilt. You boys were doing what cow-hands do, and Mister Art Pendragon wouldn't have it any other way. The job is to get your friend to a doctor. And keep those horses moving toward the Keystone."

When they were back at the wagons again, Evan Thompson checked to see that the quilts and blankets the woman had placed around Link were going to keep his head from bobbing around.

"Did you get enough pain-killer into him?" he asked.

"Yes. He'll sleep now, most of the day," she said.

"Good. All right, here's what we'll do. Garth, you and the boy line out your cow ponies and get 'em moving. You'll want to head that way" — he pointed with a huge hand — "staying a good distance north of Chimney Rock. Pretty soon you'll run onto a good trail going that way. We'll follow with the wagons, but, if we don't catch up with you by nightfall, don't worry. Keep heading west and about midday tomorrow you ought to see Fort Laramie. When you cross a little river called the Rawhide, you'll just about be there."

Link groaned and tried to move his head from side to side. Thompson leaned over to listen.

"Chimney Rock," the injured man groaned. "Got to get there. Garth? Garth? What about . . . what was that about a tower? Garth? Kid . . . ?"

Thompson put a hand on Link's chest. "Know who I am, Link? Remember me?"

"Blacksmith? You here again? What about the tower? We better head for it. . . ."

Thompson's voice was low, firm, prophetic. "Not this trip, cowboy. I came with a little journey for you to take. Now it has to wait. You're pretty broke up."

"Gonna die," Link stated, his words slurred from the elixir the woman had given him. "Damn. Middle of nowhere, too."

"No," Thompson said. "You've got more to do before you die. It looks like your ribs are caved in, your leg's broke, one arm's busted, and the other came out of its socket. Your jaw's gonna hurt a while, too. But you're going to live. We're going to take you past Chimney Rock and over to Fort Laramie. We'll get started just as soon as your partner gets the horses lined out."

"Hurts like hell, Evan," Link groaned. "Rather die right here. Jus' dig me a hole an' lead me to it, all right?"

"Not your time to go, Link. You just lay back. You're going to live and take that journey for me. The story says so. Right now all you need to do is let that medicine work. Just sleep."

Garth and the blacksmith's boy put the mare and the stud horse on lead ropes fastened to Link's saddle horse, which the boy rode. The rest of the bunch moved along peacefully, looking sweet and docile-like as if they felt responsible for what had happened and were going to behave from now on. Garth finally seemed to be able to breathe normal again, once they were all on the trail. There was reassurance in the sounds of the hoofs and the jingling harness of the wagon teams. It was good to hear Evan Thompson clucking to his horses and the boy whistling at the cow ponies and slapping his thigh to encourage them as they plodded along.

The day became warm and Chimney Rock seemed to shrink, diminishing to a featureless shadow finger of stone rising like a slender tower shimmering in the hazy distance.

The rock and sway of the wagon lulled Link into sleep where he dreamed of spires and towers, of badland hoodoo rocks, of cliffs that looked like walls laid up by a race of giants. The pain and the drug took hold of his mind like a team of horses, drawing him back through time, back to picture books he saw as a boy. He was in a room with an enormous desk and shelf after shelf of books. There was a dark, gloomy picture on the wall, a picture of a castle with high turrets. Some of the books also had drawings of castles and fair women in flowing dresses.

The wagon wheels jolted over a ledge of rocks when they crossed a creek and the turrets and castles vanished from his mind. Now the pain and the drug carried him along until he came to a towering figure in a robe of black. The robe grew bigger and bigger until it was all his mind could see. Everything was black, then a pale skull began to materialize, the head of a skeleton with a hideous grin looking out from the folds of darkness. Then he saw the bony hands holding a long, rusted scythe.

Link knew what it meant. He tried to raise his arm to

sweep it away, and pain shot through his shoulder.

He groaned into semiconsciousness. The wagon had stopped. He heard the sound of horses slobbering water from a stream. The woman came and laid a cool hand on his forehead and put a flask to his lips. He swallowed and was grateful. The wagon started, once again rocking him to sleep.

This time he dreamed of graves. Or they might have been just holes that looked like graves, for they were not quite long enough to hold a man. They could have been prospecting holes, like miners dig looking for gold, except that they were mounded up with freshly dug earth. There were no markers on them, just mound after mound.

Link woke. The wagon was stopped again. He smelled wood smoke and supper cooking and heard voices. After a time the woman came to see how he was and found his eyes open. When she asked if he needed more medicine for the pain he croaked — "No." — through parched lips, and she gave him water, instead. He began to remember things that had happened. He remembered talking to the blacksmith. That's why the woman was there. He had tried to ride a wild bronc' and it fell on him.

The smell of the cooking was too much for him, and he asked for food. The woman brought broth and spooned it between his lips a little at a time. His jaw ached like hell, but he was able to eat some bread soaked in the broth. There was pain, and a lot of it, and he wanted to ask for some more of her medicine to knock him out. But then he remembered the dreams of walls and towers and unmarked graves, and he figured he'd rather have the pain than the nightmares.

It was almost midday of the second day when Evan Thompson, driving the wagon, called back to Link that they had topped a rise and he could see Garth and the remuda in the distance. He could see the dark line of trees marking the Platte, too, and another marking the Laramie River. Suppertime would see him in the post hospital.

"The Keystone?" Link croaked through dry lips. It was more of a groan.

"Hah?" Thompson turned to look back at him. He had barely heard the cowboy's question. "Oh, the Keystone! Well, I would reckon on you staying with the soldier boys a few days, maybe a week, until Captain Paulding is sure you aren't going to get gangrene. Then we'll take you on to the Keystone."

"Manage from there," Link groaned, meaning that he didn't want Thompson to have to hang around and be an ambulance service for him. He'd find a way to get from Fort Laramie down to the Keystone on his own. The wagon hit a jolt that sent blazing pain through his shoulder and leg.

"We'll see you home," the blacksmith said. "Can't say I mind hanging around the fort at all. I can get good coal there for my forge, and, besides that, there will be plenty of work for me among the soldier boys. Always is."

Link felt the wagon slant downward abruptly and they were on the last leg of the trip into the fort. He drifted off into painful slumber again, wondering if the post surgeon would give him morphine, afraid it would bring back the dreams.

Far away to the southwest, at the headquarter house of the sprawling Keystone Ranch, a certain lovely woman with long, lustrous hair sat at her breakfast. Her husband rose from the table and kissed her and put on his hat to go outside.

"Time to get at it," he said.

"Looks like a lovely day," she said.

"Yes. Could use some rain."

"Are you staying near home today?"

"I guess so. I'm kind of looking for Link and Garth to get here with those horses today or tomorrow. Telegram said they were on their way a week ago."

That afternoon the woman was sitting on the long, shaded porch of the main house and saw two riders and a bunch of horses come through the north gate, heading toward the main corral. She recognized Garth, but the other rider was no more than a boy. She seemed to have seen him somewhere before, but could not remember who he was. Perhaps he was from one of the neighboring ranches.

She stood up and watched the north gate a long while, but Garth and the boy were the only two who came. There was no one following them, no tall man coming along behind, no tall and dark man sitting beautifully in his saddle, no man with silky black mustache.

Some time later, Art came back to the house with the news. Link was at Fort Laramie, all busted up. But he was in good hands. Evan Thompson had sent his boy to help Garth with the horses.

"Of course!" Gwen said. "I thought I remembered that boy. Will he be staying on?"

"That's the plan," Art said. "We can use him down at the forge. Shouldn't be but a week or two until Link's good enough to travel. Thompson's going to bring him home."

The following days often found her standing at her sitting-room window high in the house, brushing her hair or folding and refolding her handkerchief, watching the northern horizon in hopes of seeing a tall man riding toward the ranch. At times, she could force her mind to imagine him in an Army ambulance wagon, or riding in some kind of buggy, or even being brought home in the Keystone's own mud wagon. But that image would always fade and he came riding upright and straight and tall, hat brim level, and she imagined him looking up at her window as he loped through the north gate.

But it was two more weeks before he came. He came sitting up, cradled in two narrow mattresses that made a kind of easy chair lashed to the seat of a freight wagon drawn by two teams. A second wagon followed, driven by a woman. Gwen came out on the porch in time to see the boy running toward the wagons.

A bandage was tied over Link's head and under his jaw. A plaster cast enveloped his left arm, another his right leg. His left eye was red, the flesh purple and black all around it. The blacksmith had to lift him down off the wagon seat, and Link hobbled toward the house on a crutch. His neck was crooked to one side and he could not raise his eyes high enough to see where she stood at her window. For all of his obvious pain, however, she saw the glint of white teeth in his smile through the silky thick curtain of mustache.

Supper over, Link excused himself and went out to do his evening "constitutional", which is what he called his slow hobble with his crutch around the big barn. Sounds of activity coming from behind the horse stables caught his attention, and there he found Evan Thompson packing up his tools. The anvil and the forge were already loaded in the heavy wagon.

"Pullin' out tomorrow, I hear," Link said.

"Yes," said the big blacksmith. "I've done what I need to do here. Finished another link in the chain."

Link reached for his pocket purse. "I want to pay you

back," he said, "at least for the mattresses and the crutch. Garth says you bought them when we were at Fort Laramie. Like to pay you for your time, too. Without you and your wife I reckon I'd still be lying up there north of Chimney Rock."

"No need," the smith replied. "Put your money away."

"Well, I feel awful obliged to you."

"There is something . . . ," Thompson said, reaching into the wagon. He drew out a leather wrapper, untied it, and unrolled it on the tailboard. Inside were three stone chisels, newly sharpened. Link picked one up and examined it.

"One of these days you'll be heading south," the blacksmith said, "and you could deliver these to their owner. I took them to have the points hardened. I ground the swage down for him, too. Awful dangerous to have those fly off when you hit the chisel."

"Glad to do it," Link said. "Who's the owner?"

"An old fellow named Bernard. A stonecutter. Lives with his two sons and a daughter 'way down in Colorado. Pretty near the Arkansas River."

"And you're pretty sure I'm headed that way," Link said, rolling the chisels into the leather wrapping again and tying it with the leather thong.

"You'll make your journey, yes."

"Any idea why?"

Evan Thompson looked at the way Link's brow was furrowed and he laughed.

"You're problem is you're too serious, Link. Too serious by half. Don't worry so much about why you do things or what they mean. Don't even worry about where you're headed. Just think south, boy. Just go looking for new things."

"I like new things all right," Link said defensively.

"Sure," Thompson said. "Sure you do. And this trip will do you good. It'll give you a few months to work the kinks out. One day you'll find you're able to pick a flower with that hand. Another day you'll find you can chew a tough steak without pain. You know how colts and calves find out how to use their legs. They just run and play and build up their muscles. They explore the world. Always seeing new things everywhere."

"That seems to bring somethin' to mind," Link said.

He sat down on the stump where Thompson's anvil had been and used his one good hand to rub at his stiff leg, the leg that didn't have a plaster cast on it. It seemed like the weight of the cast and the limping kept his leg muscle hurting most of the time.

"Something about calves and colts?" Thompson said.

"No, about usin' this busted arm again. Back there when your wife gave me that pain-killer . . . ," he broke off.

"Yes. You want her to leave some for you?"

"No, that's not it. I was just wondering about it. It gave me these dreams about graves. And a tower and peculiar-looking rocks. Seemed like some kind of riddle or somethin'. You . . . well, you seem to know about such things. That ain't part of this trip of mine, is it?"

In his giant hand Thompson held a long iron bar that he was preparing to slide into the bed of the wagon. In spite of its obvious weight he held it much the way a teacher might hold a yardstick, pointing first across the creek and past the high hill on the other side, and then south and a little east.

"Your next ride takes you that way," he said, "but you'll end up right back here. You'll find graves where no one has died, and you'll change, but you'll stay the same. That's what the dream is about. Is that riddle enough for you,

40

cowpuncher?" Thompson was grinning broadly under his beard.

"Guess so," Link said, " 'specially when you consider that I'm not leavin' the ranch for a good long spell." He tapped the crutch against his cast and lifted the arm that was also in a cast, hanging in a sling. "Even if I could ride, Art needs me here. He has to go out to Omaha and Saint Louis for a time, and he's leavin' me in charge. It's the kinda job a cowboy dreams about! Just sit on the porch in a big ol' chair and give orders all day. Maybe talk to some buyers, plan some improvements, here and there. If I feel really ambitious, I might rig up a buggy so I can drive around and supervise the men. What do you think about that?"

Evan Thompson raised the heavy tailboard and fastened it with its chains, then dusted his hands on his jeans before extending one to Link.

"I didn't say you're leaving right away. I just said you're leaving. Well I'm wishin' you good luck, young Link," he said. "Come dawn, we'll be moving out, heading west this time, but I'll be back this way to see how you've done."

"Any idea how I'll know when I get there?"

"You'll recognize the place. Just look around, take whatever path seems to need takin'. When you get there, you'll know you've arrived."

"Thanks again for comin' along when you did," Link said, "and for gettin' me to the Army surgeon and all. We'd been in bad shape without you."

"Glad I was there," Thompson said.

"Probably see you soon," Link said.

"Probably." The blacksmith grinned. "Mind how you ride, now."

"Good luck to you," Link said.

Evan Thompson smiled.

Chapter Three

Hobbles

Gwen — Mrs. Pendragon — left the house after breakfast to go riding.

Her long split skirt was made of natural suede, her vest the color of spring sage over a white shirtwaist. She wore high boots and a broad-brimmed hat of light brown. In short, there was nothing remarkable or unusual about her except for her long hair and attractive figure. Even the shoulder bag in which she carried her sketching materials and lunch was of plain green canvas.

As she walked toward the stable to have the hostler catch and saddle her horse, several ranch hands tipped their hats respectfully; she smiled slightly and tipped her head in acknowledgement. As men will, they watched her after she passed, fascinated by how light and quick her movements were for one so straight-laced and poised.

Rounding the corner of the stables, she saw a half dozen cowboys lounging at the corral. Two sat on the top rail with their feet hooked under the next rail for balance; another leaned back with one foot up on a rail and his arms draped over the rail behind him; another squatted in the shade of a post and yet another sat in the dust examining one of his spurs.

Link was with them and was the center of their attention. Indeed, for a few moments none of the men noticed Gwen walking toward them; Link was finishing a story.

"So the fella who'd just lost the dogfight says . . . 'I

never saw a dog bite off another dog's head like that. What breed is he, anyway?'

"An' the Mexican, he says . . . 'I don't know what breed means, *señor*. But before I cut off his tail and painted him yellow, he was a alligator.' "

Link saw Gwen emerge from the shadow of the building and instantly wished the boys weren't laughing at that particular moment. Even though she hadn't overheard his story, there was something about the way she was standing there that seemed to say she didn't approve of it. Seeing that she was dressed for riding, the hostler broke from the group and limped toward the corrals, self-conscious at having been caught loafing. The cowboys touched their hat brims to her and moved off as well, walking with that slow sort of deliberation men have when they want to appear to be heading toward some very important work.

Link picked up his crutch and made a purposeful move away from the corral rail he'd been leaning on, but then it occurred to him that he didn't need to look busy just because Gwen had come into view. Nor did he need to limp over to where she waited for her horse just because she was there. The woman had been sort of distant lately, almost haughty. She still greeted him by name and smiled at him whenever they met, but somehow it seemed more forced, as if she were maintaining more distance between herself and him now that Art was away. Maybe she thought she'd better keep more distance between herself and him. Either way it was just about as confusing as one of Evan Thompson's damned riddles.

"Good morning, Link." She said it as if she had just noticed him.

" 'Morning," he replied. "Nice day for a ride."

"Very nice," she agreed. "I thought I would go out. Per-

43

haps I'll ride up to the water tanks in the cottonwoods and do some sketching."

He had already noticed the shoulder bag with the sketch pad sticking up out of it.

"Well, it's a nice morning for it," he said.

Standing there with his crutch under his arm and his leg bent up behind him, the other arm in a sling, he felt awkward. He was also self-conscious of the fat little notebook bulging in his shirt pocket. It symbolized his new responsibility as ranch boss, carrying Art's notebook of daily chores and ranch records around with him. Art himself had stuck it in that pocket like a town mayor pinning a badge on a new sheriff. In it were written all the things he expected to see done when he came back from his trip out to Omaha and St. Louis. *Here I am,* thought Link, *a man with responsibilities standing around telling stories and keeping a half dozen cowboys from their chores.*

But why would he feel so uncomfortable? He — and the cowboys — had been up since almost daybreak. They had seen to the milk cows, fed the corral horses, mucked out the main stables, and repaired the corral gate before she had finished with her breakfast. But he still felt like a kid caught doing something wrong. He remembered back to other summer days when she had seemed far more friendly, more cheerful, more apt to join in with a funny story of her own than to stand at a distance with that disapproving look on her face.

She turned her back to him and watched the hostler putting the saddle on her horse. Link limped closer, determined to be pleasant.

"Just tellin' the boys a funny story I heard," he began.

Without moving her feet or taking her hands from her hips, she turned her upper body sideways with surprising

44

suddenness and looked at him. There was no expression in her face, yet the movement was enough to make him feel awkward.

"Not much of a story, I guess. Then, again, it doesn't generally take much to make those boys laugh."

"I suppose not," she said, and turned back to address the hostler. "Could you also hang a canteen on the saddle?" she suggested. "I may be out quite some time."

"So," Link said, "I guess I'd better get about my day's rat killin'. You have a nice ride."

His voice sounded tentative, even to himself. She turned again, that quick swing of the shoulders, and he thought she was looking at him as if she didn't care for the shape of his hat or how he brushed his mustache. Maybe one of his shirt buttons was open.

"Thank you," she said.

Link gimped off with his crutch, headed toward the wagon barn to check on the hostler's new assistant, a kid named Tad who was supposed to be spending his time making sure all the wagons and buggies were serviceable. Especially the wagons, with roundup coming. The structure they called the wagon barn was more of a pole barn, open on the front. It was there to keep snow and rain and sun off any rigs that weren't being used. Inside, there were two freight wagons, a heavy chuck wagon, a water tank on wheels, a two-wheel cart, and a couple of buggies.

Link grimly stumped along, feeling like he was himself no more than a hired hand around the place. Everything he did seemed to somehow annoy that woman. He'd like to saddle up and go for a ride, too, maybe all the way to town, but he couldn't go anywhere so long as Art was away.

Tad was just pulling up to the shed in a buckboard behind a light team. Seeing Link, he jerked a thumb over his shoulder at the wagon bed. Inside, Link saw a man sleeping with his head cradled on a wad of old feed sacks, a battered Stetson shading his face. His disheveled clothes hadn't been washed in quite a while and his boots were worn but well-soled. Under his arm, he wore a revolver in a shoulder holster.

"Pickin' up passengers for hire now?" Link smiled, speaking softly so as not to wake the stranger.

"No, sir, Mister Link," Tad said in a whisper. "Just got in on his own, I reckon. I fitted that hind wheel with new spokes yesterday and set 'er down in the creek for 'em to swell up nice an' tight, and, when I went to get 'er this mornin', there he was. I think he's sleepin' one off."

Link sniffed the air and agreed. Whoever it was, his clothes and breath smelled worse than a saloon shithouse. He eyed the man's pockets for signs of a bottle, since drinking and whiskey bottles were strictly prohibited on the Keystone, but found none.

"Probably finished it on the back of the buckboard and dropped the bottle in the creek before he passed out," Tad whispered.

Link reached over and slid the revolver from the shoulder holster. "Thirty-Eight Smith and Wesson." He slipped the catch and opened the cylinder to dump out the cartridges, which he put in his pocket. "Just as soon not have a drunk wake up on the ranch with a loaded gun," he said. He put the gun back. "So," Link said, "any sign of anyone else down there? Maybe a campfire ring, or tracks?"

"No, sir. Not that I looked around much. Bein' new around here, I thought maybe he might be one of the hands. Thought maybe he wandered down there from the bunkhouse to sleep off the whiskey."

"Not one of ours," Link said. "Some range bum, most

likely. Those boots look like U.S. cavalry."

Tad unhitched his team and the noisy clatter of horses dragging the singletrees away brought the man awake. He sat up with one hand holding his hat onto his head as if he thought it would keep his brains from exploding. He blinked into the bright morning light.

"Where the hell is this place? Who got my horse? Who the hell are you?" His voice had the rasp of a drunk waking up dry. He had to stop and catch his breath, but he kept on staring at Link.

"Keystone Ranch," Link said, "the main headquarters. That buckboard was parked in the creek. Apparently you went to sleep in it. I don't know where the hell your horse is."

"Keystone," the man repeated. "That figgers. Man can't spit nor squat 'round here without him bein' on some damn' Keystone range. Lemme see th' head man."

"I'm in charge for the time bein'. So what can I do for you?" Link asked.

"Y'can give me my god-damn' horse back, that's what you can god-damn' do for openers."

"And where exactly did you lose your god-damn' horse and what did he god-damn' look like?" Link said.

"You makin' fun of me?" the scruffy one replied, edging his way to the rear of the wagon to let his legs hang down. He moved gingerly to keep his head from splitting open.

"Yeah."

The man's hand moved slightly in the direction of his shoulder holster, but relaxed again.

"Kind of a cross b'tween ginger an' roan. Face has a crooked blaze. It's been two days ago, maybe three, he run off with a bunch of your horses."

"Run off with 'em?" Link asked. "You mean he led 'em

47

away, or went away with 'em?"

"Dammit, bunch of your horses came nosin' around my camp and mine went off with 'em. Left me on foot for two days. Three days, maybe."

"So you an' your whiskey bottle just wandered around and ended up sleeping it off in our buckboard."

"I was followin' tracks. He come this way all right."

"What were you doin' on our range in the first place? Camping, like you said?"

"Just crossin' your range. Nothin' else."

"Well, we don't mind folks crossin' the range, as long as they keep on with their crossin' and nothin' else."

"You calling me a rustler or somethin'?"

"I guess you wouldn't be much shakes as a rustler. Can't even keep track of your own horse, let alone steal a herd of 'em."

The man scowled as he dropped carefully to the ground, wincing as his legs took the shock. "I'm gonna find that son-of-a-bitch and shoot 'im, that's what I'm gonna do."

"Sure," Link said. "Sure. First, why don't we get you up to the bunkhouse and have the cook fix you some food, get some coffee in you, and the boys can help you pick out a horse from the corral so's you can go after yours. That sound friendly enough for you?"

"Don't need no god-damn' Keystone hand-outs," he blurted. "I've had enough of your boys already. You just owe me the borrow of the horse."

"What do you mean, enough of my boys?"

"I was nearly to catch up with that bunch and get my horse back, wasn't I? An' them riders of yours came along and run 'em off again. Seemed to think it was funny to see me on foot like that."

"None of my boys should have been out there. You see

48

brands, anything like that?"

"God-damn' tracks. Tracks was all. Three shod horses, at least, heavy shoes, caulked. Good-size animals . . . for cow ponies. Your range string have shoes, any of 'em?"

"Nope. Only horses out in that direction are with the rough string. We pulled their shoes and turned 'em out two, three months ago. So how good a look did you get at these riders you claim you saw?"

"Claim, hell!" he shouted. "Call me a liar? You owe me a horse, mister, an' I'll take it now!"

The stranger jerked his Smith & Wesson from its shoulder holster and pointed it at Link, who only stood there calmly looking at him. Then Link raised his crutch as if he was pointing into the distance with it and brought it down hard, hitting the man's forearm and knocking the gun into the dirt.

"God damn!" the hothead said, "you nearly broke my damn' wrist!"

"Shortest way off the range is that way," Link said quietly, pointing with his crutch. "You just walk on out of here. We find your horse in with ours, we'll send him the same way."

Dick Elliot and Emil rode up not more than two minutes later to find Link and Tad looking in the direction of a man walking away.

"Trouble?" Emil asked. Emil seldom used more words than necessary.

"Might be," Link said. "You boys get your saddle carbines and some extra shells, pick up Jess or Lem, or both of 'em if you find 'em, and go check on the rough string. That drifter you see walkin' away said there was somebody runnin' the string and it sounded like they were on Army horses. Might be he's even one of 'em."

49

"How'd you figure that, Mister Link?" Tad was surprised. He had been as close to the stranger as Link had.

"Boots," Link said. "Flat, wide heels, and half soled not long go. He wasn't a cowboy for long, and he hadn't been walkin' very far. He sure as hell didn't walk for two days. I think they had him as a look-out, maybe lead us off in the wrong direction if anybody happened to leave headquarters to check on the horse range. He could've been watching us while his partners ran off some ponies somewhere else. But I figure they didn't count on him havin' a bottle. Figure he was out there, keepin' an eye on the buildings, but he got drunk. Probably saw the buckboard sittin' there and got off his horse and into it to lay down and go to sleep."

"But he said he was on foot," Tad suggested.

"Boots again," Link said. "The rig was sittin' in the deep part of the creek, right? Up to the hubs or better? So, how come his boots didn't look like they'd got wet? No, he rode up to that buckboard and unloaded himself onto it, and his horse strolled away. All that bull about it wanderin' off with our herd is just smoke, that's all. You boys get goin'. Oh, and tell Pat or somebody to saddle my black for me. I'll catch you up directly."

Pat was one of two hostlers whose job it was to look after the horses and stables at the ranch headquarters and do odd jobs around the big house. He saddled Messenger, Link's big black gelding, and led him to the mounting block put there for ladies to use when mounting a side-saddle.

Link didn't like the idea of using a lady-step, but saw the wisdom of it. Handing the Winchester and canteen to Pat to hold while he got on, he crippled his way up the two steps and swung his bum leg, cast and all, over the saddle. Even with Pat holding the stirrup, Link couldn't get a foot into it because of the cast.

"Well, anyway, it's lucky you found them loose overalls. Levi's wouldn't never fit over that cast of yours," Pat observed.

"Oh, lucky as hell," Link said. He slid the rifle into the scabbard and tied the canteen to the horn, then pulled Messenger around to chase after the other three men.

Obviously he wouldn't catch them. He couldn't catch a turtle, not jouncing up and down with that plastered leg throwing him off balance and one arm out of action. All he could do was put the reins in that hand and use the good one to hold onto the horn.

At the top of the little rise he stopped and looked after the three horsemen, who by now were just small, black figures making dust in the distance. He couldn't see the man on foot anywhere, but figured he was somewhere over one of the hills. The sight of the creek reminded him: *Gwen said she was going to the tanks, a pair of man-made ponds a few miles upstream. If there were horse thieves on the range . . . or if that drunk bastard decided to wander up the creek. . . .*

Link turned Messenger toward the trail leading to the tanks and bounced along at a trot, keeping the distant grove of cottonwoods in sight as his hat brim flapped up and down. The way the saddle slammed at his crotch with every step made him think that, by the time they got there, him and the gelding would have more in common than when they started.

Approaching the cottonwoods, he slowed Messenger to an easy walk and studied the trail. There was only one set of tracks, probably hers. Just to be sure, he made sweeps for a hundred yards to either side of the trail; crippled as he was, it wouldn't pay to take any chances at all. Satisfied Gwen was alone by the tanks, he rode on through the trees.

She was seated in the grass near the sluice where the

water fell from the upper pond into the lower one with a plashing that covered the sounds of Messenger's hoofs. She had her back to him and her sketch pad open on her lap as she drew. She was a pretty picture herself, sitting straight and slim with her skirt spread out, her riding hat hanging at her back, and, to finish off the scene, she was framed by a backdrop of glittering water and tall green grass.

When she finally heard Messenger and turned her head to look, it seemed to Link she stiffened at the sight of him.

"Hello, again," she said. "I see you can ride. How is it?"

"Painful," he said as he drew up to the tank and let the horse drink. "Can't recommend havin' your socks made out of plaster at all."

She sat there regarding him, and he kept the horse at a polite distance while he told her about the man found in the buckboard and the possibility there might be some horse thieves somewhere on the range. There wasn't much chance she'd run into them, since most of the Keystone horses they probably had their eye on were on the range away off in the other direction.

"I have my pistol," she said.

Two years earlier when they were on very friendly, almost playful, terms with each other, he had taught her how to shoot the pistol Art insisted she carry when on her own. She had been an excellent pupil.

Link nodded. Figures she can take care of herself. Still, a woman could show a little more gratitude to a man for riding out to warn her when his leg was the way it was. A woman might even say she was glad to see him. Instead, he felt like he didn't need to have bothered.

He didn't stay long. When he left, he made a wide circuit around the cottonwoods and over the highest hills in the area, but there was no sign of any other horsemen. All he saw, and only briefly from a hilltop, was a mirage. It looked like a lake shimmering and shining 'way off in the remote distance, a lake with a tall, slender shadow rising from it.

Satisfied that Gwen was in no danger, Link returned to the main house, and she arrived back at suppertime. The next morning there was no sign of the three riders, but at dusk of the following day Dick Elliot rode up to report he and Emil and Lem had, indeed, followed four men mounted on Army horses. Through field glasses they could see the men wore rough civilian clothes. They had followed them all night, making sure the four knew they were being followed. All next day, too, they kept trailing the strangers at a distance and didn't let them stop to camp. Finally, at the edge of the Keystone range, Dick let Emil "encourage" their departure with a few rounds of rifle fire.

"You'd better watch out for that Emil." Dick smiled. "I think he's as good a shot as you are! We were a good hundred yards off and he was kickin' up puffs of dirt right under the belly of the leader's horse."

"Oh?" Link grinned. "Just let me get this plaster off and we'll find out. One of these days."

Link's leg ached all the next day from that short ride up to the tanks. His arm itched inside the cast like someone had poured red ants in there. To make matters worse, Gwen asked him and Bob Riley to take their suppers with her at the main house so they could discuss ranch operations and go over Art's instructions. So he not only felt like a damned cripple, he had to sit there with an awkward cast on his arm, eating off fancy plates. Chewing his meat brought pain to his chin and made him wince.

Gwen's attitude didn't help, either. Once he looked up from his plate and caught her watching him. She had a little look on her face like she thought he'd injured himself just to

53

spite her. When she rose to go, Bob Riley scraped his chair back and got to his feet the way a man should when a lady stands up. Link followed his example even though he had to put a hand on the table to hoist himself up. At the doorway Gwen took a quick backward look at him with one hand on her hip.

At the top of Art's list was **ROUNDUP** in big block letters. Preparations had to be made early, for this would be one of the biggest gatherings ever seen in the territory. Men were sent out to make a sweep of the whole south range for horses, every animal of the rough string brought in and either corralled or pastured near headquarters. A half dozen cowboys were chosen to start green-breaking them, gentling six to eight for each cowboy on the roundup to use as his string.

Other men were sent out to the hayfields to cut, haul, and stack winter feed with orders to bring in as much as they could. Two more crews took wagons into the foothills to bring back firewood. Art had contracted for a shipment of coal for the furnace in the main house and for bunkhouse stoves, and it arrived one day in four freight wagons hitched in two tandem rigs. Cowboys stripped to the waist were soon black with fine dust as they shoveled coal into the bunkers.

The bunkhouse cook had his preparations to make, too. The new Dutch ovens needed to be greased and heated and greased and heated repeatedly until they were well "cured" and ready for cooking; flour needed to be boxed up and loaded into the chuck wagons; there was salt pork to slice and stack in kegs, and the medicine boxes to replenish. At the forge and at the wagon shed, the smith and the hostler kept their helpers jumping. They had to make sure the wagon teams were well shod, the harness chains and tugs inspected, the steel wagon tires on tight, branding irons and picket pins wrapped in bundles and stored in the gear wagons. And among all this activity, Link limped around on his crutch, trying to watch everything at once, answering questions fired at him from all directions, and trying to anticipate anything that ought to be anticipated.

"Hey!" Garth called out to him one morning as he was gimping down to supervise the start of a new haystack, "I thought you were goin' to sit on the porch an' sip cider and give orders. Live th' easy life of a ranch boss, y'said!"

"Just shut your cake hole, kid." Link smiled grimly. "If you're out of horses to break, there's an opening on the hay crew. An' there's an outhouse hole wants digging."

Horses milled inside the big corral, trotting in a bunch around the rails while cowboys on foot whirled big loops over bobbing necks. Everywhere you looked everything was in movement. There were visitors, representatives from distant ranches coming by to finalize the plan of operation. Buyers came, too, hoping to get an early advantage, disappointed that Art wasn't there to talk prices. Small ranchers came to find out when the roundup would start so they could get in on it. Their older sons and grown boys from farms near town came and stood around awkwardly, waiting for a chance to ask Link or Bob if they might sign on.

The plan was ambitious. All the ranchers in the whole area and all their cowhands would start to move on the same designated day, taking chuck wagons and equipment wagons and hundreds of horses high into the foothills along a hundred-mile line and out along a second line stretching east from the hills. Each foreman, range boss, and *segundo* would "string" his hands to cover as much territory as possible, riding with them to certain points and dropping off two, three, or a half dozen men at a time to search out the cañons and draws and high pastures for cattle.

The cattle would be caught in between with horsemen blocking their movement except to the east and to the south. Then, as the long lines of riders began to swing inward, the cattle would start to bunch up and find themselves walking along in ever-growing herds, first a few dozen, then a few hundred, and finally thousands lumbering along together in a cloud of dust reaching from horizon to horizon. As the big herds gathered, reps from the different brands would ride among them on horses trained for cutting, separating the cattle into groups according to ownership. Yearlings still sticking close to their mothers would be branded with their mother's mark; unbranded ones that were on their own would be cut into the maverick herd and branded with the M. Weak animals unfit for the trail would be butchered to feed the cowhands.

Link practiced riding, getting himself ready. He found he could ride a few hours a day, if he didn't push Messenger into anything faster than a walk. Some days, however, it just wasn't enough for him and he would punish his body with a long ride out to one of the hayfields or up to the high pasture to make sure everything was on schedule. It hurt, but he seemed to be healing pretty fast. By the time roundup started, he wanted to be ready to do a full day's work.

One day he felt so full of himself that he asked Gwen if she'd like to ride out to the tanks by the cottonwoods and have a picnic supper. She turned him down with a look that made him feel she was very disappointed in him. It must have been the way he said it, he figured.

That same evening after supper she made an announcement.

"All the men have been working so hard," she said, mostly addressing Bob Riley, "that I think they deserve a nice party. A picnic. We'll set up lots of tables and roast a beef in a fire pit and even bring in beer from town."

"I don't know as we have the time for all that," Link objected. "Takes time and men to put somethin' like that together."

"Oh, nonsense!" Gwen said with a forced laugh. "I'm sure you'll all be ready for the roundup in plenty of time. Now, Bob, I'll make a list of things we need from town. You find somebody to go with a wagon . . . maybe Garth? And, Link, just last evening you said the crew was about finished fencing in the haystacks. Do you suppose they could dig a big fire pit for me?"

Link scowled. "They're supposed to be digging new outhouse holes behind the bunkhouse," he said.

"Oh, that can wait. Never mind that. And who's the young man who knows beef steers so well? You know, Sam? The one who always does the butchering? Let's send him to cut out two good ones, at least, and get them ready. One of those pigs would be nice, too. We might need two fire pits. And wood. Good wood for the coals. Bob, what do you think?"

"Well, I guess oak or juniper would be best for that. I could get one of the firewood crews to locate you some dead oak from up in the foothills."

Link scowled over his coffee cup. He had come back to the ranch a broken-up cripple through no fault of his own. Before that he had been shot at over some Keystone horses. He was the one who had ridden clear out to the tanks to make sure she wasn't in danger from those range bums and hurt his leg again in the process. Now here she was, suddenly bent on showing "appreciation" to all Art's other cowpokes for just doing what they get paid to do. Her and that little smile of hers. *And* that way she had of making Bob Riley do whatever she wanted. It was enough to make a man's stomach turn over.

Link lurched to his feet and excused himself. He stuck his head through the kitchen door to say — "Good supper." — to Mary, and pegged off with his crutch. He limped and bumped his way down the front steps and kept on going straight out the gate, taking grim satisfaction in the pain he was inflicting on his body.

Chapter Four

A Feast Fit for a King

As the Pendragons' personal cook, Mary also carried the responsibility of feeding the many guests who came to the ranch, a job she took most seriously. She took particular care when it came to the growing and preservation of vegetables. "Any old biscuit-slinger can turn out meat and bread," she would say, "but you ain't civilized until you got greens to go with them." To that end she had been the instigator of no fewer than three gardens. Any cowhand she happened to spot loitering around the main ranch buildings was likely to be put to work with a hand cultivator, assigned to clean her system of irrigation ditches, or sent out with pliers and hammer to tighten up the barb-wire fences that kept livestock from wandering into the vegetables.

There were actually four gardens, if you counted the pumpkin and squash patch down by the fruit orchard. One was the kitchen garden, a good-size plot just outside the back door of the big house where she grew "small stuff" as she called it, bushels of radishes and carrots, horseradish and string beans. Another was the potato garden that the ranch hands manured and plowed for her each spring and that grew enough potatoes and onions to keep the household going all winter. One of its borders was planted in rhubarb for pie. Another side was hedged with gooseberry bushes.

Mary and Bob Riley and Link were standing at the edge of the largest garden, which she referred to as the "truck garden". Each spring she conscripted ranch hands to plow, harrow, and seed it with all sorts of "truck" ranging from lettuce and corn to cabbages and beets.

"So what all are you going to need for this shindig?" Link asked, licking the tip of his pencil and addressing it to a blank page in the notebook.

"I'm figuring we've plenty of corn and beans," Mary said, "but we oughta send Andy or somebody to town for a dozen cases of canned tomatoes. Could pick up two sacks of buckwheat flour while he's there, and I'd like some of those fancy French canned apples for pie. Come to think of it, you send Andy. He's the only one that is able to read can labels right. Some of those boys of yours wouldn't know kerosene from carrots, if there wasn't a picture on the can. Missus Pendragon is particularly fond of my French apple and rhubarb pie. And I need another keg of molasses, and tell him it better not be a leaky one like last time."

"Well," Link said, making notes, "I'll tell him to check the keg. And make sure he gets French apples. We sure don't want to disappoint Missus Pendragon."

Bob Riley looked at him. "What happened?" he said. "The boss lady kick your bad leg or something?"

"Never mind," Link said. "Didn't mean nuthin' by it."

"Let's hope not," Mary said. "I work hard keeping my household happy. Don't need anybody passin' remarks."

"I said I didn't mean nuthin' by it," Link repeated.

"Missus Pendragon wants this party to make the boys feel good for all th' work they done lately. We all need to pitch in, and that's all I'm going to say about it."

Mary put her chin in the air and bustled off to look at her onions, and the way she walked reminded Link of a fussy hen. He turned to Riley.

"If you got all that, maybe you'd better find Andy and

tell him he's been volunteered to be the grocery boy. Don't forget to tell him about the French apples and to check the molasses keg."

"OK, boss," Riley said.

"What's that supposed to mean?" Link snapped.

"Nuthin' 'cept that I'll be glad when Art gets back. As a ramrod you've been a pain in the butt lately."

Link left the garden and crutched his way toward the cook shack to see if there was any coffee left. *That darn' Gwen, anyway,* he thought. *It'd sure make it easier to run things if she'd just quit lookin' at me like I was wrong all the time.* What the hell had put a burr under her saddle was more than he could figure out. He wanted to blame Art, because it was Art who decided to go on a business trip and leave her without much to do. Maybe she was mad because she didn't get to go along.

Before he had reached the cook shack, Link had a change of mind. It wasn't anything to do with Gwen Pendragon at all. It was he. He was getting antsy as a green colt somebody penned up in a corral. These damned casts on his arm and leg were making him touchy, and what he really needed was just to cheer up.

There was nobody in the cook shack and the pot was empty except for some cold, brown sludge in the bottom. He slammed it back down on the stove and glared around for the cook so he could cuss him out for not tending to his kitchen. Still not seeing anybody, Link swung around on his crutch and pounded away toward the bunkhouse. If he had been a drinking man, and if liquor hadn't been prohibited on the Keystone, he would have been knee-walking, stomach-heaving, motherless drunk by suppertime.

There was laughter coming from the bunkhouse, along with the chatter of men playing cards inside. For some reason the sound of them enjoying themselves made him even madder. He limped on past the bunkhouse without even looking in. He kept going, clear up to the crest of the rise where the horse trail went through the sagebrush and wound down into the next valley.

It was from there, his face touched by a light breeze coming out of nowhere and his eyes searching for distance, that he saw it again: A mirage of a far-off tower surrounded by a lake that wasn't there. Link watched it until it broke into long, shimmering slivers of light and vanished. When it was gone, a deep sadness pressed down on him, for right now that tower seemed to him to be the most peaceful place in all the world.

He thought of Evan Thompson's words to him. If it wasn't that Art was still gone, if he wasn't supposed to be in charge, he'd pack his bundle and start for that mirage. Like Thompson said, it looked like some place that needed going to.

"Buggy comin'!"

Sam was the first to see it, since he was on the barn roof replacing some broken shingles. Ranch hands left their work to stare out across the fields to where the road crossed the rise. Gwen and Mary watched from the porch, and soon they could see it was Art who was driving the light buggy hitched behind a high-stepping chestnut roan. He wheeled right up to the porch steps, smiling under a spanking new Stetson. The buying and selling had gone faster than he'd expected. Finding himself with extra time and extra money, he had bought a new horse and buggy and brought them on the train all the way from St. Louis. He also had a stack of mysterious, wrapped parcels for Gwen. Some of the men grinned at this — here was the man who had settled the valley almost single-handed, fighting the weather and the land and outlaws and thieves, spending days in the saddle and nights sleeping on the ground in raw weather. Here was the same man, decked out in town clothes and driving a high-prancing fancy horse and rig, carrying piles of presents like somebody's rich uncle come to visit. No man dared call him a dude, but dudes *had* been known to wear fancy duds like that.

Cowboys and cooks, hostlers and hay crew, cartwrights and fence menders all found excuses to pay their respects at the main house that afternoon. Pat, the grumpy old hostler, muttered that they all looked like bees buzzing around a busted molasses barrel. Gwen was in the center of it, hurrying to bring him coffee and a slice of cake, hugging his arm, asking questions about St. Louis and beaming up into his face as she shared him with people dropping by to welcome him home. His return infused the whole headquarters ranch with new life, new excitement, and not merely because he had brought the news that this year's roundup would likely increase all of their fortunes. It was as if he had brought a spark of fire from the outside world, or like it was a fresh shift of wind bringing moist air to a drought. Even the news that he would have to return to St. Louis after roundup seemed to be exciting, a feeling of being connected to the rest of the country.

The next morning was almost comical.

It had long been Art's custom to appear on the wide porch of the big house each morning shortly after sunrise with a leather-bound ledger book in his hands. The crew bosses and ramrods and the hostler's crew lounging around the cook shack after breakfast would watch for him to emerge. When he did, it was the signal for them to walk up to the porch and get their orders for the day. Sometimes Art would just ask them how things were going and then send them off to their daily jobs, but sometimes he would have something big to tell them about or a major project he wanted them to get started on.

The morning after Art's return, it was different. Link filched an extra biscuit and cup of coffee while the bunkhouse cook was looking the other way and went outside to lean against the building and watch the main house. There wasn't a sign of life. The hostler joined him, then Bob Riley, then Pat limped up on his game leg. Together they just stood and looked at the main house. The shades were still drawn in the upstairs windows. Smoke rose from the kitchen chimney, but there was no sign of Art walking out onto the porch with his ledger book. There was no sound coming from the house, just lots of silence.

The four men outside the cook shack watched the house from a respectful distance as if they were keeping vigil over a shrine.

"Sleepin' in late," Riley finally speculated.

"Probably," Link agreed. That would be one explanation for the drawn shades.

"Well," Pat said by way of making the final word on the subject, "he hasn't been home in quite a while."

The hostler's boys shambled off toward the corrals, knowing they had stock to feed and horse apples to scoop up. The four bachelor ramrods turned and went back inside the cook shack to refill their cups, taking a few more glances backward to make certain Art wasn't on the porch.

It was well after mid-morning when Art finally came strolling down toward the barns, cleaning his favorite pipe as he walked. He found Link brushing Messenger's black coat.

"Beautiful morning," he said.

" 'Morning, Art," Link replied. "Yeah, should be a nice day. Not too hot."

Art patted Messenger on the shoulder. "Best-looking horse on the place," he said, mostly to the horse.

"Not now" — Link smiled — "not since you pulled in with that fancy-lookin' chestnut. Not to mention that high-tone buggy and that fooforaw outfit of yours."

"Aw, drop it," Art said. "Back in Saint Louis all that gear seemed like what a big important rancher oughta have. By the time they unloaded it at Cheyenne, it seemed kind of showy. I knew that. But what was I goin' to do, send it back on the train? Besides, Gwen likes it."

"Yeah, well . . . ," Link said, "then again, she likes *you*. No accountin' for taste, I guess."

"That's true," Art returned. "Messenger here even seems to like *you*, don't you, boy?"

The big black horse snorted and stamped a hoof.

"Going out for a ride?" Art asked.

"Just around headquarters. Lots of things to check on, what with this big party the boss lady is throwin' tomorrow. Which reminds me I got a homecomin' present for you."

Link took the fat little notebook from his shirt pocket and handed it to Art.

"Don't mind tellin' you I'm glad to get rid of it. I'm never goin' to make fun of your job again. I won't give you any trouble about anything from here on in. I'd rather chase stampedes through prairie fires than try to run an operation like this. One damn' thing follows another until you don't know what you're doin'."

"I'm glad to have somebody appreciate that," Art said. "Well, I was talkin' to a couple of the boys, and they say you did a good job. So . . . I guess most everything is under control around here, huh? Just this party of Gwen's to get together."

"Pretty much," Link said, smoothing the saddle blanket into place. "I need to check on a few things today is all. She wanted two fire pits dug, one big enough to roast a pig. I'll need to make sure the boys did it right."

"Fine," Art said. "Tonight or tomorrow maybe we can talk over what's been happening the past few weeks."

"Any time you say," Link said, giving his saddle cinch one last tug. "You're the boss. Thank God."

As strangely as Gwen treated him since he came back crippled up, the day of the party she seemed to avoid him altogether. The same thing happened as before. He was in a circle of men sharing a funny story and happened to look over to see her watching him with her hands planted on her hips, her upper body turned halfway around. Some time later he was thinking of teasing the Pinto Kid about his fancy new neck scarf just as Gwen happened to walk past where they were talking. This time she neither looked at nor spoke to him. One minute he was all cheered up and enjoying himself, and the next minute he felt like smashing crockery or throwing rocks at the house.

He didn't mind, so long as he was among the ranch hands. But if her glance caught him out in the open, such as when he was crossing from the fire pit to the porch, he felt himself suddenly nervous, instantly on edge. It made the back of his neck prickly when she seemed to be looking in his direction, or even when he saw her standing with her back stiff as a wagon rod.

Even the party itself started to irritate him, the more it dragged on into the afternoon. Gwen and her guests from town — four young women invited to add some "interest" to the occasion, as she put it — stayed mainly at the table in the shade of the largest cottonwood, chattering and sipping punch and watching the antics of the cowboys. These stalwarts of the saddle carried on like schoolboys, demonstrating how their favorite pony could be made to bow to the ladies, or competing to see who could twirl a lariat into the biggest loop. The Pinto Kid showed off his gymnastic skills by standing on his saddle as his horse pranced in a circle. Bob Riley had his hair all slicked down and a new silk scarf tied in a big bow and lounged on the grass near the ladies, regaling them with tall tales about cowboy life.

Link kept on the move from group to group, mostly repeating the same reply to the same question about his broken arm and leg. "Gettin' better, thanks. No, doesn't hurt at all any more. Just itches is all."

He saw color everywhere, from the new silk neckerchiefs on the cowhands to the summer dresses of the ladies and red bunting draped along the tables. It was like the 4th of July picnics he had known as a boy. Smells were in the air, too — as he passed by the food he caught the sharp tang of pickled cucumbers, and, pausing to smile with a cluster of cowboys talking with two ladies from town, he picked up the smells of bay rum and lavender. There was a smell of roast meat, and sometimes a whiff of just-sliced bread fresh from the oven.

The whole day was good for the men's morale and made a fine homecoming for Art, but along toward late afternoon it began to wear on Link. In fact, the more it went on, the more he wished the men would all just get back to work. It was nice to have a party, but after a while it just became a waste of good daylight. Everything pointed to a long, deep winter, and with the biggest roundup in history coming up, they'd scarcely find time to stack all the hay and cut all the firewood and shore up all the outbuildings for when the winter snowdrifts came. And there the crew was, courting women and tossing horseshoes and sucking up punch and generally acting like life was one big picnic. *Somebody ought to be making a long ride around the horse range,* Link thought, *just to make sure those range bums hadn't come back. But, of course, we wouldn't want any of the men to miss out on dessert just to catch a few horse thieves.*

It was Art who inadvertently lit the match that brought Link's mood to a rolling boil. Link was sitting on the porch railing, watching the goings-on. Close by, Pat was churning away at the ice-cream maker. The old man complained with each turn of the handle, the ice cream getting almost too thick to move. Art came up, carrying a second ice-cream maker and another bag of rock salt.

"Link," he said, "why don't you take that new batch of ice cream over to the ladies. Pat and me, we'll start a new batch in the meantime. Just take the tub and all. We'll get this other one going."

Ice cream for ladies. Art looked at his boss, all decked out in a Stetson silver belly and green silk neck scarf, and wondered if this was the same man who once had led six Keystone riders in a wild charge against a camp of rustlers, or if it was the same one who had saved four of them, when they were caught in a mountain blizzard, by breaking trail until his horse gave out and then going ahead on foot. Art Pendragon, one of the best riders and most respected men in the whole territory, carefully pouring cream into a metal tub and packing it with salt and ice. For the ladies.

Link muttered "sure", or something like that, looped the bail of the ice-cream tub over his arm — the one in the sling — and pushed off the porch with his crutch to make his way across the open yard to where the group of women was sitting. To make things comfortable for them there in the shade, kitchen chairs had been brought out and arranged around one of the small tables. It was a regular picture book tea party with fancy dresses and all.

Link's route took him within earshot of a cluster of cowboys trying to impress two young ladies.

"You see ol' Garth aboard Sunfisher yesterday mornin'? Wasn't that some ride?"

"Oh, yeah," another replied. "I reckon he's about the best bronc' buster *I* ever seen."

"Is this a wild horse?" asked one of the young ladies innocently. "What you cowboys call a mustang?"

"Oh, no." The first speaker laughed. "Mustangs run free and nobody owns 'em. What we call a bronc' is just some snake what needs remindin' almost every mornin' that it's supposed to be a saddle horse. Some of 'em are just natcherly ornery, and somebody's got to get on and ride 'em to a standstill at least once a week. And Garth, now, he's about the best."

"It would be exciting to watch," the other young lady said.

"Y'know what we oughta do," the cowboy mused, "is to have us a special day, like maybe a Sunday afternoon, and invite you girls out from town and ride our wildest bronc's for y' to watch. Lem here, he could show off how he ropes steers. Why, he can rope an' throw a calf quicker'n you can say scat!"

Link limped on past, a grim smile on his face. *These youngsters,* he thought. He remembered when he was their age, full of piss and vinegar, always ready for some excitement. He, too, had known how to make a bucking horse show off, had known how to make it look more dangerous than it was. And how to make himself look even better than he really was.

A strange thing happened as he came limping up to deliver the ice cream to the group of women sitting around Gwen. As soon as they saw him coming, a silence fell over them as if he had interrupted their privacy. If it had been a bunch of men sharing a dirty story and he had been a preacher walking up on them, the effect would have been the same. One of the other women was the first to see him. Gwen saw the expression on her friend's face and turned her head to look over her shoulder at him. She looked back at the gathering and they were all suddenly silent, some looking at their hands, some looking at each other, and none of them looking directly at him.

"Art thought you ladies would like ice cream," he said, putting the tub on the table. They'd need bowls and spoons for it, but he was damned if he was going to play waiter and fetch them.

The youngest, hardly more than a girl, got up and removed the top and looked in the tub. "Oh, yummy!" she said, dipping in with a finger and putting it to her lips.

"Thank you," Gwen said to Link.

Link heard a tone of dismissal in her voice like you'd use on a railroad porter after he set your bag down.

Art walked up to the group, smiling and carrying bowls and spoons and a pile of napkins. He'd thought of everything. A perfect host. He started to hand a bowl to Link, but Link didn't feel like staying there with these women. He didn't want to make things any tougher on Art, either. He didn't want ice cream, and he didn't want to chat, and he didn't want to be asked — for the tenth damned time — about his busted arm and leg. Suddenly he just wanted to get away.

The most obvious escape route was toward the dry field

of stubble outside the shade of the cottonwoods. Just beyond it, at the stables, there was a haze of dust and sounds of men shouting. The boys had something going on down there. Link turned on his crutch and muttered — "You're welcome." — as civilly as he could before stumping away.

As soon as he was limping through the stubble, he could no longer smell the lavender-sweet aromas of women's perfume, or the sharp, cold smell of ice cream, or even the damp, green grass of the lawn. Clumping along, he smelled only the honest smells of dust and old wheat stalks. Drawing closer to the stables, he caught the sharp and almost sweet stink of fresh horse droppings, and it pleased him. When he hauled himself up to sit on the top rail, propped against a tall gatepost, he was even more satisfied to smell the tang of a saddle someone had put on the rail nearby, a saddle still smelling damp with horse sweat.

Link was pleased to see there was only one woman standing by the corral. She was on the far side of it and he recognized her as the wife of one of the small ranchers from over in the Otis valley. Her husband was standing next to her.

Lem and the Pinto Kid and Dick Elliott were in the corral with two green horses, doing their best to get a lariat on one of them. Link studied the moves of each horse, the way it plunged, the way the back moved as the legs thudded down into the dirt. He imagined a rider up there on that animal, how the man's legs should be positioned to control the horse and still stay on. He remembered a medical book he'd seen once with a drawing of a man who didn't have any skin so you could see all the muscles and where they were connected to the bones. Link imagined the horse the same way, without its skin, and in his mind's eye he could see where the muscles would attach and how they would work. If a man could kind of be aware of that, he might know what the horse was going to do when one muscle or another one tensed up.

One of the horses was eventually roped and eared down, and Lem climbed aboard to try his luck. Link studied the arch of Lem's back critically and could see just how he should move and react in order to stay on. It didn't look easy, not by a long shot, but he could see how it all worked.

Dick came over to where Link was sitting.

"What horse is that?" Link asked. "Ranger?"

"Yup. Brought him in a couple of days ago, along with that other snake over there, Brownie."

"Brownie?" Link said. "Not much of a name for a killer horse. Or are you just funnin' me, calling that droopy old skag a snake?"

"He's a snake all right," Dick said. "Trust me. I don't even know why we keep him around here. Every time a man gets on him, he goes to twistin' and spinnin' and tries to break the corral down. And when y'do get him lined out and ready to work, he's just likely to start a stampede. He's scared of tumbleweeds, doesn't like to swim, and I think he's even night blind."

"Makes a good rodeo for somebody, then," Link said. "That's all he's good for?"

"That's about all."

"I figured you waddies to be down here showin' off for the girls. What happened?"

"Aw, nuthin'. They all went in the house to freshen up or somethin', and we never saw 'em again. We'd been talkin' about bronc's, and Lem bet us he could stay on Ranger, so we come down here to see about it."

"Tell you what," Link said, hauling his bad leg over the rail so he could climb down. "Soon as Lem has that Ranger horse wore out, why don't you catch up ol' Brownie and let me have a shot at him. If none of you boys objects, that is."

"Hell, no!" Dick laughed. "I always wanted to see a cripple throwed off a killer horse."

Ranger wheeled and pounded until the corral dust rose in thick clouds, trying to unseat Lem. Cowboys whooped encouragement and slapped their hats at the bucking bronco whenever it got near the rail. The odor of sweat and horse droppings now mixed with the smells of earth and rose to the nostrils on shimmering heat waves. To Link it all seemed about as peaceful as things could get. Looking off over the corrals and over the road and irrigation ditch, far out in the distance, he even imagined for an instant that he saw it again, the silvered mirage. No need to go anywhere. Right here was where he needed to be.

Old Brownie proved to be predictable, at least at the start of the ride. Link found that the horse would first put his hoofs together and hump his back, then spin to the left. After a pause, Brownie would lash out with both hind hoofs like he was kicking some imaginary wildcat. Then there would be another pause and the hoofs would come together to do it all over again.

Link also discovered that the casts on his arm and leg weren't as much of a handicap as he'd thought they would be. He used his neckerchief to lash the arm down to his belt, and, together with the sling, it was pretty much impossible for it to bounce up and down. The cast on his lower leg let him grip the side of the horse harder, too. As he was settling into the saddle, he even joked about it.

"You boys oughta try usin' plaster chaps sometime!" He laughed.

"You ready?" Dick said, holding the horse's head. He'd

blindfolded him with his jacket.

"Let 'im go and jump back!" Link laughed. "He's a real killer, y'know!"

Brownie was not a flashy, cowboy-crushing, widow-making mustang bronco. His leaps and moves were patterned and predictable. Link could picture in his mind how the horse's muscles looked under the skin and matched his own moves to those of the bronc'. It was all a rhythm, like square dancing with a partner who's able to match your moves.

"Ride 'em, Link!" came a cry from the corral rails.

"Whoopee! Look a' that crippled cowpuncher ride!" came another cheer.

"Ride 'em out, Link! Ride 'em to a standstill!"

But Brownie had one other trick that Link didn't anticipate. The horse had been through it many, many times, this irritation of some wiry two-legged creature strapping a saddle on him and climbing on. Sometimes he could twist himself quickly enough to get rid of it, at least get rid of the cowboy. Sometimes a quick flick of both back heels would toss the offender over his neck and into the dirt. But if that didn't work. . . .

Brownie came down from kicking, but this time he didn't gather his hoofs for a spin the way Link anticipated. He lined out instead, put his neck down and head forward, and went running full-tilt along the rails of the corral. At full speed he suddenly hopped with his front hoofs and swung sideways to smash the saddle — and with any luck, the cowboy — into the fence.

Link lost the rhythm and knew the ride had gone south. The only thing he could think to do was try to raise his bad leg out of the way, to swing it up so it wouldn't crash into the rail. He heard rather than saw the crash as Brownie's shoulder hit wood, and he felt rather than saw his own departure from the saddle, his good hand dropping the reins to fend off the rail coming at him, the *thwunk* noise of the plaster cast striking, then a loss of orientation as sky and rail and earth seemed to spin and wheel around him, then a sharp, ugly pain when his elbow, sticking out from the cast, smacked the lower rail. Then came utter blackness.

The next thing he knew, there was cold water running into his eyes. Lem was kneeling over him, swabbing at his forehead with a neckerchief he had soaked in the horse trough.

"You all right?" Lem asked.

Link groaned. The cast on his arm was twisted and the arm was on fire. His head felt like it had been squashed out of shape. There was a moist, hot pain running along his side under his ripped shirt. He looked up at Lem and said the only thing a cowboy can say under those conditions.

"Yeah, I guess so."

Lem and Dick helped him to his feet, collecting his hat and scarf for him. He limped over to sit on the edge of the horse trough.

"What can I do for y'?" Dick asked anxiously. "Y'gonna be all right?"

"Go to the forge, would you, and get me a big pair of shears or nippers. I need you to cut this cast off."

His friends protested that the doctor was due to return to the ranch that week, and that he had left orders for Link to leave the arm in a cast and sling, but it didn't matter to Link. All he could think of was getting it off before it twisted his skin right off his arm. When the big shears had been brought, and the cast had been cut away, he was grimly pleased to find how well the arm was healed. He rubbed the skin, which was bleached whiter than his other arm, and flexed his fist over and over. There was a long gash along his ribs, but nothing seemed broken and it wasn't bleeding too much. He considered cutting the cast off of his leg, but thought he might as well let it go a few more days since it didn't hurt. Too bad.

Word of the accident got to the main house quickly, and Art was soon there with his hand on Link's shoulder, peering anxiously at the arm. For a moment it was like the old days when the two of them rode together and fought together.

They brought Link his crutch and helped him limp to the shade of the bunkhouse where he dropped down on the bench. Art brought him a cup of coffee and sat down next to him.

"What the hell made you think you ought to start breaking broncos today?" he asked, more amused than critical.

"*That* I don't know." Link tried to grin and discovered that it hurt. He must have hit the railing with the side of his head.

Art looked around at the other cowhands.

"Maybe you boys could find somethin' to do," he suggested.

They left without a word. If Art was about to rip into Link, they didn't want to be around. Art waited until they were out of earshot before he spoke again.

"I watched you leave the party and figured you had to let some steam off. Don't know who turpentined your underdrawers, but I know you did a damn' good job while I was in Saint Louis. And you were the best man to do it."

Both men studied their boots.

"Been thinking, seein' you kinda down in the mouth," Art continued. "That trip of mine did me a world of good, just gettin' away for a while. Maybe you ought to think about doing that same thing."

"All the same to you," Link said, "I don't care a whole hell of a lot for Saint Louis."

"You know what I mean," Art said. "Take yourself a trip somewhere. Change your scenery."

"You been talkin' to Evan Thompson?"

"Matter of fact, yeah. He said not to be surprised if you had to get clear of the place for a while."

"I tried takin' a trip, remember?" Link said. "Me and the new kid went after th' horses and I got shot at, shot a man, broke myself all to hell and gone, and came back wearing plaster Levi's." He grinned, even though it hurt.

"Yeah," Art said. "Well, if you don't need a furlough and you're just goin' to go on *lookin'* for ways to bust yourself up, maybe we better assign you to be rough-string rider. Permanently."

Now both men laughed and the tension drifted away on the echoes.

"Nah," Link finally said. "It's pretty clear I'm not goin' to be any use on the roundup. If it's all right with you, I think I *would* like to draw my pay and pull stakes for a while. Maybe ride down and see how ol' Pasque is doin' with that Mexican spread of his. Evan Thompson wanted me to look up a fella, too, down along the Arkansas River."

Art now studied his friend's face. "You're not thinkin' of doin' something dumb, like huntin' those horse thieves, maybe? That's the direction they took."

"I'd keep an eye out for 'em, sure. One of these days, Art, we're gonna need to deal with that bunch once and for all. Havin' 'em on the range is like havin' a little grain of sand in your sock. Sooner or later you

77

gotta do somethin' about it."

Art looked out over the peaceful country, his country, sweeping all the way up into the distant hills. "I know." He smiled.

Both of them sat silently, just looking at the horizon.

"So when you thinking about leaving?"

"Tomorrow," Link said. "Might as well make it tomorrow." Link looked where the afternoon sun was slanting through the cottonwood grove. He looked southward and a little east.

Tomorrow.

Chapter Five

> Down the Valley of the Shadow,
> Ride, boldly ride.
> *"Eldorado"*
> EDGAR ALLAN POE

The following day Link set out early and rode south.

Leaving bunkhouse and stable behind, he crossed the creek flowing from the cottonwood-shaded ponds where Gwen liked to go. He rode up the hill and turned to look back at the headquarters ranch with its sprawl of buildings and network of fences, its patchwork quilt of plowed fields and enclosures. He rode across one rise after another until he crossed Bear Creek toward late afternoon and came to the end of Keystone land. He paused at the gate where Garth had set fire to the grass.

Next to the gate he could barely make out the old campfire circle where the kid had attempted to forge a new hoop for the barb-wire gate. Wherever there had been fire, new, thick, green grass waved in the light breeze. Some of the pine trees showed blackened branches, but, otherwise, it was as if the fire had never happened. The grass came back better than ever.

This was where Link wanted to make his first camp. After unpacking and stripping the saddles from the animals, he let Messenger loose to graze, knowing the black would not stray far. But he was unfamiliar with the pack mule, so he put it on a long picket rope. He cleared out the old fire circle and discovered the heavy metal strap Garth had described. The kid had intended to heat it and bend it into a hoop for holding the gate closed, until the fire got away from him.

Link took his rope and went to the trees up on the slope for firewood. Hopping from tree to tree on his crutch, he broke off dead branches and looped them with his lariat so he could drag them behind him. After he collected enough for his evening fire and morning coffee, he stacked them next to his bedroll so he could sit and feed the fire throughout the evening without getting up. He covered his saddle and the packs with a small tarp. It was a good camp, orderly and clean, and he was pleased with it.

He began the next day's ride by leaving the Keystone range and closing the gate behind him. From now on he would seldom know who owned the land across which he traveled, but there would be no problem — in that country and in that time a man, well mounted and neatly outfitted, was welcome to cross any range unmolested and often unchallenged. A Keystone man was welcome anywhere he went.

He crossed Horse Creek and spooked a herd of pronghorns that dashed up to a hilltop to look back at him. In a chokecherry hollow he flushed some prairie chickens. All the day long he saw life everywhere, rabbits in the sage, small birds in the thickets, a king snake sunning on a cattle trail, heavy bees rising from the wildflowers, prairie dogs squeaking from their mounds. He came across a maverick yearling and momentarily felt a twinge of regret at having left Art and the boys at roundup time.

"Hi-yah!" he yelled, and the yearling jumped with all four hoofs at once and plunged into the brush and was gone. Link rode on. All was silent except for the squeak of his saddle leather and the thud of Messenger's hoofs. He set his face toward the sun and rode on and forgot about feeling guilty.

Link came to an arroyo and made a detour to go around the head of it. There he stopped, and out of force of habit he considered whether another hard rain would extend the gully farther uphill. He sat with one hand on the saddle horn and the other stroking his mustache, figuring how a couple of men might collect some of the dead trees nearby and drag them into the gully to stop the washing. He was deciding whether to place the trees across the watercourse or in line with it, their branches upstream, when he brought himself up short and smiled in self-amusement. He was still thinking like a foreman who spent all day being bossed by a little notebook.

"What are you stopping for?" he asked Messenger, and prodded him into a walk. He was letting the horse find his own pace and his own path, taking care only to keep drifting south. They came down out of the low hills and came up against a railroad right of way, where Link discovered that the mule was frightened of stepping on the sleepers or even onto the crushed rock ballast. He also discovered that Messenger had little patience with pack mules. At their first attempt the mule balked on the lead rope as soon as it felt the crushed rock underfoot. Link turned Messenger around and they crossed back over. This time the black horse pushed the mule by chesting it and prodding with his head. When that didn't work, Messenger resorted to a few high kicks from his forehoofs and showed his teeth and snorted. The mule dashed frantically across the deadly rails and ties.

"Mules," he said to Messenger when they were once more under way. "Lotta people say they're smarter'n horses, but they're scared of their own shadows, aren't they, boy?"

Coming to where the dim trail branched, Link chose the way that led a little east of south. It eventually took them to a two-track trail of sorts, which became a wider, more traveled road after a while. Along toward late afternoon it brought them to a town called Live Oak. He stopped to buy supplies and under other circumstances would have taken a room at the hotel, treated himself to a bath and a barbershop shave and an evening in one of the local saloons. But he wasn't in a mood to rub elbows with strangers, not just yet. After securing his canned goods and the bag of oats under the pack-saddle cover, he rode east again, and camped at a creek out of sight of the town.

He would camp once more before crossing the South Platte, where he would again see the familiar, distant mirage.

Link passed through uncounted fences and skirted a handful of towns in the next few days. The old open range was getting settled fast, although he could still find miles and miles of rolling grassland where a man could go for days without hearing a human voice. Some men, he knew, savored such isolation. As for himself, being too far from other people for too long a time made him kind of moody. He had bypassed more than one town and had ridden around more than one ranch, but, after a week of it, he found himself kind of wishing he could have someone to ride with, someone to talk to.

That was why he rode toward the sound of the bell.

He was going along with Messenger in an easy lope, just for exercise. Messenger's hoof beats combined with those of the mule and the sound of the saddles so that at first he wasn't sure whether he had heard the bell or imagined it. Coming up over the next hill, he heard the sound distinctly and saw where it was coming from. It was a bunch of horses, ten or twelve, being hazed along through the grass by a young boy mounted on a docile old cow pony. One of the mares was wearing a bell.

Link knew why it had sounded familiar. On the big spring and fall cattle drives, when a half dozen outfits might work together, each outfit had its own string of thirty to forty horses. In each string a reliable mare was chosen to wear the outfit's bell, a mare that would stick around the wagon and not get homesick for the ranch and wander off. The other horses from that ranch would stay with her, getting accustomed to associating the bell with their own horse pals. Link had spent more than one night on horse guard with darkness so thick the only way to keep track of the horses was to listen for the different sounds of bells.

He made sure the boy saw him and then rode toward him, going along easy and coming up behind the horses so as not to upset them. The boy looked Link over carefully, and Link noticed he held his reins in his right hand while his left hand rested near the butt of a big old cap-and-ball revolver hanging in a deep holster from his belt. The boy's hat was too big for him and shapeless. His coveralls were neatly patched and his gingham shirt was sun-bleached. The lariat he had strapped by his knee had seen much better days. But he sat his old saddle with boyish dignity and met Link's smile with fearless cordiality.

"Howdy," he said.

" 'Afternoon," Link said. "Been on roundup?"

"Nah," the boy said. "This here's the P Bar T cavvy. The old man's gonna feed 'em until spring an' breed some of th' mares with our stud." The boy patted the fat bedroll he carried behind the saddle, and indicated the grain sack hanging beside it. No doubt it contained his food. "Old man sent me to fetch 'em. Been on the trail two nights now."

He was clearly proud of being a real cowboy, packing his own food and being trusted with this cavvy of tame mares and geldings. Link smiled at the thought of this slip of a kid lying awake in his blankets out there in the dark, out in the lonesome hills, listening to the bell mare grazing somewhere nearby. Out alone like that, a boy would probably be scared and excited at the same time. He himself had known such nights when he was a boy.

"Had any trouble so far?" Link asked.

The boy smiled proudly at having a fellow cowhand ask him such a question in such a way. "Nuthin' to speak of," he replied casually. "The other night I seen an' ol' lobo sneakin' down a dry gulch towards the cavvy while I was grazin' 'em. I got off a couple of shots."

"Hard to hit a wolf on the run," Link observed. "Don't even see too many wolves nowadays."

"Yeah. This one was a wolf, all right. Too bad I missed 'im."

"So, it's far to where you're going?" Link asked.

"Figure to be home tonight," the boy replied. "You're welcome to ride along, mebbe have grub with us."

"I'd appreciate that. The name's Link." He extended his hand, and the boy shook it solemnly.

"Davy," he said. "Davy Dunlap. Our spread's not but about a long gunshot from here."

The boy was trying to talk like a trail driver, with words like "spread" and "grub" and "cavvy". Link saw that his heart was good and his invitation sincere, and he rode along with him, letting the boy do the work of hazing in any horses that showed sign of quitting the herd. In between times, they talked together about bucking horses and smart horses they had known, or about Link's experiences with cattle. Link showed him his guns, and the boy told him the family history of the old cap-and-ball Remington he carried. Link mentioned his accident and pulled up the leg of his California pants to show the cast.

"Darn' near can't get the top of my boot over it," he said.

"Cow broke my arm, once," Davy said. "Tryin' to get her in the stall for milkin' and she knocked me right over the manger."

They made quite a sight together. Messenger walked with a nice arch to his neck and a proud lift in his hoofs, his rider tall and straight and lean, dressed in neat, dark clothes and carefully shaped Stetson, the thick, black mustache waxed to points. Next to him, the boy's old horse held its head as if the hackamore were made of lead. It tried to switch its tail from time to time, but its days as a tail switcher were long behind it. The kid rode his saddle straight up and held his reins loosely in one hand. Someone had taught him horsemanship. He would like to have worn his old black hat level with the horizon, but it was a bit too big and kept slipping back on his head. The gun belt was also a bit big for him, and, seeing as he had no hips to speak of, it tended to shift around on him as he rode.

As the afternoon wore on, the boy asked more and more questions about "cowboying" as he called it. It was his ambition, he explained, to leave the family farm with its meager herd of cattle and head farther west, maybe north towards Montana. Oh, he didn't expect to get a good job cowboying right away, he was thinking maybe he could find work helping to drive a wagon around a ranch at first, then probably they'd let him wrangle. He could already stay on, if a horse decided to buck with him. He could use an axe pretty good, and knew how to sharpen one. Knew how to hitch a team and grease a hub.

He was in the middle of this recitation of his skills when a pair of horses, two chestnuts larger than the other horses in the bunch, took it into their heads to lope away.

"Hey!" the kid shouted, wheeling his horse to chase them back. "Hey! Hey!" With a shrill whistle and several slaps with his soft lariat, he got them back into his cavvy. When he rode back to resume his place next to Link, he noticed something he had not noticed before.

"That there's a Keystone brand!" he exclaimed, pointing to the simple tapering rectangle on Messenger's flank.

Link pretended a scowl. "Might be," he said. "But I'll give you a piece of free advice at no charge, wrangler. Out here on the high open range it just isn't considered polite to notice the brand on a man's horse. Might be it isn't his, you see. Or might be he isn't where he ought to be. Or he might be up to something legitimate, but ain't none of your business."

"Oh," the boy said. "Y'mean like . . . well, I know you ain't no horse thief. I knowed that right off. So y'might be . . . say, you ain't some kind of stock detective are y'? Lookin' for those four horse thieves?"

"What do you know about four horse thieves?"

"Aw, everybody knows. Back at Webster's ranch where I picked up this here cavvy, it's all they talked about. Aw, damn, there they go again!"

This time one of the big chestnut geldings was on top of the bell mare, his teeth clamped on her neck right where the mane meets the shoulder. She whinnied in fright and rolled her eyes, trying to twist away from him while lashing out with her hind hoofs. He took another bite at her shoulder, his ears laid back low, trying to put a foreleg on her back. She screamed and kicked, throwing the rest of the small herd into a panic.

"Hi-yah!" Link yelled, charging Messenger into the mêlée. "Hi-yah! Quit that!"

He whacked the gelding a hard blow with his coiled lariat and pushed his horse between it and the mare. The mare kicked again, the blow catching Link on the thigh. On his bad leg, too. He pulled the reins over hard, getting himself clear. "Oh, damn!" he muttered. The pain made him cramp over in the saddle.

The boy rode in to whip the gelding away from the bell mare, and much to his credit he also managed to keep the two wild outlaws from running off. He stayed on one side of the bunch and Link stayed on the other, gritting his teeth from the pain and pressing his hand to his thigh, and between them they pushed the loose horses along at a fast clip so as to keep them too busy to fight with each other.

"Say! We're nearly there!" the boy said. "Yes, sir, there's the Dunlap place all right."

They topped a low rise, and the boy rose in his stirrups to point out a set of buildings down in a green swale below them. A man walking between the barn and the house paused to wave in their direction.

"There's my ol' man down there!" the boy said. "I tol' him I'd bring this bunch of broomtails in OK! I *tol'* him so! Well, sir, you come on along, Mister Link. We'll get this bunch corralled, and then you and me'll get washed up and tuck inta a good supper."

Link grinned at his new friend despite the throbbing ache in his leg. He wouldn't mind a good supper. He wouldn't mind at all.

The little cowboy's old man, Carl Dunlap, turned out to be slightly on the shady side of thirty, a homesteader with a wife and the one boy, gradually building up a ranching and farming operation. The moment they shook hands, Link knew here was a good man. And if Dunlap was likable, his young wife was a downright breath of spring. Sarah Dunlap chirruped over her son's wonderful accomplishment in bringing all those wild horses all that distance, praised her husband for raising such a splendid boy, exclaimed what a lovely evening it was, and how nice it was to have a visitor " 'way out here." Even before he had a chance to dismount, she made Link feel as welcome as a rich uncle coming to stay a while.

After the men had seen to the horses and had washed up at the pump, they went into the tidy little house and sat down to some of the best beef and potatoes and gravy Link had ever tasted. Even the greens tasted good, fixed with vinegar and salt the way he liked them, and her dessert of wild berry pie was a downright treat. Link's little sidekick shoveled the food up like a boy who had never seen food before and had no hope of seeing any ever again.

The following morning Carl was out early and busy with his chores before breakfast. Link's bed in the barn consisted of a couple of quilts on top of a couple of feet of straw, and it was so cozy and warm he couldn't bring himself to get up. It was nice just to lie there, listening to the morning sounds and watching the yellowish light from the rising sun coming through the cracks between the boards.

He heard the milk cow being moved into the milking stall at the other end of the barn, her bell clanking and Davy making low, clucking noises. He was probably luring her along with a handful of green hay. There was the sound of a corral gate being opened with a squeak of its wooden pole turning in a steel hoop, then the sound of a barn door latch being dropped into place.

From farther away came the sound of someone cutting kindling for a stove. It was that nice, clean sound of a hatchet hitting straight-grain wood and the thin kindling strip coming off with a musical *"barroinng!"* before dropping to the ground. He caught a whiff of wood smoke, letting him know it was time for a polite guest to roll out and turn to if he wanted breakfast. The cool morning air hit his bare chest when he pushed the quilt aside. Link shivered all over, rewrapping the bandage over his thigh before struggling into his pants. While he was here, he thought, he might as well cut the cast off his leg. It was a damn nuisance.

He was still shivering as he buttoned his shirt. Carl had left him a basin and ewer of water the night before, so there was cold water to wash his face.

Coming out into the bright morning, Link turned toward the corral and saw Messenger was already taken care of, his nose thrust down into a manger full of fresh hay, looking about as happy as a horse can look. Carl was nowhere in sight. Davy was making his way across the farmyard to the house, lugging a pail of milk in front of him with both hands.

Sarah Dunlap came out and down the steps to help the boy with the pail, and, as she did so, she waved an invitation to Link to come on up to the house. He didn't need to be asked twice. A few minutes later, he was seated at the kitchen table, cup of coffee in hand, watching her as she whipped pancake batter and greased a big frying pan for the eggs and a big square skillet for the pancakes. Link figured she was one of those women of Welsh descent, dark-haired, kind of short, perpetually energetic, always in motion, never without a big smile running from cheek bone to cheek bone. As she worked, she chatted happily about what a beautiful day it was going to be and the way the chickens were laying and what a good milk cow they had. She didn't ask her guest his name or his business.

"Have to tell you again" — Link smiled over the rim of his coffee cup — "supper last night was the best I've had in a long, long time. Those mashed potatoes . . . there's a cook back at the Keystone who'd give a year's wages to know how to make mashed potatoes that good."

"Thank you very much." She beamed. "My mother taught me. She was always proud of her potatoes, let me tell you."

"I feel a little guilty here, having breakfast without doin' any chores," Link said.

"Don't you worry about that," came a voice behind him. Carl and Davy had come into the kitchen, all scrubbed and wearing the expression of males who anticipate being spoiled.

Spoiled they were, all three of them. Link finally pushed his chair back a few inches after forking the last mouthful of flapjack into his face. He picked up his cup to enjoy the last of his coffee. He patted his stomach appreciatively.

"Ma'am," he said, "I've had flapjacks all over this country, made by everybody from miners to missionaries, and I never had any as good as those. They are about the best I ever ate."

"Thank you again," she said. "It's nice to have a visitor to cook for once in a while."

"Speaking of that," Link said, turning to the man of the house, "I'm wonderin' if I might take advantage of your hospitality another night. I could use the rest, and so could the animals. I'd be more'n happy to contribute to the cigar box, do chores, or whatever."

The man leaned forward with his elbows on the table and his coffee cup between his hands. He seemed to be sizing Link up, searching his face to see what kind of man he was. Finally he spoke. "Tell you the truth," he said, "I've got a favor I might ask of *you*. If you happen to be headed southeast, that is."

"Well," Link replied, "don't want you thinkin' I'm a range bum or anything, but I'm kinda headed in any direction the wind blows me. Kind of ridin' the grubline a while, lookin' the country over."

"The boy thought you were huntin' those horse bandits."

"Only if I run across 'em. I'm still ridin' for the brand, watching for good breed stock to buy for the Keystone, anything like that. What's the favor?"

"It's those two geldings from the P Bar T. I can see already that they're troublemakers, and I just don't need 'em around here. They look to me like animals that'll eat a ton of hay and need to be rode every day, besides. They're not even good for . . ." — he gave his wife a sideways glance, and she smiled — "for, uh, not quite fit for breeding, you know what I mean?"

"Yeah," Link said. "Know what you mean."

"Fact is, those two happen to have been bought and paid for. Not by me, though. I agreed that Davy could bring 'em along this far, and the new owner would come get 'em. I'm supposed to send word, but if you'd happen to be heading that way, it's only a day and a half, two days' ride. Maybe you could see your way clear to drop 'em off."

"Sure," Link said.

"Aw, on second thought" — the homesteader almost

blushed — "it's a heck of an imposition even to ask. Just forget I said anything. Have that last pancake there."

Link saw Sarah Dunlap looking at him and shot her a wink. "No," Link said, "I don't want to make any more work for your wife."

"Work? That there pancake's already made, just sittin' there on the griddle for you."

Link grinned. "What I mean is, if I ate jus' one more flapjack, your wife'd have to get out her needle and thread and go to work lettin' out the waistband on these pants. But if there's a sip of that coffee left. . . ."

The two men rose and went outside into the crisp morning. Link pulled on his Stetson and looked off to the south.

"Whereabouts is this place that owns the geldings?" he asked.

"That direction," Dunlap said. "They call it Hacienda Challa something. But don't feel y'have to do this for me."

"No, I think it's just what I want, some kind of job. Got nothin' much else to do."

"That being the case," Dunlap said, "I'd sure appreciate it. Let me just step back in and get a piece of paper. I'll draw you a map."

He sketched out the location of his own place and a few hills and arroyos and a creek Link would come to if he headed south and east.

"After a while you'll see a couple of buttes in the distance, box buttes. Twins, almost. Now, the road is pretty clear, but you'll see it turns to go around the right hand side of the buttes, the west side, like this . . ." — he sketched it on the map — ". . . but there's a smaller road that branches off an' goes between 'em. That's the road you want. Head between those buttes and you come to a dry wash. Up the wash there's some stone fins, rock formations settin' up on edge. And a sign or two sayin' 'No Trespassing'."

Carl Dunlap explained that the dry wash would take Link to a clear-running stream and that, if he followed the stream up, keeping to the two-track wagon road, he would discover a big, open valley hidden behind the buttes, a valley where a small stream had been split in half to run around an island. On the island was the dwelling of the man who had paid for the horses.

"Can I go with Mister Link, Pa?" Davy had been eaves-dropping from the porch. "I never seen that place, and you told me about it lots of times. He might need me for those broomtails. They're mighty cantankerous. I'd sure like to see that place."

"No, can't spare you," his father said seriously. "We need to get the pasture ready, and the last of the hay brought in. And I need you to ride fence, besides."

"Ridin' fence?" Link said. "You know, that's how I got my start at cowboying, Davy."

The boy beamed with interest.

"Yep," Link said. "No bigger than you. A rancher said he'd hire me if I could ride fence. Before you know it, I'd learned how to splice barbed wire with the best of 'em, and how to set posts good and solid, too."

"I can do that!" Davy said. "I'm a good fence splicer, ain't I, Pa?"

"Sure are." Dunbar turned back to Link. "I might better tell you about the holes."

"Holes?"

"As you get closer to the place, you might see what look like graves. The ol' man dug 'em. He digs 'em all the time. He's just a harmless old goat, keeps to himself and digs around the hills and buttes for rock. Got these two grown sons, both of 'em quiet and harmless and I guess they're sane enough. Then there's a daughter, grown-up, kinda shy and spooky."

"What are the graves for?" Link asked.

"Well, according to one of the boys, the ol' man was digging a cellar or an outhouse hole or something a long time back, when they were just babies, and found rock under the grass all through that area. It splits off into squares, like limestone does. He got to quarrying it up, and directly he started piling it into walls and stuff like that, and before long he has his castle goin'."

"Castle?" Link repeated.

"Not really. You'll see a tower, though. And these holes like graves everywhere. He's harmless. Just likes to pile up rock. He digs around until he finds some flat rock under the ground, then he rigs up his big ol' tripod and his block and fall, and he winches and levers the rock up out of there. Leaves a hole just like a big grave."

"Wonder if he ever loses animals down those holes," Link mused.

"Some are filled in, mounded up like real graves. 'Course, on any place you're bound to lose some stock and want to bury it. Still looks spooky, though. His boys don't know much more about it than anyone else, just that the old man's been doin' it all their lives. They hire out, breed horses, mostly. They get by."

"Tell me more about this tower. You seen it yourself?"

"Yeah, about two, three years back. Like I said, the old man's wheel seems to be missin' a few spokes, but he's a good stonemason. He cuts the blocks to . . . oh . . . about two by three foot, maybe smaller, and he's laid 'em up in a tower that's maybe thirty feet to a side."

"Round, is it? Like one of those silos?"

"Nope, square. It was about two stories high when I saw it, but it didn't look finished yet. I think he and the girl live in it. The two boys, they each got themselves a log cabin."

"Well," Link said, "you've sure got my curiosity up to see it. Funny thing is, I think I had a nightmare or two about a place just about like that."

"Believe in dreams, do you?"

"I don't know. I got thrown and hurt pretty bad up by Chimney Rock. Knocked me cold, an' I guess I was out for a couple of days. That may be why I had these nightmares about a big rock stickin' up, or some kinda tower. Chimney Rock was probably the last thing I saw before hittin' the ground."

"Might be. Man gets some strange dreams, for sure. Sometimes a good thump on the head does it, too, or so I hear."

"Well, I'll tell you what," Link said. "You throw in another night's feeding for me and my animals, and I'll wrangle those outlaws up to their new owner for you."

The lady of the house had been listening from the doorway. "Fried chicken tonight," she said, "provided you have your appetite back by then. We don't want you bustin' your britches!"

"I'll make sure of it!" Link smiled, turning. "Where's your axe and how many cords of wood you want cut?"

Mid-morning once again found the rider topping a ridge above a ranch and once again he looked back at the place he had left. This far away from it there was no odor of livestock, no clacking chickens or yapping dogs, no slamming doors or breezes raising dust in the farmyard. This far away it was all peaceful and clean and quiet and ideal. He saw the tiny figure of Davy Dunlap running across the yard away down there and felt a little pang of sympathy for the boy. By the time he was old enough to realize his dream of becoming a genuine cowboy, the range would probably be all closed up and boxed in with barbed wire.

The pack mule jerked on one lead rope as it tried to get to a clump of grass, and one of the geldings jerked on the other as it tried to bite its companion. Link ignored them and shaded his eyes into the morning sun. He knew what he was watching for before it materialized and came into focus out of the morning haze, the image of the tower all fuzzy and hazy at first, and then becoming distinct and dark against the shimmer of the mirage lake. He wondered if Messenger could see it.

"Let's go," he said to Messenger, touching his heels to the horse's flank. They went down over the hill and out of sight of the watching boy. They were three horses, a pack mule, and a rider dropping away into the haze-filled purple valley, riding toward the two buttes.

Chapter Six

Meadows trim, with daisies pied,
Shallow brooks, and rivers wide;
Towers and battlements it sees
Bosom'd high in tufted trees,
Where perhaps some beauty lies,
The cynosure of neighboring eyes.
"L'Allegro"
JOHN MILTON

It was all as Carl Dunlap had described it, the freight road bending off to the west around the two buttes, the dim wagon track entering the cleft between them, the cleft eventually opening out into flat land. Link came to a well-made fence; the board nailed to the gatepost read **H-C Ranch**.

After the fence the scenery began to change. Link had been riding through sandhills and dusty wasteland, but now he was in a more fertile valley where there were cottonwood groves and willow thickets with a few yellow leaves still clinging to the branches. The road turned to follow a creek rimmed with tall grass. The grass was bent over and matted but still dark green. As yet there was no sign of a tower or house or lake.

Link stopped and climbed down to ease the pain in his leg. One of the geldings had gone crazy on him again, making five or six times on that two-day trip, kicking him so hard across his bum leg that it was now oozing a little blood through the bandanna he had wrapped it with. It was swollen as though some of the bleeding was under the skin.

He found a rock to sit on and kneaded at the stiffness while the animals went after the grass like starved goats. He stood up and walked around a little, hobbling painfully. The day before, when that chestnut snake had tried to climb up into the saddle with him, Link put his hand to his Colt and wondered how much he would have to pay the owner for a dead horse.

"To hell with it," Link muttered, sitting down again and sticking his leg out in front of him. He took out his sheath knife, pulled up the leg of his pants, and started sawing away at the cast. Eventually, after he'd cut himself twice and used up just about every cussword in his vocabulary, it lay at his feet in white shards and scraps of old gauze. The leg was white and looked skinnier than the other one, but the bone felt like it was healed. He spent several minutes just scratching it, reveling in the relief it brought. He couldn't do much about the swelling — that would have to take care of itself, one way or the other — but he was damned glad to have that plaster off.

Sitting there, scratching at his leg and listening to the animals tearing up mouthfuls of grass, he heard another sound. It sounded like the *chink-chink-chink* of a steel bar hitting rock. It came from the hill to his right, like someone working in among the pine trees. Might be that stonemason busy at his quarrying.

Link tied the pack mule and two geldings to a tree and painfully clambered back up onto Messenger. The big horse picked his way up through the pines with his rider dodging the low branches, and directly they came to a tiny clearing. In the clearing he saw a deep, rectangular hole, a rawboned team of draft horses, and an antique hearse. A long-handled shovel and a long, rock bar stood upright, stuck into a mound of earth. The old black hearse had a tarp rigged on one side like a lean-to for sleeping, and Link saw that its original carriage wheels had been replaced with the wheels and running gear from a freight wagon of some sort. A long cargo box had been built under the body. Beyond this strange vehicle and the sorry-looking team Link saw a little campfire circle, a chuck box, and a sougan rolled out on the ground.

Messenger's ears tilted toward the trees.

"Not much of a place for a grave, is it, boy?" Link said to the horse. "Damned gloomy, if you asked me."

Then he heard the same thing Messenger had, the sound of somebody hurrying through the trees. He saw him, too, just a quick glimpse of movement.

Well, whoever it was, whoever had camped there to dig that hole, it was none of Link's business. Nobody was around to lay claim to those two damned geldings, and that was all he really cared about right at the moment. He turned Messenger and went back to collect the other animals. They would go on up the track and see what was there.

Before long he stopped to let the animals drink. The stream of clear, pure water ran swiftly between its grassy banks. Willows came down to the water's edge along with cottonwood and chokecherry. Upstream, above some riffles, Link saw something making small silver rings in the mirror-like water between mats of fallen, yellow leaves. Brook trout were softly lipping the surface for the last insects of autumn.

The horses and the mule showed no interest in resuming the journey and seemed content to stay there with their legs and noses in the stream. He resorted to his quirt to get them lined out and moving again.

The next thing he saw was a cabin beside the track. It

was just about the most tidy cabin he'd ever seen anywhere. The log walls had been adzed and trimmed by somebody who knew his way around a broad-axe, the logs coped to lie upon each other with scarcely a perceptible crack, straight and plumb with slender stripes of white chinking. The corner dovetail joints were closely fitted and angled so rain water would run out of them. The roofline was straight as a ruler, the shingles as carefully cut and matched as you would find on any house in a city. Out behind the cabin was a good corral, a sturdy log barn, another building Link assumed was for storage, and an open front shed with a blacksmith's forge in it.

On the wide, covered porch of the cabin there sat a man of medium height, smoking a pipe. He rose casually from his rocking chair, knocked his pipe ashes into a clay bowl on the porch rail, and stepped down to the tie rail.

"Good day to you!" he called.

"Good day," Link replied. "Nice-lookin' spot you got here."

"Thank you much. It suits me. You're welcome to light down and sit a spell."

"Thanks. Might do that. I'm lookin' for a place called Hacienda Chalma or somethin' like that. Fella named Bernard?"

"Hacienda Chalana." The fellow chuckled. "It means 'ranch of the horse-dealers'. At least, that's what it means in the lingo that passes for Spanish hereabouts. Tory's my name. I'm Bernard's son. Father lives a bit farther on. Old Tim's probably told him you're coming already."

"Old Tim?"

"The gravedigger. He came hurrying through here a minute ago, making signs that a horseman was coming. He's a mute, you see. You mustn't take it personal if he shies away from you. He's pretty harmless."

"So that *was* a grave he was digging, the one I saw back yonder. Sorry to hear somebody died," Link said seriously. "Relative?"

"Oh, nothing like that," Tory said. "Old Tim just digs graves. Digs them for women, or so we gather from what he manages to tell us. A lot of the time he gets one dug, and then doesn't like it for some reason of his own. Just leaves it, sometimes even half finished. You'll see them all over around here."

Tory walked over to the two geldings and examined them closely, running his hands over the necks and withers and picking up hoofs to look for damage. The animals stood perfectly still for him, allowing him to check their teeth and eyes and ears. At first, Link was surprised they didn't offer to bite, or kick, or at even shy away from him. Here, he realized, was one of that rare breed of horsemen who seem born to be with horses, a man that horses trust by instinct.

"Nice of you to deliver these boys for us," Tory said.

Link saw that the man was looking with some curiosity at his swollen leg and blood-stained pants.

"Why don't we turn them into the corral along with your own animals, and then see about this wound of yours. I imagine it hurts like fury."

"Hate to say it, but you're right."

They started toward the corral.

"Sure is a nice place you got here," Link repeated.

"I'll wager you've been wondering what we'd want with a couple of half crazy geldings 'way out here."

"I figure that's your business," Link said.

"That's the word." Tory smiled. "Horse business. My brother and I, we breed horses. We're working to develop a strain of heavy saddle mounts, a thousand to fifteen hundred pounds. And you're wondering what good are a couple of geldings to a breeding outfit, so I'll tell you. No good at all! But we'll train them to be a good wagon team. Then we intend trading them to a man we know. He'll give us the use of his stud in return."

"Horse tradin'," Link said.

"That's the word," Tory said again. "Come on. Let's get that leg looked at."

He took Link to a small, neat workshop next to his cabin. In addition to a workbench and rack of woodworking tools, the little building housed a narrow bed, a washstand, and a wardrobe made of wooden crates covered with a gingham curtain.

"Sit down there," Tory said. "Let's doctor that leg."

Link sank down gratefully on the bed and didn't protest as Tory tugged off his boots. He stood up again to struggle out of his California pants and his drawers and stood there in his shirt and vest and Stetson. Tory peered at the huge discolored patch surrounding the ugly scar.

"Broke the darn' thing a while back," Link said. "I was just gettin' around without my crutch when I got kicked on the same leg. Twice, in fact. I don't mind tellin' you it hurts."

"I can see that. You've got some bleeding going on under the skin there. Sit down while I go get something for it."

Tory returned with a steaming kettle, a pile of clean rags, a skinning knife, and a small earthen jar. Link gritted his teeth to hold in the scream tearing at the inside of his throat as Tory made three slices across the worst of the swelling. With his big hard hands he squeezed and pressed until Link thought he was going to vomit right through his pent-up screams. But he swallowed it back and kept it in, and he knew he was within two heartbeats of fainting into blackness when Tory finally stopped. As he wiped ointment from the jar into the wound, Link's gut felt empty and his head felt like all the blood had drained out of it. Spots and rainbows and bright flashes of light danced around the small workshop.

"That should help," Tory said, wrapping clean cloth strips around the leg. "I'll get you some bigger overalls to wear. Shouldn't wear anything tight over that for a while. We'll need to drain it again tomorrow, too."

Link groaned and fell back on the bed. He would have given a month's wages — if he was drawing any wages — for a pint of whiskey.

"No alcohol around here," Tory said as if reading his mind. "But you'll feel better directly. Now I'm going to get you those overalls and see to your horse and mule, and then it'll be about suppertime."

"Suppertime?" Link asked dazedly. He couldn't imagine being able to eat any time soon, not without having it all come up again.

"That's the word." Tory smiled. "You could use something to eat. I'll bring in your pack and saddlebags, if this shed suits you as a place to sleep."

"Fine," Link said, and passed out.

He woke to find the little building almost dark. He swung his feet to the floor, grimaced at the throbbing pain in his leg, and looked out the small window. There was nothing to see except a mist like old gray flannel covering the landscape. Wet and cold, it slid against the sash and rolled down the glass in little droplets. The door opened and Tory entered, followed by swirls of mist that twisted around the door frame and dissipated along the walls.

"Feeling better?" Tory asked. "Nearly time for supper, if you're hungry."

"Starvin'," Link said, surprised to find he actually *was* hungry. "Looks like the weather changed."

"Indeed it did. We get these little clouds pretty regular, 'long about evening. They come up the valley out of the south."

Tory gave Link time to comb his hair and mustache and do what he could to make his clothes presentable, then led the way out to a covered cart hitched to a single horse.

"Hold on a second," Link said, returning to the shed for Evan Thompson's roll of leather with the chisels in it.

"Got somethin' here for your father," he said, climbing in.

The cart had one large, leather padded seat and two oversize wheels. The top was a folding frame covered with leather. The jet-black horse standing in the shafts was such a horse as Link had never seen before. Its neck was thick and arched, its chest wide and deep. When the two men had climbed up into the seat and Tory lightly flipped the lines, the horse moved off with legs lifting high and sharp at the knees.

"Bred him ourselves," Tory said, nodding toward the black animal. "Turned out pretty good, too. By himself or coupled in a team, he can keep that pace all day long. I've got him broke to a saddle, too."

Link looked at Tory with surprise. The horse had to stand at least fourteen hands high and must have weighed over a thousand pounds. It was bigger than Messenger, and Messenger was considered to be a tall horse. The idea of using it for a saddle mount seemed almost ludicrous. A horse with that much muscle couldn't be much good when working with cattle, where a pony had to be quick and wiry.

"You're surprised," Tory said. "We hope to breed down in size, a little, and get a little less muscle in the shoulders. Not much use for such a horse around cattle. The Army likes them for cavalry mounts, though. Well, here we are!"

They stopped in front of a long, low porch where the dark mist dripped from the eaves. Link could see, dimly, that it was a log building that seemed to be attached to a wall made of quarried stone. He took his bundle and gingerly stepped down. Tory drove off to put horse and cart under shelter. While waiting, Link took a closer look at the stone wall running off into the soggy gloom; he thought he could just barely make out a corner farther down. He couldn't see any windows.

He heard a latch rattle, and, when the door swung open, Link was confronted with himself. That is to say, the man who opened the door would have been Link's twin had he been born with dark hair rather than light, and had he grown a full mustache rather than a beard. Even with the light hair and beard, the man standing before him was the same height, same weight, even had similar nose and eyes. Link had the sensation of looking in a mirror at himself wearing a blond beard.

"I'm Lavaine," the mirror image said with a smile. "Welcome to Chalana. Come on in out of the weather, won't you?"

Link was ushered into a parlor made over into a dining room. The brother who called himself Lavaine led him to the head of the table where an old-looking man sat. His back was bent from years of hard work, but, when the men approached, he made an effort to straighten up enough to look up at the visitor.

"Father," Lavaine said, "this is Link, from the Keystone

Ranch. He's brought us those two geldings I told you about."

"Welcome," croaked the old man.

"Evan Thompson sent these for you," Link said, setting the leather roll next to Bernard's plate.

Bernard's eyes lit up and a cracked smile found its way to one corner of his mouth as he untied the thong and unrolled the leather. He lifted each chisel in turn, eyeing the new points, running a callused thumb over the newly ground surface and trying the edge.

"Good," he said, picking up the first chisel again. "Good. That blacksmith knows about stone chisels. Look here, boy." He held it up to Lavaine and pointed at the edge. "See that bevel? Won't get nicked with the first blow, that edge. Thompson knows his business."

A thin young woman glided silently into the room with a platter of freshly sliced bread that she set in front of her father.

"Elaine, this is Link. He's delivered those horses for us. You remember. Father Nicholas said he'd be coming? Link, like you to meet our sister Elaine."

"Ma'am," Link said, nodding his head slightly. Elaine smiled and said he was welcome but nothing more. When Tory joined them, Link noticed a relaxation of the atmosphere.

"You've met Father and Elaine?" Tory said. "Glad to get your chisels back, Father?"

The old man held up the leather roll and grinned.

"Well, then," Tory said. "Let's eat. Link, if you'd take that chair there. . . ."

Throughout supper, Elaine kept her large eyes fixed either on her plate or on her lap. When she wanted something, the bowl of green beans for example, she would extend a thin arm and unfold the long, thin hand at the end of it until a long, thin finger pointed at the object in question, whereupon one of the men would hand it to her. Tory would rise and go to the kitchen whenever more food was needed, or to fetch the buttermilk pitcher. Elaine ate with a slow, methodical rhythm, lifting her fork almost as if she were meditating while eating. Bernard remained silent, bent over his plate, holding his spoon like a trowel he was using to carry mortar to his mouth.

After everyone had finished, the brothers carried the plates to the kitchen. Bernard moved to a rocker by a window. Link remained in the parlor, examining the pictures of horses hanging on the walls and the collection of guns in the open rack. Elaine folded the napkins and put away the napkin rings, and, after she had straightened the chairs around the dining table, she gave him half of a faint little smile and glided away through a door that Link assumed led into the stone part of the house.

"Now, Mister Link," Tory said, returning from the kitchen and indicating that Link was to sit in one of the several armchairs, "the thing is, you are to stay with us a while, at least until that problem with your leg is resolved. We offer a modest wage, simple honest food, and you have seen my guest accommodation. Or Lavaine has an extra room at his house, if you'd prefer."

"Awful nice of you to offer," Link said. "What kind of work are we talkin' about?"

Lavaine and Bernard entered the room and took the two remaining chairs.

"Horse work," Lavaine said. "Mostly. Tory says your leg needs rest, but maybe you could see your way clear to haze some of the ponies once in a while, when we move them from pasture to pasture, and perhaps help me in building a couple of . . . uh . . . breeding corrals. We all help out with the feeding and mucking out, of course."

Link was looking at Lavaine's beard. He ran his fingers over his own chin. He needed a shave. Maybe he would let his beard grow. . . .

"You're a Keystone man," Bernard said suddenly.

"Yeah, that's right," Link said. "But I'm obliged to let you know that I quit there, at least for now. Had what you might call a case of restless feet. Nobody's mad at nobody, but I just felt like I needed to be somewhere else for a while. I'm obliged to let you know, though, that I might take it in my head to go back. Sort of quit, but I'm still ridin' for the brand. Just so's you'll know."

"I'm sure that wouldn't be a problem," Lavaine said. "And I'm going to be honest with you in return." He looked at Tory, who nodded in agreement.

"In short, we want you to stay a while because we might be in need of your gun."

"My gun?"

"Some weeks ago," Tory said, "a distant neighbor of ours . . . the man I mentioned as having the stud horse . . . began suspecting that some of his bred mares were being driven off and kept in some remote place until they foaled. They returned with sore hoofs, showing signs of having had their foals."

"I've heard of such things," Link said, an angry furrow creasing his forehead.

"He thinks a gang of rustlers is driving off his mares, and then rasping their hoofs down to the quick so they won't wander far. When the foals come, the gang weans them early, puts their brand on them, and hazes the mares back toward their home range again. We've found mares, some of our own and some we can't account for, limping on bloody hoofs, half starved."

"Anybody who'd do that to a horse. . . ."

"We feel the same way," Lavaine said. "And we're afraid they're looking at our place next. Rumor is the gang has a hiding hole somewhere in the mountains, and they come out looking for likely stock, ranging pretty far afield."

"They might've come as far as the Keystone, too," Link agreed.

"People say this gang's been working the whole territory for several years now. So you see why we might like to have an extra gun around the place. Perhaps you could act as a kind of horse guard, if it comes to that. For as long as you could stay."

"Done," Link said. "I'll do what I can."

The cloudless morning came up bright and dazzling over the little valley. Link rose, stripped, washed himself all shivering with cold water from the pitcher and basin, then rubbed more of Tory's ointment into his leg and rewrapped it. After he was dressed and combed — having decided against shaving — he followed the scent of coffee and bacon to the back door of Tory's cabin and entered the small kitchen where breakfast was waiting. Tory suggested another day or two of rest for the injured leg, and Link wasn't about to argue with him.

"It's a nice place to rest," he said. "This valley is downright peaceful."

"That's the word," Tory agreed. "Peaceful."

After breakfast, Tory supplied him with a stout walking stick, and Link walked out in the morning air to exercise his leg. He walked up the road toward the strange house, taking note of the tightly strung fences running here and there to separate the valley into horse pastures, the haystacks and pole sheds where animals could shelter against winter winds and snow, the small irrigation ditches bringing water to the pastures. It was almost a miniature of the Keystone, only with the great sprawling spread brought into a few forested acres.

The narrow road curved off up the valley, presumably going to Lavaine's place farther on, and avoided a bit of lower ground where the stream divided. Someone — Link guessed it was Bernard — had built a stone dam across the creek. Higher up, a stone diversion made the creek split so it would run around both sides of a rise about a half acre in area. The house stood on this mound. It was either a two-story log house built onto a stone tower, or a stone tower with a log house attached to it.

The island on which the house stood could only be reached by way of a stone bridge. Link realized that he and Tory must have crossed that bridge with the cart when they went to supper, but he hadn't noticed it because of the mist and all.

The quietly flowing stream was like a mirror reflecting the tall tower attached to the house. About two and a half stories high, it was built of quarried stone blocks. He saw narrow, deep windows on the second floor — or at least he guessed it was the second floor — and a set of smaller square windows above that. Probably another room up there. A couple of windows stood open; sunshine glinted off the others.

The log part of the house was larger than most, but otherwise just an ordinary, well-made log house. The wood was dark with age and moss grew on the roof shingles. The tower's stone walls were also stained and streaked, so he couldn't tell which section of the place had been built first.

The morning had an eerie silence to it. No one was

moving about; no chickens scratched in the dust around the front stoop; no dogs or cats rested in the morning sunlight; there were no birds of any kind anywhere in sight. Even the stream flowed without sound, and Link wondered briefly if that's why it had been dammed up, to keep it from making noise. A movement at the tower caught his eye and he turned in time to see a window being pulled shut in one of the narrow openings. For a moment he thought he saw a face looking at him from behind the glass, but he could have been wrong.

Link turned and limped back down the road. He wanted to check and see if Messenger and the mule had been fed and watered. He might give Messenger a good rub-down and go over him with a brush. Then he figured he'd sit on the porch and clean his guns.

The warm sun felt good on his leg as he sat in the shelter of the porch out of the breeze. Link stripped the bark and leaves from a slender whip of willow, then took the cylinder out of the Colt and used the twig to push an oiled scrap of rag through the barrel. He swabbed each chamber of the cylinder next, and even unscrewed the grips to oil the hammer spring. While he was at it, he took the cartridges from his belt and cleaned specks of green tarnish from the brass.

The sound of harness chains came across the pasture. A few moments later, old Bernard came into sight, leading a draft horse pulling a chunk of stone on a cart. Link again thought of that book he had seen somewhere in his youth, the book showing the castles. One of them used to show a heavy-looking old hay wagon with wooden wheels, looking like whoever made it didn't have any tools except for an axe and hammer. Bernard's cart was hewn from logs, or so it looked from that distance, and had six small wooden wheels, like rounds sawed off the ends of logs. A pole stuck up on the far side, with what looked like a rope attached to the top of it. Probably some kind of brake. The whole outfit looked old and foreign.

The stone on the cart was a big rectangular block of light tan. Probably sandstone or some kind of — Link couldn't remember the name of it, but he'd seen light-colored rock like that in the Río Grande country once.

Old Bernard, bareheaded and bald, his dome shiny in the sunlight, plodded along with the horse. In his rough, brown poncho, he could have been a stonecutter from some distant and vanished age hauling another block to add to the castle walls.

When Bernard and his stone were out of sight up the road, the deep silence returned and Link's thoughts drifted toward the Keystone. While the brothers' place was quiet and restful as a cemetery, he was feeling the need for sound and movement. He wondered if the Keystone boys were riding the rough off some bronc's this morning, or maybe they were up on one of the high ranges culling beef cattle. They might be bringing in that horse herd from Rickard's Flat — Link could imagine the shrill whistles of the riders hazing the running horses along, dashing out with reckless speed to intercept a bunch quitter, whipping coiled lariats against their chaps to keep them moving. He imagined the smell of dust thrown up in swirls by the running herd, and the smell of the horses themselves. He imagined the nickering and whinnying of mares trotting with their heads high and nostrils flared, looking for their colts as they ran.

He remembered how it was to ride back into the main ranch after a pounding day of hard riding, loping into the corral, stirrup to stirrup in a pack with a dozen good men, then the whole bunch of them busy stripping off saddles and rubbing down their mounts, carrying saddles and bridles and ropes and gear into the barns, all of them talking at once about horses they'd seen that day and talking about how good it was going to be to sit down to supper.

And Link remembered when, on late afternoons like that, after a hard ride, he would end up looking toward the Pendragon house. Always that. There was always that moment, coming out of the corral or out of the barn, headed for the bunkhouse and a good wash-up, when he would look toward the main house. He invariably looked at that one particular window on the second floor, the corner window, because sometimes she would be standing there. It would only be a movement of curtain and a quick flash of yellow hair, or light catching a white dress behind the glass, but it was always enough to give his heart that flutter, that little bounce along the blood veins of his chest.

Link's fingers mechanically put the Colt back together, holding the cylinder into the frame while inserting the cylinder pin, without looking at what he was doing. He was looking up the road instead, the road leading around the corner and down to where the stream flattened out into a reflecting mirror and where a square cold tower of stone rose on an island. He was wondering who she was, the thin silent woman of Hacienda Chalana.

Chapter Seven

Field and Tower

Winter was late in coming.

Mild days without snow gave Tory and Lavaine and Link time to sort the horse herds, repair drift fences, and stockpile feed for winter. The brothers and Link quickly formed a bond of trust, that sort of unspoken understanding between men who work comfortably together. When he had nothing else to do, Link liked to watch them working with the horses. Before riding one, they would spend time visiting with it, talking to it, running their hands over it, softly caressing its flanks and muzzle as they walked it around in the fenced pasture.

Lavaine in particular could take a half-wild horse and touch it and talk to it and make it accept him. Within a week the animal would accept the saddle and bridle readily, and he could get on and ride it like a kid's gentle pony. With the two seemingly intractable geldings he took a bit longer because he wanted to be certain they would be a trouble-free buggy team. One by one he walked them and walked them for hours, holding them by the headstall, speaking low into their ears and breathing onto their faces. After two weeks of visiting with them and walking them, he gradually relaxed his grip on the headstall. Finally he could let go of it altogether and they would follow him like dogs trained to heel.

When they got to that point, he and Link put light buggy harness on them and patiently, slowly maneuvered them into position between two large draft horses, veterans with years of pulling experience. They learned to walk together, even to turn in unison. A few more days of those lessons and Lavaine hitched them with a draft horse between them. When the calmer, older horse stepped out smoothly, the geldings had no choice but to walk along. Finally the day came when the new team could be hitched together in full harness without flinching or moving a hoof. At first, Lavaine drove them with a buggy. Then he made them pull a hay rake until they got used to the rattle and clatter of it. He got out the long chains and taught the team to skid logs. He hooked them to his father's rock cart loaded down so they could barely make it move. In this way, he lessoned them in teamwork and rhythm. Sometime after Christmas, in February he thought, weather permitting, he would deliver them to their new owner and return with the stud.

The first real snow set in after days of gray clouds that only spit out sparse, hard grains of snow. Then it began in earnest with feathery flakes coming straight down like a lace curtain hung outside the window. Link and the brothers built up a blaze in the parlor fireplace after breakfast and were content to sit and look at books and watch the snow pile up beyond the covered porch.

Link's thoughts were of Christmas at the Keystone.

When Link first went to work for Art Pendragon, the fledgling territory presented a seemingly endless supply of challenges, the sort that thrilled the blood of young men. With Colt and Winchester they kept the range and foothills free from renegades and rustlers and marauders. There appeared to be a constant need for three or four riders to take the trail together on the way to help neighbors, even if they were only struggling to get a roof on a dug-out before winter or find where their cattle had strayed. Every winter they would be called on to ride out, two men side-by-side, on the trail of a pack of wolves or a cougar that had developed a taste for young beef. But then came Christmas. Always before Christmas came a peaceful time, a time when there was nothing to do except small chores around the headquarters ranch.

It was a time of grand dining. On any given day Gwen and Mary were either giving a dinner party or planning for one. Guests came from all over the territory, some from outside the territory. The house was extravagantly decorated in garlands of evergreen and ribbons and tinsel. Right next to the grand entryway a big basket overflowed with small beautifully wrapped presents, mysterious little gifts. Not a single guest left Gwen's house without carrying one of these presents to unwrap on the way home.

By comparison, Christmas at the house of Bernard and Elaine was scarcely noticeable. Link and Lavaine brought in an evergreen tree that they hung with homemade paper decorations and a few glass and porcelain ornaments Lavaine brought from his cabin. Elaine looked at the tree without comment, then went away and returned with a half dozen extra tall candles to set on the mantle and in the window.

Bernard, just as silent as his daughter, didn't seem to notice any of it at all. He sat day after day, either reading from an enormous leather-bound book or sketching in a big portfolio. His favorite spot was an armchair near the west window where he could stare out at the frozen stream.

"Mother died some years ago," Tory explained. "I'm afraid he's been this way ever since. We had just finished the log house for her and diverted the stream to flow by her favorite window."

Link wished he had presents to give. He wanted some

way to bring smiles to the old man and to Elaine, if only momentarily. He wanted some way to show Tory and Lavaine that the past couple of months meant something to him. He considered making Tory a gift of his best razor, since he was no longer shaving his beard, but he had nothing to give to the others.

On Christmas Eve, Elaine and Tory prepared a special supper. After supper Lavaine produced a bottle of brandy and the brothers persuaded Elaine to join in singing Christmas carols — just a few — while Bernard sat in his chair by the window. Once, Link thought, he saw the old man smiling to himself.

It was Elaine who provided presents. With a narrow-lipped, shy smile she brought them out. For her father, a pair of thick leather gloves to protect his hands as he worked with his stones. She had cut them from elk hide and laced them with sinew. There was a heavy, knitted cap for Tory, with an intricate snowflake design in horsehair woven into the crown. Lavaine unwrapped the brown paper from his and drew forth a new vest, a fancy one such as a man might wear to a party or to church. He examined it solemnly, almost reverently. With just a touch of shy pride in her voice, Elaine explained to Link that the material was from one of their mother's fine silk dresses.

For Link she had taken a long strip of another pattern and had made him a fine scarf, binding the edges with fine needlework and embroidering it with three flowers. On either end she had added fringe and had embroidered an outline of the tower. She unwrapped it and draped it across her hands to display the design, then timorously took it to where Link was sitting and placed it over his head to lie on his shoulders. It was an awkward scene, the thin girl-woman trying to smile without showing her teeth, bending

117

toward him but careful not to touch him, the tall, broad-shouldered man with flowing mustache and silky dark beard bending toward her with matching stiffness and caution. Her lips made a narrow slit when she arranged the silk around his neck.

Neither of them looked into the eyes of the other.

"I hope you'll have occasion to wear this," she softly said, her voice almost inaudible.

"It's real nice," Link said. "You must've spent hours doing all this needlework. It's real nice. Thank you."

Elaine said she knew it wasn't as grand as the embroidery he probably was used to at the Keystone Ranch, but that perhaps he could wear it to church or to dances. Link said no one had ever given him such a really beautiful scarf like it, not ever. A smile escaped from her heart onto her lips, but she turned it away and dropped her eyes to hide the sudden shining there. Head down, she retreated into the kitchen.

When Elaine reappeared, she brought coffee and Christmas cake. She did not stay to join the men. Old Bernard ate his cake quickly, crumbs falling over his coat, and then retired for the night. Lavaine put another log on the fire. Tory filled his pipe and lit it.

"So," Link began, "I heard your father started his stone walls on account of digging a grave. That would have been for your mother, I guess."

Tory blew smoke toward the rafters and gave Lavaine a look that seemed to concern which of them was to answer this. Then he spoke.

"That's the story we generally tell, yes. The old man did start building the tower about the time our mother died. But the grave was the work of Old Tim."

"Oh, yeah," Link said. "The gravedigger you told me

about. The one who uses a hearse for a camp wagon. I haven't seen him since that first time, come to think of it. But I've seen his handiwork, though. There's a fresh hole not far from the gate to the south pasture."

"He's shy of you," Lavaine explained. "As long as you're here, we won't see him much. But he'll go on with his work. You know," he said, turning to Tory, "that reminds me . . . we might just drag that dead deer carcass over to Tim's latest hole and bury it before it attracts more coyotes. It's starting to smell pretty bad."

"Good idea," Tory agreed.

"But this gravedigger," Link resumed, "he isn't digging to find building stone?"

"Oh, he finds some, certainly. Sometimes comes to get Father to crack it and lift it out of one of his holes. But that's not what he's after. No, he's just a man who digs graves. For women, he says."

"I thought he was a mute," Link said.

"If you ask him who a grave is for, he draws a figure of a woman in the dirt. But sometimes we use them for an animal that's died and he doesn't seem to mind at all."

"I think he appreciates it when we fill in one of his graves and mark it," Lavaine added.

"So he stays out there all winter somewhere?"

"He has a pretty comfortable dug-out back in one of the side cañons," Lavaine said. "There again, that's fine with us. I think just having somebody living out there might discourage trespassers. He'd come and get us if he saw anybody prowling around."

"So your father just got an urge to build himself a tower, huh?"

"That's the word for it," Tory said. "Just had him an

urge. We both know it's for Elaine . . . but we never mention that."

"Elaine?"

"Because of the 'affliction'. At least she calls it that. Not supposed to get excited. That's why she never wants to go into town, for instance, or have friends. Anything like being afraid, or maybe laughing too much, or getting upset . . . not supposed to do it. She can work and take short walks, even ride a little. But . . . underneath all that quiet of hers, she's pretty emotional."

"High-strung," Lavaine said.

"That's the word," Tory said.

January came with enough snow to bury the range grass and pile up deeply in the thick trees of the north-facing slopes. After that came a thaw to melt most of the snow from the open places. February brought drier, lighter snowfalls sifting over the pastures. Before the month ended, winter called an early halt to deeply cold days and snow-gray skies.

Behind the tower, old Bernard worked without speaking except to mumble to himself. With rollers, levers, and hoists he patiently nudged blocks of stone into place along the foundation wall of a new room. Coming from hanging wash on the line, Elaine watched her father a while and sighed a deep sigh. She brushed back an errant lock of hair and looked out over the winter fields and frozen stream, but her brothers were nowhere in sight. Neither was Link. She sighed again and carried the empty wash basket back to the wooden tubs on the porch. She looked at the sheets swaying wetly from the line, at the shirts of her brothers now clean of perspiration and dirt and animal blood, at her father's shirt and second best pair of bib coveralls hanging there like a sun-bleached, impotent scarecrow.

When she looked down at her thin fingers gripping the handles of the laundry basket, she nearly wanted to weep. Lye soap and boiling water, starch and bluing had left them looking like skinned rabbits, swollen and blood-red. The washboard had taken one thumbnail, all of it.

She hung the basket on its peg and eased her back by putting her hands on her hips and pushing them forward as she looked up into the sky. Now to finish the washday by emptying the warm, gray, soapy water from the boiler and tubs. She did it with a small bucket, as she had not the strength to lift the tubs full of water. She would dash the soapy water over the porch boards and scrub them. On her knees. She'd lug the empty boiler and tubs to the river to rinse out the lingering taste and smell of lye soap, then fill the boiler and the kettle with water, put them on the fire, chop more sticks for the stove, and begin to boil the pota toes.

She was grimly glad she had peeled and cut up the potatoes the night before, even though she did it by lamplight. Her eyes hurt. Her hands hurt. Her back hurt terribly, and so did her neck. Chopping the first armload of kindling for the stove that morning and then bending over to lift it, she had again felt that dulling rip of soft pain coursing up from her waist and under her left breast. But it was gone now and there was no time to think about it. The hour of supper was approaching and so too were the men who had been out working hard all day.

Elaine took up her small bucket and dipped it full from the first washtub. Perhaps at supper Link would tell them another story about the Keystone Ranch or somewhere else he had been. Maybe he'd tell that story about the giant again, the one that came to the Keystone one Christmas.

He would give her a smile and thank her for supper — he never failed in that — and she would take the story and the smile with her up the stone steps to her room.

Kneeling to her scrubbing, she looked again over the stream. This time she caught sight of Link and his horse Messenger trotting across the field. The horse's nostrils blew out frosty clouds and his neck arched like one of the Greek sculptures in her picture book. The man in heavy coat and wide Stetson sat tall against the late winter air.

Where the railroad crossed the Platte a few miles above its confluence with the Missouri, it was the second day of waiting. The ice was off, but gray winter still hung over the plains and hills.

The floodwaters were now only a memory asleep in the dank mud and brown débris that lay in windrows along both banks, marking the highest reach of the torrent. Teams of men in flat-bottom skiffs used boat hooks and poles to push mounds of sodden branches away from the bridge supports. High above them, hanging in the skeleton of the trestle, another crew finished hammering together scaffolding to stabilize the rails and ties until new pilings could be driven.

Two days of waiting, and another two before the stalled train could cross the river and continue the westward journey. To Art Pendragon, who stood at the edge of the flood-brown churn of water, the Keystone Ranch had never seemed so remote. Now it seemed like just a distant idea, just the way it had when he first conceived its creation — the massive main house with lawn and low, stone wall seeming to float above the ground like a mirage house with a mirage background of barns and corrals, more of a painting than an actual place.

That was how he had imagined it for years before it was built, and that was how he had built it, and now that was how he was imagining it again.

Art poked at the icy mud with a stick. He couldn't seem to put people into this imaginary place of his mind. No one came out onto the wide porch. No riders went jogging past the corrals. No one walked across the yard. Not even Gwen seemed to be there anywhere, the woman he always thought of as his bride even after four years of being married. And yet, he could remember all kinds of activity at that house. There had been his homecoming, complete with a two-day party for the hired hands. Then Link getting sullen and leaving. Then he himself leaving on another damned business trip back East.

Whatever happened, he wondered, to the old days when it was just himself and a half dozen other men working their cattle from horseback, covering miles of range with not much more than a bedroll and canned beans?

Art jammed the stick down into the mud at the water's edge and studied it, hoping it would tell him the river was still dropping. He listened to the shouts of the foreman at the bridge and heard an engine pushing the steam pile driver into place, then the chugging and the steady rhythmic rise and fall of it as it *whumpfed* pilings into the mud beside the sagging trestle. Débris floated past him — boards, limbs, logs, shed doors, and broken crates — and occasionally an entire tree slowly drifted by, turning over and over in the water, the bare roots clawing now at the sky and now vanishing beneath the muddy surface like a lethargic windmill or a rip saw blade coasting to a stop. Steamboat pilots called them sawyers, and deckhands were stationed at the bow to fend them off with long, iron-tipped poles.

Art's eyes followed one sawyer drifting downstream. He

imagined it turning and rolling that way all the way to the Mississippi, then on into New Orleans. New Orleans — the name carried the idea of glitter and glamour, of crystal chandeliers shining through goblets of old wine and throwing ovals of burgundy-colored light on lace tablecloths, of fine and venerable violins stroking wonderful strains of music across wide and polished floors. In New Orleans, come evening, men of gentility and manners would be conversing with women of infamous beauty.

He could, he thought, board a steamboat and go there. As easily as getting back on the train to Wyoming and the Keystone, he could get on a downriver boat to New Orleans.

Downriver was an older country, a civilized place. There a man of imagination and leadership could form another empire for himself, different than the one in Wyoming. It would depend upon shrewd dealings and integrity and personal ability, and in that respect it would be the same, but whatever it was — a lumber business, a bank, an investment company — it would have nothing to do with the whims of rainfall and blizzards and cattle disease and cattle thieves. Down there an ambitious man could have his pick of skilled, experienced helpers for his enterprise — the French craftsmen, the meticulous Spanish artisans and clerks, the Jews and Germans with their knowledge of buying and selling. Why return to a dependence on drifters and cowboys with only one name, or no name at all, men who rode in with little more than a six-gun and rope and asked for a job riding herd on a thousand head of expensive beef?

The slowly revolving sawyer drifted out of sight, and Art turned to look upstream past the sagging railroad trestle and the pile driver. He tried to imagine where all the water was coming from, all this flow and flow going ceaselessly toward the gulf, unimaginable volumes of it moving by day and by night. A man could get a horse and a pack animal and follow it upstream. The West had changed since the war, with people living everywhere it seemed, but a man could still set out with a gun and a few fixin's and trace that old river right back into history, back to where the mountain men had wandered free, back to where there still might be found wild Indian tribes willing to trade for goods, where the game was plentiful, and there was land free for the taking.

Up there a man would have little or nothing to show for a year's living, maybe a pack of furs if he was lucky, but everything he did have would come from his own work, his own dependence on himself. No one would look to him for anything, and he would return the favor. Himself and maybe a couple of partners, strong and reliable men, taking a living from the wilderness. It was the old idea again, the old dream.

Art heard the shriek of a steam whistle. The pile driver was being pulled back now so the work gang could walk out on the trestle and hoist and pry the bridge timbers up onto the new pilings. Art nodded his head silently, submitting to the fact that his trip home was at the whim of others. If that big Irish gang boss up there let his men break a rail, or for some reason just decided to let the whole job wait another day, then the owner of the biggest and most powerful ranch in Wyoming would, by God, have to sit on his hands some more. That short kid up there, the one being lowered on a rope to help guide a pole jack into place — he could fall, or get twisted up in the hoist ropes, or let his hand get mangled in the jack gears, and the train and Art would wait another day.

But, he told himself, the foreman wanted that train running again. There would be no unnecessary delay, not while the railroad was paying that gang boss to get things back on schedule. By tomorrow the crew would have the sleepers back in place and would have the rails spiked down and the cars would be carrying Art west again, back to Wyoming, back to the Keystone.

Art sensed a presence behind him and turned to confront a man in his mid-thirties whose appearance he would have called preposterous had it not been for the earnestness of the man's eyes. Clearly the character did not regard himself as preposterous, only individualistic. He sported a generous mustache and a thin streak of goatee. His hat brim was the widest one made by Stetson and was canted over at an exaggerated angle. He had leather fringe everywhere, from the epaulets on his leather hunting shirt and the gauntlets on his enormous gloves to the sleeves and hem of his shirt. The boots he wore were shiny black and reached to mid-thigh and were fitted with delicate English riding spurs. His neck scarf was identical to the yellow ones worn by U.S. cavalry on parade, except that it looked to be silk.

He stood, or perhaps posed would be a better term, with the butt end of his heavy-caliber Winchester rifle on the ground and his hands clasped together over the muzzle. Art saw no need for a man to be carrying a rifle, but he also saw that the man would seem incomplete without it.

"William F. Cody," the man said, as if answering a question. "And you?"

"Art Pendragon," Art replied. "Wyoming."

"Ah! The name of the Keystone Ranch is not unknown to me. I myself am in possession of a modest ranching establishment near the town of North Platte. It is, in fact, to that very place that I am now endeavoring to return."

"Same with me," Art said. "Here I was taking a chance, going back East in February, thinking the train might get stopped by blizzards. Didn't figure on an early thaw drowning the bridges."

"You have possibly heard of me?" Cody continued. It was the question, not the man that sounded preposterous. Anyone in the West who could read, whether it was newspapers or Buntline's dime novels, had heard of Buffalo Bill Cody and his exploits. Pony Express rider, Indian fighter, hunter, his name at times seemed to be synonymous with "Wild West".

"Must be kind of tame for you, just living in a little place like North Platte," Art said.

"Believe me, sir, the same notion has crossed my own mind more than once. But let me tell you . . . trusting your discretion to keep this information confidential for the present time . . . that upon my return to North Platte there will be a considerable surge of excitement. Projects are afoot, sir, great things. I should not be surprised to see, in the none-too-distant future, this very railroad crowded with important persons wending their way to our little community."

"Oh?"

"Oh, indeed. 'Awe' could be more apropos of the coming situation. Perhaps you heard of a Fourth of July celebration in Colorado some years ago. Cowboys roping steers and that sort of thing. One young man apparently was crowned as the Champion Bronc' Buster of the Plains, or something like that. And again, in Cheyenne there in your own district, the anniversary of our nation was celebrated with a display of manly talents, including the riding of wild steers and shooting at targets."

"Didn't get there myself," Art said, "but I heard about it."

"You will hear a great deal more this summer!" Cody exclaimed, his voice getting louder as he warmed up to his topic. "For I can now tell you, in strict confidence of course, that certain civic leaders have solicited my assistance in assembling what promises to be the grandest, the most unforgettable Fourth of July celebration ever seen this side of the Mississippi River."

"Quite a blowoff, then?" Art asked.

"Blowoff scarcely describes it, my friend. Why, we intend bringing in the wildest assortment of mustangs and broncos ever seen, and these fierce steeds will be challenged by the best cowboy riders from all over the territories. We will demonstrate the buffalo hunt with a running herd of no less than two hundred bison. My friends from the various Indian tribes will perform their barbaric rituals in public for the first time. Prizes of great value will be offered in shooting, sir, both in stationary and flying targets, pistol, rifle, and shotgun. The North Platte G.A.R. has formed a band to lead a street parade in anticipation of this event and to play at the arena during the performances. I can say with all surety that news of this great celebration will do much to raise the reputation of the frontier West in the eyes of our Eastern brethren."

"Maybe I'll get some of my boys to ride out there myself," Art said. "We might just show your flatland farm hands how real cowboys can ride."

"That's the spirit!" Cody said. "Come one, come all. Bring your chuck wagon and bedrolls as well, for the town's ordinary accommodations will be bulging with customers."

They both turned at the sound of a train whistle that tooted twice, paused, then twice more. The steam pile driver was being shunted onto a makeshift siding and the westbound train was calling the passengers back.

Mr. Cody took his leave with a flamboyant sweep of his hat. Art climbed up the embankment toward the cars. *This 4th of July get-together might be just what the Keystone boys needed. Everything was getting to be too routine around there. It'd be like a spring tonic,* he thought. *Just getting things ready to go to this shindig would perk the boys up. Afterward, they'd talk about it clear through the winter.*

He'd do it. He'd let the boys have time off to get ready for it. They could practice shooting and roping, or whatever. Any of them who wanted to go, he'd pay for the provisions and provide the wagons. *Let's see* — he began to figure in his head — *going to North Platte, it would take maybe two weeks total. They would need two or three wagons for bedrolls and equipment. Better figure on three horses per man, maybe take Pat along as hostler.*

Art walked through the passenger car and found his seat again. He opened the window, although he knew he'd have to close it when the train started moving since the air was still cool outside, but for now the fresh air felt good. After the train started, he would locate Buffalo Bill's car, get more details from him. The Keystone riders *would* be there. They'd celebrate the 4th of July in high style. *And* they'd show those prairie clodhoppers a thing or two about riding and roping.

The Keystone riders. The words felt good, held sort of silent and secret in the mouth like that.

In the long weeks between February's end and the onset of spring, the horse ranch between the buttes became a place of slow routine and perpetual boredom. Link spent days in his small shed, feeding sticks into the small stove, whittling sticks into toothpicks, reading the same few books over again, sleeping. It was a relief to struggle into a borrowed sheepskin coat and wrap his ears against frostbite and go out to help with the chores, although each man began jealously to guard his own chores lest one of the others do them and leave him with nothing to occupy his time. Each time he went outside, he seemed to feel Elaine watching from her narrow window.

After the thaw began, there was more work to do and they could range farther afield to check fences and doctor the livestock. Link made a circuit of the whole range where the brothers ran their different herds of horses. He drew crude maps and studied the terrain carefully, sometimes riding over onto a distant vantage point to look back. After a week of it, he was ready to take Tory and Lavaine out and explain his idea.

"Here," he said, pointing at a pasture meadow behind a rocky hogback, "here's a perfect place for those horse thieves to get at your mares and not be seen doing it. There's another such spot a mile farther on, up there."

He took them to a larger flat, where the grass wasn't quite as promising.

"Now, this is a place one man could look after. What I'm thinkin' is that, if you put in some drift fences like I've shown on my map here, you can keep your herds where you can keep an eye on 'em. Wouldn't need to watch 'em day and night, but you could ride out every other day or so and check on things."

"I see," Lavaine said. "He's right, Tory. Look . . . we fence off that hogback meadow, and that bay herd will graze up and over into that other one."

"Those damn' rustlers need time," Link explained. "I figure the way they work is to camp near a place, study it,

130

figure out which mares to take and what direction to go. Takes time to push a herd of horses off a range, too, especially if they keep tryin' to turn back. So you just don't use any pasturage where you can't check on it pretty regular."

Riding back, Tory brought up the subject of rustlers once again.

"You a pretty good shot, Link? You seem like you ought to be."

"Fair, I guess," Link replied.

"How about showing Lavaine and me some of the tricks? You know, watch us shoot and tell us how to get better at it. I can bring down a deer with a rifle, and so can Lavaine, but when it comes to pistols, I don't think either of us could even hit the ground."

"Practice," Link said. "Takes practice."

"That's the word," Tory said. "Practice. What say we find a place away from the house and get started? Need to be quite a ways off . . . don't want to upset Elaine with any gunfire."

They returned to the house for the noon meal, after which Link went to his small shack for his rifle and the extra boxes of ammunition in his saddlebags. When he came out, he saw the two brothers already starting to walk toward the low rise of ground to the west of the house and he followed. From time to time all three looked back to gauge the distance between themselves and the stone tower where Elaine stood at her window, hands clutching each other over her heart, watching them walk away with their revolvers on their hips and long rifles in their hands. Spaced well apart but walking together in concerted rhythm, they looked at the same time romantic and terribly dangerous.

Chapter Eight

On, ye brave,
Who rush to glory or the grave!
"Hohenlinden"
THOMAS CAMPBELL

They practiced each afternoon, the brothers becoming more proficient with every shot. When Sunday arrived, they observed the Sabbath with inactivity, Tory and Link sitting and reading, Lavaine braiding a headstall. Elaine went to her tower room after breakfast and returned in an hour to help Lavaine prepare a Sunday dinner of chicken and mashed potatoes, with pie for dessert. When Link complimented her on her attire, which was her best Sunday dress, her pale face took on noticeable color and she smiled down toward her plate. Later, in the quiet of her room, she repeated his compliment to the girl in her mirror.

The next day, the men resumed going out to the swale across the hill to practice shooting at a circle drawn with charcoal on a stump.

Link showed the brothers how to draw a revolver with a smooth, deliberate movement, using the weapon's solid weight to steady it. He showed them how to steady the forearm in the curve between waist and hip and squeeze off a shot. The trick was not to look at the gun but to look at the target and imagine the line between it and the gun barrel. The trick was to let the hand rather than the eye tell the mind exactly where the gun was pointed. And to be steady. Bring it out of the holster, let the weight keep it from jerking up and wiggling around, keep looking hard at the target, let the hand follow the eye, squeeze off the shot.

"That's the trick," Link said as Tory swung the Colt smoothly out of the leather and put a bullet dead center in the circle.

"Trick. That's the word for it." Tory laughed.

They practiced over and over until the brothers acquired the elusive "feel" for a bullet's trajectory and could tell where it was going even without looking at the gun. They moved on to flying targets, Link hurling slabs of pine bark into the air for them to shoot at. At first, all the shots went wild as the brothers tried to watch the flying target and the sights on their revolvers and their own hand all at the same time. Patiently Link showed them how to steady the gun with the forearm held against the body, as before, how to fix the eyes on the wood, how to swing the upper arm to bring the gun up in a firm arc until the mind said "now". He could do it every time, bringing the gun up in an easy arc and cocking it while the barrel followed a hard, green pine cone thrown by one of the brothers. They saw how the upward swing of the steady arm and the pointing gun paused just as the cone reached the top of the arc and hesitated. At that instant gun and hand and arm, target and trigger all became a single, sharp explosion: bits of pine cone flew away in all directions. The brothers saw how the thing was done, and before long they could do it themselves.

After that they practiced with more concentration, but less often. Spring was coming on fast and there was other work to do. They rode the hills and meadows, sometimes together and sometimes alone, keeping the cattle where they should be and checking on the horse herds. Sometimes, Link and Tory roped cattle for doctoring or to check the brand or just to put them where they were supposed to be. One old cow that was wise to the ways of ropes dodged Link's loop a half dozen times and he ended up catching her by one horn, which led to a wrestling match to get his rope back.

Tory rode up alongside as Link was untangling his rope and pulled out his Colt.

"I could shoot her for you," he said with a grin. "That way you could check why she has that limp in her leg and maybe even get your rope back."

"Don't think I didn't think of that," Link said.

"One of these days, we'll give you a few pointers about heeling a cow. That's the best way to handle 'em, heeling."

What Link liked best was chasing the small bands of horses scattered across the brothers' range. One herd of eight was his particular favorite: the bunch had a habit of straying around the end of the long drift fence and getting themselves onto an open ridge several miles away. There was a stud with this group, and Link figured he liked to be up there on that ridge where he could spot anything approaching his mares. Every time he saw the stud up there on the ridge in the distance, Link kicked Messenger and they'd go on a fast trot through the edge of the trees and up and down steep draws, staying out of sight until they could come up behind the band.

Then the race was on.

Messenger could anticipate every move of the running mares as the stud led them swerving this way and that way. He'd cut them off before they got into the trees, and then race them to a long draw and beat them to the other side. From there he could turn them back toward the drift fence. For his part, Link held on and waved his coiled lariat, shouting and whistling as the big black pounded back and forth over the half-frozen ground, guided more by instinct than by the reins.

Sometimes, the band of horses would get into the trees and then it became a breathtaking game of headlong tag in among the aspen and lodgepoles. Messenger jumped over deadfall, galloped in one direction to swing back suddenly and surprise the running mares, sometimes trotted around a thick stand of trees to surprise the runaways on the other side. Link loved it when they broke out into the open once more and Messenger would make a sharp galloping turn in one direction or the other, leaning at a perilous angle as his hoofs tore into the ground. Link leaned with him, balancing easily, horse and man intent on their quarry.

On one such day, Link and Messenger had galloped the band down off the ridge and Link looked back to see if he had missed any. There was a rider up on the ridgeline, his arms up as if he were looking through field glasses. Forgetting the stud and mares, Link pulled Messenger around and spurred him into a run up the ridge. The big black was tired from hard running, but to him the other horse looked like the start of another good chase. Clods of earth flew as his big muscles took them up the hill.

But the other rider was not having any of it. He spurred his horse and headed down into the timber, off the ridge and off the brothers' range. Link chased him as far as the bottom of the wooded valley, then broke off. There was being brave and then there was being foolhardy, and to chase a single rider into heavy cover where his pals might be waiting seemed foolhardy.

When Link told Tory and Lavaine about the incident, the three of them made a circuit of the entire range to search for campsites or any other signs of strangers. They found nothing, and the next couple of weeks went by without evidence of any strange horsemen. Tory went in search of Old Tim to learn if he'd seen anything, but the mute gravedigger only shook his head sadly.

"Reckon it was just one of 'em makin' a reconnoiter," Link said over supper. "Maybe he'll go back and tell his pals to try some place where there ain't three guns watchin' over things."

It was Lavaine's idea that one of them should go to town and shop for supplies, particularly more ammunition to replace that which they had shot up in practice. It was decided he would be the one to go, partly because it was his idea and partly because it would give him a chance to test the new team he had been training. It would take him the better part of two days to get there, and two to get back. Meanwhile, Link and Tory would hold the fort.

"Why don't you get yourself a good barbershop shave and haircut while you're there," Link joshed, flipping Lavaine's beard with his forefinger. Lavaine was putting his bedroll and food sack behind the wagon seat.

"Maybe I'll save my money to buy *you* a razor," Lavaine returned, feinting with his hand as if to pull at Link's luxurious growth.

From the porch Elaine smiled without changing the line of her mouth, amused to see the two bearded men joking with one another and glad that one of them was staying behind. Lavaine, looking past Link's shoulder, saw Elaine lift a white hand to him in farewell. He replied with a wave, but, when Link turned to look, Elaine's gaze was once again upon the floorboards.

The soft breeze blowing out of the west brought memories to Link, memories of February and March Chinooks on the Keystone, steady winds coming down out of the mountains and across the range like someone had opened a door from a warm room. He remembered how horses and men would stand looking into the wind with nostrils flaring to receive scents of thawing earth and fresh evergreen. He remembered one Chinook in particular, his second year at the Keystone, when Gwen Pendragon came out onto the porch in a dress of deep blue and stood facing the mountains as if inhaling the magical warmth into her soul. He had not meant to be near the porch and he had not meant to stare, but he had been and he could not help being captured by the sight.

Link drew a deep breath, and, when he exhaled, his shoulders sagged. Down here where the country was mostly mesas and sand, a warm wind was only another wind.

He looked toward the stone tower and saw a window open on the second floor. He could just barely make out a dark figure standing inside. Must be Elaine, wearing a black dress, framed by the narrow rectangle. He waved, knowing she was watching him. He saw her white hand move in reply, and she leaned out the opening to point down the road.

Lavaine was returning.

The team came along smartly, heads high, hoofs lifted proudly, positively strutting despite the loaded wagon they pulled. The trace chains jingled and the singletrees danced in rhythm. The horses were brushed, gleaming, and Lavaine wore a new shirt the color of sunrise and a new tan Stetson. Like the warm westerly breezes up north, he seemed to be a promise of spring and new life coming along the road beside the stream. Link remembered Art Pendragon returning to the Keystone like that, changing a drab day into a bright one.

It was almost like a Christmas, with Tory and Lavaine

and even old Bernard exclaiming over every parcel and box as it was unloaded and carried into the house. The father shuffled back and forth with a wan smile, taking some of the packages into his room and sniffing to locate the one that had his fresh supply of pipe tobacco in it. Elaine lugged sacks of sugar and cans of lard into the kitchen, followed by Tory with a sack of flour on either shoulder.

When they came back, Lavaine gave Elaine a bundle wrapped in brown paper.

"Got most of what you asked for," he told his sister. "Look, here's that red thread you wanted so you could fix mother's party dress. And more yard goods, pins and needles, and such."

"What's this?" she asked, holding out a smaller package also wrapped in brown paper.

"Smell it!" he said.

She held it to her nose and smiled.

"Soap," he said. "Real French soap. McCarthy made me a good price on it, and I knew you'd like how it smells."

Lavaine showed the men all the ammunition he had brought, then the keg of nails for carpentry, a new saw, and rolls of fresh, strong harness strap.

"But look at *this!*" he exclaimed, pulling a stiff cardboard poster from between two boxes of canned goods. "This is the best surprise of all!"

Tory took the red, white, and blue placard and read it out:

!!! Old Glory Blowout !!!
July 4, 1882
North Platte Nebraska
A Committee of North Platte Citizens Including
W. F. "BUFFALO BILL" CODY

**Invites one and all to a celebration
Including Prizes for
Horse Racing, Bronco Riding, Steer Roping and
Shooting**

♦ ♦ ♦

**Exhibitions of Frontier Adventure
And Cowboy Skills**

♦ ♦ ♦

Lavaine's eyes glittered at hearing the words again.

"Prizes!" he said. "Between Link's shooting and our roping, we're certain to bring home some easy cash! And better yet, Tory, better yet, there's bound to be horse buyers at a wingding like this. We could take our best saddle horses and our best teams and drum ourselves up some business. They'll be clamoring to have us breed horses for them. This is our chance, what we've worked for all this time!"

"You're right," Tory said, contemplating the poster as if it were a crystal ball. "Even if the three of us only won enough prize money to pay expenses, just taking some horses to such a show could be the making of us. Link, what do you say?"

"Sounds like what you've been building up to, no doubt about it. Sounds like what they call opportunity knocking."

"Opportunity. That's the word for it!" Tory said.

"Only, I'll stay here and look after things," Link added. "Somebody has to."

"Nope," Lavaine said. "I already thought of that. Me and the priest stopped off at the Nordanger place on the way home, and young Wen said he'd be more than happy to come stay here and feed the stock and take care of things."

"Priest?" Tory said. "Father Nicholas is back?"

139

"Yeah. I met him at the junction and he said he was on a visit. We rode along until we spotted Ol' Tim, then the *padre* dropped off to chat. He should be along shortly. Anyway, Link, you've gotta go to North Platte with us. Word in town was that all the big ranches will be sending cowboys to compete for these prizes. Including the Keystone, for sure. You gotta go, if just to see your friends again."

"Not so sure they want to see me," Link said quietly. "I left there just about roundup time when they needed me and, well, I'm just not ready. . . ."

"Say," Lavaine said, "wouldn't it be fine if you came ridin' in and they didn't know you? With that beard and all? I mean, what if you came ridin' in and whupped 'em at ridin' bronc's, or shooting? Wouldn't *that* shine, though!"

"I'll give it some thought. But I'm thinking, right now, we oughta just get you boys practiced up and ready to go. Like you said, it's a real good chance to get yourselves some long-term customers for your horse breeding."

"You're right," Lavaine said. "And think how much better it'd be for me and Tory to be known as the brothers who bested all the cowboys in the whole region at roping and riding! Yes, sir, this is our big chance!"

Lavaine had brought packages for Link — two new shirts and two sets of drawers, some socks, and saddle soap and such — and, as Link was taking them to his shed, he saw Old Tim's strange hearse approaching with two men on the high seat. A riding mule was tied on to follow behind. The human pair was even more mismatched than the team. Old Tim was dwarfish, stocky, and heavily bearded like a miniature Father Christmas figure. The other was a man who'd tower above any man of normal height, broad in the shoulders like a prize fighter and thick through the trunk like a wrestler. He wore a black Stetson, black trousers, and a black shirt beneath a stained buckskin hunting frock. Around his neck — what there was of it between his hulking shoulders and keg-sized head — he wore the black and white collar.

Priest and gravedigger seemed absorbed in conversation as the hearse rolled into the yard, although Link understood the gravedigger to be mute. Still, and without wanting to stare, he could have sworn he saw the priest's head bobbing as if in answer to something the gravedigger said. Link deposited his packages in the shed and stepped back outside.

The priest jumped down lightly and went around to untie his mule, which he led to the watering trough just outside the shed.

"Mister Link," he rumbled in a deep voice. "Late of the Keystone Ranch."

It was not a question, nor was it an introduction. It was only an expression of fact. Link stood quietly, having no reply.

"Father Nicholas," the priest stated simply. "I met your friend, the one they call Pasque, during his first journey southward. And, of course, I've known Art Pendragon since first he came to the territory. His housekeeper, Mary, is, you know, of the Holy Faith."

"I didn't know."

"Yes. Shall we wash and see what's for supper?"

Supper was a lively affair with Lavaine doing most of the talking. He seemed determined to tell the whole story of his trip into town, mile by mile, and all the things he saw there, all the people he spoke with, and the trip back home again. He described horses he had seen and how none of them could hold a candle to the proud-necked big animals he and

Tory were breeding. When the talk got around to the Old Glory Blowout, Father Nicholas expressed his own brand of quiet enthusiasm.

"The committee has glorious plans for this Old Glory day, glorious," he said in his big, deep voice. "I have heard there are already three new saloons rising along the main street just for the occasion. Cowboys from the Green River to the Arkansas are hoping to get there to show off their talents. I expect the town should also be preparing a larger hospital to accommodate those cowboys whose conceit exceeds their skills. Mister Cody certainly does not plan to provide any half-tame livestock, I can attest to that. Nothing but the most furious bucking horses and dangerous steers."

"You'll be there to give last rites to the losers, I expect," Lavaine joked.

"I'm afraid not," the priest replied. "That would be the jurisdiction of the local parish priest. I expect I'll be somewhere between here and Santa Fé, converting sinners and consoling the faithful. But tell me about your experiments with your horses. What have you produced since last I was here?"

Link rose and excused himself. He wanted to step outside, not because of any disinterest in the brothers' breeding program but because of this talk about a cowboy blowout. He knew Art Pendragon: there would be Keystone riders there, *and* they'd be challenging all comers. The certainty of that fact hammered home another fact he had not cared to face up to this point, and it was that he no longer knew if he was one of them. Or if they would want him to be.

Elaine was his other reason for getting out into the cool, evening air. The introduction of Father Nicholas to the dining table had made them shift their seating arrangement so that Link found himself next to Elaine, who seemed to blush each time he asked her to pass something and who seemed to give off a flush of heat at one point when their hands happened to brush together.

After a half hour, Father Nicholas joined him on the porch. "Your Keystone friends send you greetings," he said.

"But they don't particularly want to see me," Link replied.

"No. Pendragon is . . . well, let us just say he is troubled. He senses there are broad changes afoot in the land and does not know what to do. He senses you are somehow part of that change, and it troubles him that he cannot see where you fit in. The man has deeper worries than most people would credit."

"Maybe I'm not part of anythin' any more," Link said. "If things are changing, it's because the cattle business and cowboyin' has got dull. Seems like it's all bookkeeping any more, and routine. I can't see where's there's any spirit left in it anywhere."

"Will you go to North Platte?" the priest asked. "Your old comrades will be there. It might be that they would surprise you at how much spirit they can show."

"No, I don't think so. Don't get me wrong, I'd jump at a chance to take 'em on in some friendly shootin' or ridin'. But mostly it's that the boys need to go drum up some business, so somebody needs to stay here and look after things. Lavaine says he got a neighbor to help out, but it'll take two of us. Maybe you didn't hear, but there's a gang of horse thieves workin' the territory."

"I know them."

"You *know* them?" Link turned to face the priest and found himself looking level at the man's clerical collar. And

Link was himself a tall man.

"Their chief is a man I have known nearly as long as I've known Pendragon," Father Nicholas said. "Their base is an entire county, well hidden in the mountains from any pretension of law or government. Cattle and horses flow through their hands like quicksilver. Dozens of men, some with families."

"I've only seen one and heard of four of 'em, I think," Link said. "Unless maybe the ones we choused clear up to the badlands were part of the outfit."

"Small bands, foraging far afield. But you don't need to fear for this place so long as they know I am here. Rest assured, Link . . . here between the buttes is probably the safest place this side of the heavenly gates. Young Wen will manage just fine. Besides, one of you is *not* going to North Platte. Or should I say one of you is going and at the same time staying here?" Father Nicholas smiled at his own riddle. "In any event," he said, "you would like to go and engage your comrades in their contests. You also know, deep in your soul, that Missus Pendragon wants something from you, something which could cause great trouble between you and your friend Art. The choice is yours, whether to stay here avoiding it, telling yourself you are indispensable here. The problem is, the Keystone needs you. Art Pendragon doesn't realize it, not yet, but he needs to have you riding for the brand. Not hiding in this valley."

Link's forehead went into a furrow and he pulled a hand down across his beard — a habit he seemed to have picked up from Lavaine. The priest said no more. Wishing the cowboy a good night, he turned and returned to the house.

Father Nicholas stayed the night in one of the tower rooms. The next morning he saddled his mule, saying he wanted to ride around and look at the most recent additions to the horse herd. Link went some of the way with him in order to ride some fence and look over the cattle for one to butcher. They separated. Not finding what he wanted, Link turned Messenger back toward the house. He took a route through an open pasture and was riding up the opposite slope when he saw the hearse. It was standing beside a new hole, and Old Tim and the priest were kneeling there.

Father Nicholas made the sign of the cross, repeated the same sign over the grave, then rose and placed his hand on the gravedigger's bare head, looking upward as he did so. He had blessed the grave and now was blessing the grave-digger. The sight sent a long chill wiggling down Link's back. Was this why the priest was here? The new grave could be something to do with his remark that one of them wasn't going to North Platte. Maybe one of them was going to die. But how could the priest know that?

Old Tim rose to his feet and slid his shovel and bar into the back of the hearse. Father Nicholas spotted Link, waiting there, so he collected his mule and rode to meet the cowboy. Together they rode back toward the house.

"Tim feels better when a grave is blessed," the priest explained, as if that were an explanation for a man constantly digging graves where there were no corpses to put in them.

"So who died? Or is somebody about to?"

"We all die, Link. Each in his own time, according to the will of God. The man you see driving his hearse is not the only one who is always preparing graves for people. In a way, each of us has dug a grave for someone we know, if only in our minds. There's always someone for whose death we are always preparing."

"Maybe," Link said.

They rode along in silence, then Link spoke again. "I

145

thought maybe what you said about one of us not goin' to North Platte 'cause he would have to stay here might mean one of us was goin' to die."

"I see. But who can tell the future? Only God can tell who goes and who stays."

During the following days the big priest rested. He and Bernard sat at Bernard's favorite window, looking out at the stream and conversing in hushed tones. He walked around the tower and up into the rooms, running his hand over the joints and squinting at the corners as if making certain they were square and plumb. He walked or rode out onto the horse ranges or into the trees where he seemed to be as interested in the horse herds as in Old Tim's graves. Link had the impression he was inspecting the place like a cavalry colonel looking over an outpost.

One morning Link awoke and dressed and stepped out of his shed in time to meet the first rise of the sun. Father Nicholas's mule was not in the corral. Father Nicholas was not at breakfast.

Later that day, in the dust of the road, Link saw the mule's tracks pointed south. The tracks followed those of a wagon, a wagon that left wide, flat tracks with its iron tires. Link studied the tracks left by the team and it didn't take him long to figure out what they meant. Old Tim and his hearse with the mismatched team was traveling south, and Father Nicholas was riding behind.

Chapter Nine

As the Priest Predicted

"No! Hold it!" Tory shouted across the corral. "You've got your honda on the wrong side of your loop again. What did I tell you about that?"

The tables, as they say, had turned. Whereas Link had patiently instructed the brothers in the fine points of offhand marksmanship, they were now schooling him in the use of the lariat. Not that the cowboy was a novice: as a little boy living on the edge of a small town, Link started roping before he could ride, swiping his mother's clothesline to lasso the neighbor's terrified cat. With his first pony and his first real rope, he became the nemesis of stray dogs. But it was not until he met these two horse gentlers that he fully appreciated the artistry of the lariat.

"Step back another two paces," Tory said. "There. That's about how far you want to be from the steer. Now go ahead and build your loop."

Link gripped the stiff rope where it doubled behind the honda and gave it a vertical flip. The loop opened up.

"Now twist your elbow back like I showed you," Tory said.

Link brought his elbow back with his arm pointing upwards. It was an unnatural position, as if he were trying to throw something left-handed, but the loop flattened out and stayed open as he whirled it over his head.

"Point!" Tory yelled.

Link pointed his index finger down the doubled rope. "Throw."

When his finger came into line with the snubbing post, Link extended his arm the way they had showed him, not trying to "throw" the loop so much as just letting it fly away from his fingers as he kept his arm out straight and pointing toward the post. The loop slowed, then settled over the post like a butterfly landing on a flower.

"Good," Tory said.

"My damn' arm hurts," Link said, rubbing his shoulder. "If snubbin' posts were cattle, I'd have a thousand head penned up by now."

"Time we moved on to the real thing, then. Where'd you put that canteen? Lavaine, let's bring in a couple of steers for Link to practice with."

The live animals posed more of a challenge, especially to a roper on foot, but Link kept at it. Doggedly he built loop after loop, chaps slapping as he went striding through the corral dust after a steer. When he was in the right position, the loop would sail out, snagging the horns or settling around the neck. While he walked up the rope to turn the steer loose for the next try, Tory offered his critique.

"Your honda twisted too far over the rope that time. You do that on horseback an' you'll have your rope in a figure eight quicker'n scat. Just let it slide out of your fingers, like this . . ." — he demonstrated with his empty hands — "and don't be throwing so hard. It'll fly on its own if you give it the right toss."

Link knew most of this already. But a working cowboy doesn't stop to think about his technique. He just tosses a loop at a steer, and, if he doesn't catch it, he tries again. Tory made him care about each throw, like throwing knives at a target or shooting a rifle. He said it was like hunting with a single-shot rifle — one miss and you go hungry.

Elaine sat sewing in her little chair where the bright afternoon sunlight came through her narrow window. As she mended seams and darned socks, she watched the men practicing with the cattle in the corral. What distance blurred and made indistinct, her imagination supplied with clear detail. She imagined she could see the face of the tall man with the dark beard whirling the rope. She pictured his eyes shining with the pleasure of accomplishment as he expertly looped a steer. She imagined the grace and power in his arms as he pulled the rope taut and put a hand on the head of the range-wild beast to release his loop from the dangerous horns.

Her eyes left the work her hands were doing and gazed out at the horizon. And she went on imagining, envisioning a magnificent ranch where all the rooms were bright with sunshine from big windows, where yellow flowers danced on white wallpaper above damask bedspreads and coverlets. She saw it as a manor house like the one in her book, a grand mansion overlooking a cattle kingdom. There would be dozens of men like Link and her brothers, full of the joy of comradeship, living in a brotherhood of skill to which few men even dare aspire. She imagined Link with his flashing smile and wonderful eyes standing tall in their midst. Such worlds did exist, she knew, but they were worlds to which she would never go. Her thin lips drew tight in a smile at a sudden ironic thought: if her brothers were successful, their horses would go to live at such ranches, but she would not. Her brothers might even be invited to stay as guests wherever they went to buy and sell their livestock.

But herself, never.

Elaine looked down to her lap. She took up a pair of coveralls to mend, then let them fall again, and flexed her work-reddened fingers to get the stiffness out. With a cracked fingernail she scraped tallow from under another fingernail, a reminder of yesterday's afternoon spent making candles over a hot stove. The hot pan had left a blister on the web of her thumb.

Impatiently she dropped the coveralls to the floor and seized up a stocking of her own that needed darning. She was sick of men's heavy pants and men's heavy socks. She wanted to hold something delicate and feminine in her hand. But her rough fingers caught on the fabric as she slid the darning egg into the toe of the stocking. Her skin felt like the scales of a thick fish, rasping against the stocking, her dress, snagging everything they touched. The thin fingers with which she gripped the needle felt swollen like sausages, but in truth they were only numb and callused and reddened with work.

Her hands dropped into her lap. She raised her eyes and gazed through the window again, her thoughts taking themselves away from the dark tower. In the corral, the three men and two steers continued to circle each other warily, and the laughter of the men drifted up to her window to trespass on her silence.

"All right," Lavaine said, "let's see if Link can make the next five catches without a miss. If he does it, we'll let him start practicing from horseback."

"I don't know why I'm doin' all this rope work," Link complained. "I told you, I'm not goin' to this North Platte blowout. No, sir. You boys need to go, and somebody needs to stay here."

"All right, all right," Lavaine said. "Don't go getting testy. We're doing our share of practice. It helps to have you around to try our techniques on. Right, Tory?"

"That's the word for it. Technique. We let you do the

150

work an' we study the results."

Tory built himself a high, vertical loop, wrist-flipped it into a horizontal loop over his head, and expertly sailed it over the horns of a steer that was pacing around the rails.

"That's the word for it, technique. They say you never learn a thing until you teach it. Hey, Link, what do you know about heeling?"

"Before I ran into you two *hombres*, I would've said I knew what it was about, but now I ain't so sure."

Tory laughed and retrieved his lariat from the steer. "Then it's time we worked on our team roping. Give you a lesson or two tomorrow, maybe. Say, right now, let's see how good you do with a stampede!"

Yelling and whistling and using the end of his rope as a quirt, Tory began whipping the steers into a frenzy. Their eyes rolled back to show white and their necks went stiff as they pounded around and around the corral in a blur of flying dust.

"*Whoopeee!*" Lavaine yelled. "Cowboy! Cowboy! Get 'im!"

"*Yeee, hah!*" Link whooped, whirling his rope high and running sidewise across the corral to sail the loop toward the horned heads sticking up out of the whirling dust cloud. "That one! *Yeee, hah!*"

The loop dropped on the biggest steer. The steer wheeled and came for him, head down and horns slashing. The brothers sprang to the fence and scrambled up out of harm's way, leaving Link hiding behind the snubbing post, facing a wild-eyed brute bent on murder, all three men laughing like schoolboys.

"Go him, cowboy!" one brother shouted.

"Toss him, toss him!" shouted the other.

Link played with the enraged beast the way a small boy

might tease a puppy. He reached out from behind the post and gave its horn a twist, danced away to dodge the slashing head, popped the steer's flank with the rope's end and skipped away, presenting himself as a target, and then nimbly escaping, laughing all the while. The two men on the top rail hooted advice and encouragement, between howls of laughter, encouraging both of the combatants.

The sound of laughter caused Elaine to lift her head. She stood up and let the sewing fall unnoticed to the stone floor. Silently she watched the men at play, her cool eyes regarding the muscle and agility of Link engaged in mock combat with the steer. If an artist had been there, he could have painted her as a woman of ancient Crete watching an athlete wrestling a sacrificial bull.

She stepped back from the window, away from the pool of bright sunlight into the deep shadows once more. As she listened to the shouts and whistles of the three men, her fingers moved along the line of buttons on her dress, methodically undoing each one until the dress fell. She plucked at the lacing of her chemise and the ribbons holding her stockings. She undid the waist of her drawers, which slid down to join the other clothing heaped at her feet.

Nude, she stepped forward, taking two tiny steps toward the rectangle of bright sunshine. But the sunshine would be denied the touching of her, for with unblinking eyes she turned again toward the gloom. She walked to a carved chest, an old-fashioned immigrant trunk, and there she sat down, scarcely noticing the coolness of the old leather against her bare buttocks. She brought up her knees and wrapped her thin arms around them and rested her chin there and gazed unseeing into the dark, far corner of the room.

More weeks of shooting and roping followed. The

152

brothers had little idea what kind of cowboy skills would be tested at the North Platte Blowout, so proceeded on the confident assumption they would be ready for anything, no matter what. Several times a day they urged Link to change his mind and go with them, and each time he shrugged off the invitation.

"One thing you won't shine at, I'm thinkin', if this hoorah is anything like the Sunday fair back home," Link said, chuckling, one morning as they were saddling up to check on the horse herds.

"What would that be?" Tory asked, tightening a cheek strap. "Quilting? Paintin' flowers on crockery?"

"I can even bake a pretty mean pie, if it comes down to being one of *those* kind of July Fourth contests," Lavaine said, wrapping the loose end of a latigo strap out of the way.

"It's broncos." Link grinned. "You two are about the best horse gentlers I ever saw in my whole life, but, so far, I ain't seen you on a bucking bronc'. Unless you count that little bitty crow hop that Apache took the other day when Tory got on."

The brothers looked at each other. Link was right. Ever since their first foals, they had tamed horses by easy, gentle steps. If they brought in a horse that had been too long on open range and was "green", they always had time gradually to accustom it to the blanket, then the saddle, then the bridle, and finally the rider.

"I guess you might be right, but it's too late for you to help us do anything about it," Tory admitted as they rode out, three abreast. "But while we're on the subject, I wonder if you'd thought of something else about this blowout deal?"

"What's that?"

"Well, it's . . . well, it's that I wonder if you'd thought

about the fact that we'll be competing for prizes against some of your friends, men you rode with. Here you are, helpin' us get ready to make your own outfit look bad."

As they jogged along, Link thought about that.

"Seems to me like it's all right," he said finally. "First off, you boys need to build a reputation and there's no better way than to take some big outfit like the Keystone and knock 'em into a cocked hat. And second, maybe Art Pendragon needs to see whether his boys have gone soft or not. That's the one thing that makes me wish I was goin' with you, the idea of knockin' some heads together and showin' those wild buckaroos that they're lettin' themselves get too civilized."

"Sounds like you're talking about fist fights," Lavaine observed.

"Come to that, maybe I am. I'll bet the three of us could take on five or six of them in a good ol' bare-knuckle brawl, and come out top dogs."

They hadn't ridden far when there was a sound of hoofs coming up fast behind them. It was Wen Nordanger, all the way from the Nordanger family ranch on the other side of the buttes, anxious to start drawing pay as a horse nurse while the brothers went to the blowout. Wen came with a suggestion: his father would offer to board their band of pregnant mares while the brothers were away from Hacienda Chalana and watch over them if they began to foal. In return, he would accept payment in the form of a foal or future stud service. The advantages of Nordanger's plan were obvious — the four of them began that same afternoon to cut out and herd together the most promising of the bred mares from their various bands.

Two days later, the band was assembled, including not only the best of the bred mares but a number of "aunt" mares that would be there during foaling to give comfort and support to the ones giving birth. With the Nordanger family watching over them, it would be far easier for Wen and Link to watch over the place and they could go up to North Platte knowing everything was in good hands. On the third day, Lavaine and Wen loaded provisions into their saddlebags and began trailing the horse herd north out of the valley.

Link went on practicing the new rope tricks the brothers had taught him. Whether it was a steer penned up in the corral or a loose cow he encountered out on the range, he couldn't resist the excitement that came from kicking Messenger into a racing gallop toward the animal, leaning forward, his weight on the stirrups, building a loop as they ran. It was grand and free and fun. His arm and his leg were sound and whole again. Messenger was sleek and muscular and eager. This, Link thought, was the life he wanted. His first choice would be to go back to riding for Art Pendragon, but, like the priest said, there was something in the air, some kind of change coming. Sometimes, alone with himself and far from the ranch, Link let himself admit he wanted to see Gwen again. He also confessed his fear that he liked her *too* much.

That part of life was where women complicated everything. Men would tell each other they needed to be with women, even brag about how hard up they were after months away from town. What they really lived for, though, was just to be among men. Just do the riding and the hard work and talk about it at the end of the day, get up the next day and see what else needs doing. That's why Link liked the work at Hacienda Chalana. It was good to work with the brothers, and there wasn't any temptation to spend time trying to figure out how to go to town and get next to some woman, just because some bunkhouse Romeo started talking about it. The only female here was the pale woman who watched from the window. And even she had a way of making him feel uneasy. He felt her watching whenever he was anywhere within sight of the tower standing on the island in the stream. It felt like the shadow of something very ancient, suddenly falling across his thoughts.

A week went by and Lavaine did not return. Two more days passed and Tory often paused in his work to ride to the top of a rise and look off down the road. Elaine, laying the table for supper, would step out onto the porch, a plate forgotten in her hand, and look into the distance for her brother.

Two more days, and Link volunteered to ride out in search of him. The matter was debated and decided. If Lavaine did not come by morning, Link would take the trail.

The morning arrived and Lavaine did not, and so while Link saddled Messenger and rolled up his slicker to go behind the cantle and strapped the rifle scabbard into place, Elaine and Tory prepared a sack of food for him. He was all but ready to step into the stirrup when Bernard came limping down from the tower and across the stone bridge to where the three were standing.

"There," the old man said, pointing. "Comin' there."

They first saw the tall priest astride his big riding mule. A minute behind him came Old Tim's odd hearse with its mismatched team dragging along as if headed to a friend's funeral. At the bridge the hearse pulled up, and through its hazy glass windows they saw the figure of Lavaine lying full length beneath a blanket.

Elaine gasped. Her thin hands sprang to her cheeks. She

looked aghast at her brother's form, then looked into Link's face as if searching for help. The look in her eyes was so pitiful, so like a bewildered kitten, that Link put out a hand to her shoulder in comfort. Tory could only stand, head tilted forward, staring in disbelief.

"What . . . ?" he said.

"He's not dead," Father Nicholas said quickly, to assure them, dismounting and tying his mule to the hitching rail by the bridge. "Not dead."

Elaine rushed to the back doors of the hearse, flung them open, and climbed the step to crawl in beside her brother.

"Then what happened?" Tory said.

"I believe it's tick fever," said the priest. "He has all the signs. He's a sick young man, that much I know. When they arrived at the Nordanger place, he found a tick embedded just under his thigh and pulled it out. Next morning he was feeling light-headed, couldn't bring himself to eat anything, and by afternoon he was flat on his back with fever."

Link stood a little apart, not knowing what to say. He remembered the priest's prediction and now here he came, bringing Lavaine home too sick to stay in a saddle.

"One of you will not be going," he'd said.

They carried Lavaine into the house and put him to bed in Bernard's room. The old man wouldn't have it any other way.

"Can you do anything for him?" Link asked.

Link knew about tick fever. He'd seen it in other men, back at the Keystone and before that in Kansas. A man who got it was going to be a long time getting over it. His joints and muscles would ache for weeks, and it would be months before he felt strong enough to do a day's work. Men would work, despite the weakness, but you could see how feeble they were.

"As soon as I saw the fever in him," Father Nicholas said, "I rubbed him down with *cebadilla* and wrapped him in blankets to make him sweat. I think it will help speed the process of recovery."

"*Cebadilla?*" Link said. "What's that?"

"Deer's ears," Father Nicholas said. "A plant you find growing in the mountains. The Spanish *curanderas* swear by it when there's a case of fever. Also good for head lice."

"The Indians and Mexicans are always showing Father Nicholas how they cure people with plants," Tory explained. "Between praying and plants, he can pretty much fix anything that's wrong with you, body or soul."

"Very useful, the native knowledge of plants," the priest said. "But it takes caution. Your *cebadilla*, for instance. Some of the old people insist that it is a cure for the headache and for the cold in the head. Some take it like snuff. Others pound the roots into powder and put it up the nose before going to sleep. But too much of it can prove fatal. For myself, I use it only to rub on the body to induce sweating and draw out a fever."

Tory and Link and Father Nicholas stayed at the bedside a while. When Lavaine seemed to be sleeping comfortably, they went out and the two men walked with the priest as he led his mule to the stable. Old Tim was already rolling away, the hearse going back the way it had come. Bernard went to the back of the stable to load tools into his wooden, wheeled cart.

"Wen Nordanger is following. He should be here by dinnertime," Father Nicholas said as Link and Tory came up to him. "Now we need to decide the issue of North Platte, do we not?"

"What d'you mean?" Link said.

"Lavaine cannot go. Someone needs to go with Tory. It can only be you, Link. You must see that."

"C'mon, Link!" Tory said. "You said you'd like a chance to go up against your *compadres* from the Keystone. Well, now it's come. We'll go and whip 'em at ropin', and you can do the bronc' riding and get into the shooting contests. Why, Hacienda Chalana will come away looking like the best damn' . . . 'scuse me, Father . . . the best darn' little horse ranch ever!"

Father Nicholas stayed on at Hacienda Chalana, installing himself in Lavaine's cabin. Watching his daily routine, one would almost think he had always lived there. He rode his mule to every corner of the brothers' range. He hunted for medicinal plants and plants to use in cooking. He spent many hours in meditation and prayer, sometimes alone and sometimes with Elaine or her father. Link avoided getting into long private conversations with the priest, even though he gradually reconciled himself to the idea of going with Tory. As the day drew near when they must make their start for North Platte, he still had one hesitation, which he voiced at dinner.

"I just wish they wouldn't know me," he said. "I wish I had a magic potion like in the storybooks so I could enter the contests without anybody knowin' who I am."

"Not happy with being you?" Tory asked.

"That's not what I mean. I'd just like to be somebody else for a couple of weeks."

"Why's that?"

"For one thing, I don't want to look like I'm ridin' against the brand."

"Well, you would be!"

"Yeah. Be better if it was someone else doin' it, though.

159

A rider never likes to get shown up by another man he used to work alongside."

Father Nicholas chuckled at their conversation. Having finished, he wiped the corner of his mouth with a corner of his napkin, a surprisingly dainty gesture for so huge a man, blessed the table and crossed himself, and asked Link to follow him outside.

They stood at the end of the bridge, watching the light fade from the western sky.

"Link," he said, "do you remember what Evan Thompson told you? Didn't he say the story was working itself out?"

"I remember."

"Ever stood on a high place just at sunrise, looking east?"

"Sure," Link said.

"What did you see?"

"What do you mean?"

"What's it like, looking east at sunrise?"

"I don't know what you're gettin' at. It's like a new world startin' up, I guess."

"What happens? What do you see?"

"At first you can't see anythin'. Sometimes you're on roundup, and maybe you got the dog watch. Everybody's asleep except you an' the nighthawk, even the cattle, and it's black as the inside of your hat. It gets a little lighter, and you can see a little, but it's nothin' but shadows."

"Then what? I can't say I ever stood night watch on a herd!" Father Nicholas chuckled.

"Well, pretty soon you hear the cook maybe. He'll be stirring up the fire and bangin' around with the pots."

"And the light?"

"Oh. Well, all of a sudden it's all bright everywhere. Everything is sharp. One time, near Pine Bluffs, it got so bright I saw the outlines of trees on the horizon. Every tree. Whatta you call that?"

"Silhouettes?"

"Yeah. Only the sun was so bright I could just about see every leaf and twig."

"There's your answer, then," Father Nicholas said. "You ought to think about whether you're seeing things clearly."

The priest smiled at Link's puzzled look. Then he grinned.

"You don't need to be anyone else. You are looking ahead to North Platte and you are seeing yourself walking those streets. *You* see the man who left the Keystone, a man clean-cut but crippled up and confused. At North Platte they'll see a somewhat heavier man, a man with a thick black beard flowing from cheek bones to collar. Even as they begin to realize who you are, they'll see you in new light. 'There's Link,' they'll say, 'but he seems changed.' "

Link was suddenly aware of another presence, listening to them, and he turned to see Elaine standing there quietly.

"Perhaps if Link changed his clothes," Elaine half whispered in reply to Father Nicholas. "He could wear some of Lavaine's clothes,"

Link didn't know if he had ever before heard her say his name. She said it with a softness that in any other woman could be taken for coyness.

"Certainly," Father Nicholas said.

"He could use another horse, too. Leave Messenger here and ride Lavaine's. Or why don't you ride Rico?"

Link knew the horse and liked him. Rico was a big *palomilla* the brothers had brought in to breed with the Dutch horses.

"That'd work," Link said. "Good-lookin' animal, that."

The next day, Elaine went through Lavaine's clothes and

found two yellow shirts, much more colorful than anything Link had ever worn, and the new fancy vest she had made for him. She also brought Link her brother's pride and joy, a silver-belly Stetson with wide, flopping brim. Lavaine had shaped it to make the front part of the brim fall down over his forehead, shading his eyes. It didn't feel right to Link, who had always worn his hat with a crease in front and the sides curled up.

It was early evening again.

Lavaine raised his hand in a feeble signal, and Elaine took the supper tray from his lap. He sank back weakly on the pillows.

"All right," he whispered. "I ate something. Now do I get to see what he looks like, my new twin?"

"That's the word for it." Tory smiled. "He's just gone to change into one of your shirts, that bright one. He'll be back here directly."

And Link was there directly. But he was a far cry from being the person who had come riding up to the brothers' ranch so many months earlier. He was heavier, for one thing, the weight showing in a rounder, softer face. Not that there was much face to be seen — the low hat brim shielded his eyes and the full beard and mustache effectively covered the rest of his face.

Elaine did not like the change, but she said nothing. She could still remember him as he looked when he arrived, the tall, slim, dark Keystone rider with the soft, flowing mustache. But she had the consolation of knowing that all of this would be over in a month, or two months at most, and he would be back.

He would be back. She repeated the phrase in her mind, for it had a magical effect upon her. Thinking of when he would return was a thought that softened her eyes and relaxed the set of her mouth. Her Keystone rider would be back, her brothers would have found buyers enough to keep them in business for years, and the ranch would be on solid ground. Things would be better, happier, even if she could never leave.

"All right?" Link said, looking down at himself.

"It's almost eerie," Lavaine said from his couch. "If Link's beard was the same shade as mine, it'd almost be like I'm two men."

The sick brother drank some water and fell back on the pillows.

"It's . . . it's eerie seein' you in my shirt and vest like that. When you and Tory leave in the morning, it'll be like I'm goin' and stayin' here at the same time."

"I have something for you," Elaine said. Once again there was something in her voice that startled Link, something that worried him.

She left the room and returned carrying a neckerchief she had made for him out of yellow silk, a big square folded from corner to corner. She held it out so they could see her embroidery; upon the silk she had worked a design of the intertwined H and C of the brothers' brand, together with an outline of the tower at each corner.

"You need something to match your shirt," she said shyly. "I stayed up late making it. You shouldn't wear your Christmas scarf, but you need something."

With a nearness that disturbed Link's senses almost as much as her sudden tenderness, she came to him and stood on tiptoe to put it around his neck.

"For luck," she said. "Wear it at the contests."

"I will," he promised. It was a promise he would keep. He said it quickly, saying it clearly and in a full voice. He wanted her to step farther away from him and stop looking at him with those imploring eyes that way.

Link returned to his shed and changed back to his own shirt, putting the bright yellow one and the neckerchief into his saddlebags. Or rather into Lavaine's saddlebags, for along with the sick man's horse he was taking his saddle, boots, duster, and all. Elaine, with that same look, solemnly promised Link to look after his saddle and gear while he was gone. She also promised him she would take care of Messenger.

"I'll brush him every day," she said softly, her eyes searching his face, "and I'll clean his saddle and bridle with saddle soap and rub them with neatsfoot and keep them covered so no dust will get on them. When you come back, they will be like new for you."

The herd of horses they had picked to show off at North Platte were in the corral. A roundup tent, cooking gear, and blankets were in panniers ready to be loaded onto the pack horse. They had breakfast at first light, and by the time the rising sun peeked over the eastern rim of the world, it saw them lined out and pushing their little cavvy northward. Link looked back once at the tower with the sunrise shining on it, and at the stream splitting and going around the island on which the tower stood, then turned his face toward North Platte and looked backward no more.

There was another witness to their departure. The grave-digger saw them go, sitting on the high seat of his curious hearse. After a time he clucked to his team and snapped the lines, and his horses stepped out, trudging northward in the dusty wake of the two cowboys and their herd.

Chapter Ten

Those Who Ride and Those Who Wait

Many miles to the north of the two mesas and some distance west, in the upstairs room of another house, another woman stood gazing from her window. Like the sun-filled room and like herself, everything she saw beyond her walls was orderly and correct. She considered the split-rail fence surrounding the tidy yard, the graveled roadway passing beneath the imposing gateway, the clusters of painted and shingled outbuildings. A few milk cows grazed in a green pasture and a few saddle horses stood dozing in the sun in another fenced pasture. No amount of morning brilliance could illuminate a single flaw in any of it.

To the east she saw the far plains rising and falling, each small hill and bluff made distinct by a morning haze in the valleys. There was mystery about that vista; every time she looked out in that direction the light had changed to show yet another unexplored bluff or the shadow of an unvisited leafy grove. She paced across the room toward the door, thinking of asking Pat to saddle a light horse for her so she could take an impulsive gallop beyond the Keystone fence. Then remembering she was in her nightdress — the lavender silk Art liked so much — she turned back. She wanted to go riding, wild and free, yet she also wanted to remain where she was.

She returned to her window ledge and gripped the painted wood until her knuckles whitened.

Art and eight of his best riders had ridden to the Independence Day Blowout a few days early in hopes of staking out a choice campsite somewhere near North Platte. Gwen had been invited to go along, it was true. Art had asked her several times. His mind, however, was more concerned with details about wagons and horses and supplies. Emil had also asked her, very politely. He had urged her to come along and watch the Keystone cowboys put all other riders and ropers to shame. She found his enthusiasm as charming as his invitation, but could not help noticing that Art and Emil and the others were champing at the bit to get away from houses and soft beds — and women — and pit their skills against those of other men. It was in their carriage, in the very tone of their voices; the men were eager for competition and recognition, for the world of men.

Gwen twisted the wide sash of her lavender silk nightdress into a knot. All year long she was the one who invited Art's cowboys to dine in the main house, the one who sat and smiled at their stories of man-killing broncos and crazed range bulls. It was she who went to the bunkhouse with her medicine chest and murmured sympathy over their wounds, she who put a gloved hand on the corral rail and, with a smile, rewarded a cowboy's victory over a bucking horse. And then they read that one ridiculous poster, that garish promise of prizes and cheap acclaim, and in a circus-like display of male vanity, they go trooping off into Nebraska like schoolboys running to play at foot races and wrestling contests.

Ridiculous.

Yet, why should she remain cooped up in the house? She picked up the brush and stroked her hair, her eyes fixed on the eastern horizon where the hazy bluffs and hills met the light-blue morning sky. A burly figure of a man came into view beneath her window, walking toward the house. She raised her window and leaned out, the sun catching her loose hair as it fell forward over the casement.

"Bob!" she called. "Bob Riley!"

The man looked up at the window, seeing first the cascade of blonde hair and then the face of the boss's wife.

" 'Morning, ma'am!" he said cheerily.

"Bob, any news from town? Did you find the things you needed?"

"Yes, ma'am." Bob Riley smiled. Riley was the foreman in charge at the headquarters ranch. He was one of very few men who could feel comfortable talking to the boss's wife this way, with her upstairs and in her nightgown and all.

"Anyone new in town?" she asked.

"Just a tinker," Riley said. "At least he's the only one I saw. I bought a bunch of geegaws off of him, and a new pocket knife."

"Oh," she said. "I just thought perhaps you'd seen . . . new houses being built, or new stores."

"The tinker said there's a new family out south of town on Coal Creek."

"That's nice."

"Oh, and he said there's a new man working for John Peters. The tinker thought he looked familiar. Kind of tall, dark, big mustache. John's gettin' more work from farmers these days, so he had to hire somebody to help sharpen plows and discs and the like."

"Did you recognize him?" Gwen felt a little flush rising to her cheeks and her eyes involuntarily looked off in the direction of town.

"Didn't see him. I stopped off at John's to pick up those heavy harness tugs he made special for Mister Pendragon, but didn't see any new man. Guess he was off somewhere. So that's all I know, what the tinker said."

Bob Riley wished Gwen a good day and entered the back door to get a tally book off Art's desk. Gwen stepped back into the room, where the walls seemed closer than before. Perhaps she might buy some new wallpaper — or curtains — something to surprise Art when he came home from his Independence Day fling. At least she could go into town and look at samples. A few days in town would be nice. She could stay with her friends, catch up on news, shop for all sorts of little things she had been needing.

She probably shouldn't be going, but, if the man working at the smithy *were* to turn out to be Link, Art would want her to speak to him and persuade him to come back to the ranch. They were short-handed, after all. Art himself said good men were getting scarce. She really should find out, just to be sure.

Gwen opened both her closet doors and considered her wardrobe as she dressed. She would take the new riding outfit, since her friend Amelia always liked to go riding. She ought to take two outfits, just to be safe, the deep red riding skirt as well as the light tan one. This shirtwaist that she had worn only once, and the one in striped silk. And the other striped one, the one that fit a bit more tightly. She needed to take her riding boots and her fancy boots as well as her button-up shoes to wear to supper. Sitting down to polite supper in town also meant she needed to take the white dress, and her best petticoat.

When she stepped into the kitchen, Bob Riley was there, lounging against the pie safe, coffee in one hand and one of Mary's cinnamon rolls in the other.

" 'Morning!" he repeated. "Beautiful day shapin' up out there, so far."

She smiled at him and agreed that it did, indeed, look like a lovely day. She poured herself a cup of coffee and cut half a cinnamon roll that she put on a plate and took to the table. Settled in her chair, she spoke again.

"Bob, I've decided to ride into town for a few days. I'd like to look at some wallpaper and curtains and things. I'll be staying with Amelia's family. Can you spare one of the men to drive me?"

"Yes, ma'am, I'd guess I could find somebody I could manage without for a few days."

"Fine. If you'd have him hitch up the buggy and team? I like the one with the two seats and light-colored wood, the one with the yellowish top. You should ask him to put in several blankets and a tarp or something for shelter, just in case. And some feed for the horses. I'll pack a food box. Oh, and I'll have a trunk that I'll need help with. Now, who do you think I should take along?"

"Take along? Let's see. We got ol' Lou, if Mary don't need him around the house. Or Jess could do it, although he seems to have some religious reason not to go into town. Emil and Mac and Moore went with Mister Pendragon. There's Pat, but he'd just gripe about everythin' along the way the whole time. Not much of a traveler is Pat. Sam's around some place. I think he's ridin' fence with Tim, but we could find 'em."

"What about the Pinto Kid?" she asked. "Or Garth, he's a very nice boy."

"Both gone with Art," Bob Riley mused. "Too bad Link hasn't come back. He'd be the natural choice. Real good company, Link. 'Course, he'd be gone to the North Platte shindig with the others, I guess."

Gwen lowered her eyes and sipped from her cup. She would rather not have his name mentioned, at least not until she had spoken with him and brought him back.

"Will Jensen," she said.

"Oh, sure!" Bob said. "Sure, Will would do fine. In fact, he'll be real glad for a chance to get off the place. Him and some of the others drew straws to see who'd go with Mister Pendragon, and he lost. Couple days in town would be good for him. I'll find him. And I'll have somebody get your buggy ready."

The woman had the house girl help her carry a trunk from the lumber room to the bedroom. Just having the open trunk sitting there, just taking clothes from the closet caused some of her gloom to vanish, some of the imprisoning weight to be lifted. She shook out a petticoat and noticed her hands trembling slightly as she folded it. When she drew her best silk stockings between her fingers to straighten them, it was as if she had forgotten how fine they felt, and so she drew them slowly between her fingers once again. Ignoring the girl who was quietly folding dresses into the trunk, Gwen picked up her chocolate-colored riding hat, the one with the wide, stiff brim and braided leather chin string. She stood at the mirror, appraising herself with the hat set at this angle and that. Set straight and level, the way such hats are worn by Spanish *señoritas,* it looked very well. Tipped over her right eye at an angle, however, it looked more challenging and even — even flirtatious.

Was it two years ago, or three, when she and her friend Julia had ridden into town with Link and Kyle? She remembered now that she had worn a hat very much like this one, and Link had admired her in it. He had even mentioned how that certain tilt of that particular hat might "give a man ideas, if he was that sort of man." He blushed as soon as he said it, and they had laughed over it. Quite merrily, in fact.

"Get my hatbox from the other room, will you, Annie?"

she said. "I'll take this hat along, and that large one with the red band and feather."

Link and Tory made good time, even where the open range gave way to sprawling ranches. From ranch to ranch they went, hazing the horses along dry arroyos and dim wagon tracks and down dusty roads. One ranch family would lend them corral space and somewhere warm to sleep and would recommend the next ranch to them, drawing maps of the roads to follow and the fences to avoid. The final stop, recommended by the previous night's host, was a small spread only three miles from North Platte. It was an honest, sturdy homestead ranch. There were no frills about it, just a small solid house and modest barn, a full watering trough, well-scrubbed outhouse, and a tightly built corral.

Link and Tory agreed to the owner's price for feed and corral space and were shown to a small room attached to the back of the barn. There were two bunks with clean straw pallets, used when extra hands were needed on the place. Link spread his blankets on his bed and lay down gratefully.

"This suits me fine!" he said. "Pure comfort."

"That's the word," Tory said, flopping down on his own bunk. "Tomorrow, we'll ride into town and see what this July Fourth lash-up looks like."

Most of the year it was no more than a seldom-used racetrack situated on a mile-wide stretch of alkali soil between the river and the railroad tracks. Tumbleweeds driven along by dust devils blundered into the corral rails, freed themselves, rolled around the cattle chutes, and eventually came to rest in a prickly mass against the board fence of the racetrack.

A week before Independence Day, 1882, the place underwent transformation. Men and boys armed with pitchforks made a bonfire of the tumbleweeds, along with all the winter's detritus of broken boards and empty boxes and paper. Old manure was scraped up and taken to Olander's oat field nearby. Corral rails that had fallen during the winter were spiked back into place and a few wagonloads of sand were brought from the river to spread in the racetrack arena.

Red, white, and blue bunting seemed to flow to the racetrack from some apparently inexhaustible source, magically showing up draped all along the board fence and all over the cattle chutes and the announcing box. The bleacher seats fairly dripped with it. High, slender poles were strapped to corral posts and from these there flew flags and banners, snapping in the Nebraska wind to announce the coming event. Behind the bleacher seats — now grandly referred to as the "grandstand" — there was a sound of hammering where vendor booths were being cobbled together. Some were still in the framework stage, while others were already roofed and enclosed with canvas. Once again the red, white, and blue bunting was draped everywhere. Hand-painted signs over the booths advertised **LEMONADE, ICE-CREAM, SOUVENIRS, COLD BEER** and some said simply **FOOD**.

Committeemen from the North Platte Independence Day Blowout went around in light buggies or on foot inspecting the results. Each day they became more impressed with the number of cowboy outfits camped in the river bottom and on the hilltops. There seemed to be tents and chuck wagons everywhere they looked. Even ranchers several miles from town were making a nice bit of change renting corrals and pasture land.

There was talk among committee members of having to hire another deputy or two just to keep order. There was also a short-lived but heated debate over the possibility of charging spectators for the privilege of entering the half-mile long racetrack arena with the high board fence all around it. The motion was defeated; they settled on charging higher entry fees and keeping a larger percentage of the revenues. After all, there would be maintenance costs and a certain amount of damage to the facilities.

Buffalo Bill himself made a daily ride among the camps, more to be seen than to see anything. A showman from his oversize hat to his knee-high boots, he pranced along on a gorgeous white stallion like a general reviewing an encampment of troops. Many of the men he knew, or seemed to know, or thought he recognized from one of the crowded saloons. These he hailed with — "Hey, Buck!" or "Hi, Charley!" — from the throne of his white charger. The name was usually the wrong one, but no one minded. Just being recognized by Buffalo Bill gave a man status among his peers, even if Bill did mistake his name.

Many men remembered meeting Buffalo Bill during the crowded saloon evenings in North Platte. Others were pretty sure they'd met him, but whiskey does have a way of blurring the memory. He never restricted his largesse to one establishment, but circulated from one smoky, noisy barroom to another all night long, a wavering squad of followers in his uneven wake. Mr. Cody was free with his cash and generous with his credit, so in a very few evenings of camaraderie and strong drink he acquired many new friends named Buck and Charley.

Another man who drove his buggy out from town each day to keep track of things was the appointed announcer, arena marshal, principal judge, and self-appointed general *factotum*. He took himself seriously. In a leather notebook he jotted down men's names, names of their outfits, and a record of which events they intended to participate in. Like the rest of the committee, he was a little alarmed by the numbers of cowboys and spectators the Blowout was attracting. But the revenues were gratifying. The grocery, liquor, and haberdashery business had never been better.

It was this dignitary who stopped his buggy at the edge of the grounds to welcome Link and Tory to North Platte. They reined up and sat in their saddles surveying the layout while Mr. Parkton talked.

"You boys come far? We've got outfits here from *all* over . . . Kansas, Colorado, Wyoming, you name it. Got a few Texas boys here, too. You're going to meet Buffalo Bill himself, I imagine. You heard of him. So where you from, did you say?"

"South," Tory said. "Southern Colorado. Out by the Kansas border."

"Long way to come, a long way," Parkton went on. "But there's plenty of men here have come farther. 'Course, they might have other business brings them here, because this is one bustling little town, yes, sir. I'm not about to say that our little Fourth of July show is the only reason people come here. Say, you look like all-around cowboys to me, for sure. All-around cowboys. You got any events in mind, in particular I mean?"

"My friend here is thinking about bustin' broncos," Tory said. "And the shooting contests. What else you got?"

"Bronc' buster? You do look like you could handle a tough outlaw horse, yes, sir. The town's arranged for the very best, the very best. In fact, you boys should want to stop over at the big horse corral later on." He pointed toward a distant corral. "You might see the bucking stock when it comes in. Just got word they're on the way, a whole herd of bad ones never ridden before. Right off your own Colorado flats, yes, sir. Now, about those other events. You just stop off at the announcer's stand down there, and there's a man who'll take your names and give you a program of events. What's your main interests, uh . . . ?"

"Tory's my name," he said. "We're off the H-Bar-C Ranch. I was thinkin' of steer ropin', mainly. Might get in on a turkey shoot if there is one, and any horse races that are goin' on."

"Horse races for sure. Plenty of them. Well, you boys see the man at the announcing stand, and I'll see you later on. Don't miss the buffalo exhibition!"

After paying their entry fees, Tory and Link left their horses tied to a rail at the announcer's stand and walked to the corral east of the arena where the rough stock would be kept. They got there in time to see the horse herd coming in the distance and found themselves a place on the top rail among the dozens of other cowboys who had climbed up the fence for this first look at the wild broncos they hoped to ride. Link looked across the corral and saw a familiar sight perched on the rails opposite him. What first caught his eye was the big, floppy, black chaps lavishly decorated with elaborate silver trimmings; next he saw the flashy red shirt and oversize scarf, the gold embroidered vest, the Stetson with its wide silver band.

It was the Pinto Kid. And right next to him, wearing ordinary working chaps and a gabardine vest over a plain homespun shirt was Link's old partner, Moore. Garth was standing on the ground, peering between the rails, and next to him was Art Pendragon himself.

"Hi! Get along! Move, you hayburners! Heeah, jump! Get in there!"

The first of the broncos came dashing full speed for the open gate, saliva streaming from open mouths, flecks of sweat foam flying, eyes wide and wild. The three riders hazing them were showing no concern for the herd at all, whipping the flankers with rope ends and quirts to keep the animals packed tightly together, so tightly that the horses jostled each other and kicked each other's legs as they ran. Dust swirled up, and Link could feel the pounding of their hoofs through the rail on which he sat.

Other cowboys, ranged along the rails, waved their hats and whooped and hollered at the sight of so many outlaw bronc's.

"*Wahoo!*" one yelled, near Link, "that one's mine, that one with the milky eye and scar on his shoulder. Oh, he looks like a mean 'un!"

"I'm for the mouse-color one, me," said another excitedly. "Lookit him kick, will ya? That's a real mustang, that is."

"Hey, waddie!" called a third, yelling at one of the drovers, "just you cut that there white one out for me right away, and I'll ride 'im till the sun goes down! *Whoop!*"

"Hell!" the first one yelled out again, "swing that milk-eye over here to me, and, soon as I'm through with him, I'll ride that man-eating roan next! Hell, I'll go right on through this bunch by dark, so you might as well just go back for more!"

Link said nothing, but studied the horses as they wheeled in running circles around the corral. Many of them had been injured, some by other horses and some by men. Too many seemed to have scars on their shoulders, and fresh ones at that; somebody had ridden them recently, and had raked them from neck to belly. Most had vicious rope burns on their necks and legs. These were outlaws, no doubt about it. Whoever had agreed to acquire them for the North Platte Blowout had culled the dry draws and poor range for them, and then gave them just enough water and feed to get them here.

He looked at the three drovers sitting on their horses by the gate, giving themselves a rest and waiting for the bunch to settle down so they could open the gate and ride out. One looked familiar, somehow. He saw Link looking at him and he looked back without a glimmer of recognition for the stocky, tall man in the black beard. Link let his mind drift backwards and remembered. It was the same *hombre* he had run off the Keystone, the one they found sleeping off his liquor in the wagon.

"Hey, Tory," Link said. "Look at that fellow on the chestnut and tell me if you know him."

Tory looked. "Nope," he said. "Can't say I ever saw him before. But that one with him, the one with the blue scarf, I had him in my sights once. Found him camped pretty close to one of our best bands of mares and sent him packing. That hooked nose is hard to forget."

They were interrupted by a sudden commotion next to them. The one Link recognized had ordered a small boy standing near the gate to open it and let them out, which he did. But when it came to closing the big gate again, the boy chose to ride on it, as boys will, and between being light of weight and lacking the inertia necessary to get the gate completely closed, the boy let two of the wild horses get past him before he could slide the latch.

Tory and Link and a couple of other hands leaped to the ground to help head off the runaways, but it was too late. With loud curses, two of the drovers wheeled their horses and set out in pursuit of the escaping outlaws. The one Link remembered from the Keystone incident turned his horse and tried to run the boy down. He leaned from the saddle and took the boy by the scruff of his neck and began shaking him violently.

"Damn' little son-of-a-bitch kid, lookit what you done! I'm gonna lay you over this saddle horn and give you a whuppin' you ain't never gonna forget. You won't set down for a week. . . ."

His ranting was suddenly interrupted. Coming up on one side of him, Link reached up and ripped the kid out of his grasp and set him safely down next to the corral fence. On the other side, Tory put two hands under the tough guy's stirrup and gave a heave, sending him crashing over to land at Link's feet. His horse made a frightened whirl and ran off through the spectators. He faced Link, quirt in hand.

"That'll cost you, cowboy," he said. "Now you get the beatin' first, then the kid."

"That right?" Link said.

Wild horse herd forgotten, some of the cowboys crowded the top rail next to the gate while others made a wide circle around Link and the drover. This was better than any bunch of broncos could be. One of the other drovers returned, having seen the commotion, and jumped down to elbow his way through the onlookers. He reached for his revolver, but someone behind him had already slid it out of the holster and passed it back through the crowd. It went from hand to hand until the last man simply dropped it in the horse trough.

Link tugged his hat — Lavaine's hat — down tight. He took out the heavy, leather gloves folded over the belt of his chaps and drew them on. The drover merely stood there with his legs well spaced, quirt at the ready, and studied his opponent. It was becoming clear to the drover, and everyone watching, that the tall, bearded stranger was a man who never backed down from any other man. Ever.

He made his rush. The quirt slashed down, but Link seized it with breathtaking swiftness and used it to pull the drover straight into a flat, hard punch to the face. The drover staggered, but was held up by the wrist loop of the quirt. Again he was pulled in, and again the punch came like someone driving a fence post into his face. He now knew that his nose was broken. He knew he couldn't use his right arm so long as this bearded devil held the quirt. He twisted to try a haymaker swing at his antagonist's head, but it only wrenched his shoulder. The other one dodged the swing, easily, and returned it with another hard, straight punch into his face.

As he was slumping to the ground, unable to see through the haze of blood in his eyes and scarcely able to realize that he was falling, his partner stepped in to help. Tory also stepped forward, but Link waved him off.

"No need," Link said.

This one had seen the pile-driver punches and was wary. He circled, keeping a hand extended as a guard, keeping the other one cocked into a fist. He would just wait until that tall, shaggy son-of-a-bitch came in to make his punch, and he'd parry it away and do some punching of his own.

Link came. He came tall and straight in the back, gloved hands held at his chest, muscles at the ready. *Too easy,* the drover thought. *This is gonna be so damn' easy. . . .* His extended left hand was almost touching Link's fist, holding him off, when he threw his best Sunday punch. All it encountered, however, was air; Link dodged like a snake, dropped into a low crouch, drove that fence post of a fist deep into the man's stomach. He doubled over, turned away to protect his face and stomach, felt the second fist plow into his kidneys. With a groan he turned again and swung wildly, grazing Link's shoulder, but Link simply finished him with a brutal slash to the side of the face. He went to his knees and stayed there a moment before toppling. His last thought was that he'd ruptured something because there was blood running down his pants leg. But it wasn't blood. He'd only pissed his jeans. He passed out.

Art Pendragon and Moore and the Pinto Kid had toprail seats for all of this. While the hubbub was settled down, Art turned to his two *compadres*.

"That tough guy in the yellow bandanna look familiar to you two?"

"Why, should he?" the Pinto Kid said.

"How about you, Moore?"

"Maybe. That way of punching sure looks familiar. Like Link used to do."

"But you don't know this fellow?"

"Don't think so."

Art mused. He knew that man, knew him by his moves, knew him by the way he stood up straight and relaxed as the drover came for him. He knew who he was, all right. But he didn't think he'd say anything more about it. He'd just see what Link was up to and let things take their course. If it was Link, and he was sure it was, maybe somebody had sent him to give the Keystone cowboys a little shot in the arm by challenging them to shine like they used to. Might be that was why he was here.

Chapter Eleven

All at last were assembled in the city
on the high day of the festival. . . .
HISTORY OF THE KINGS OF BRITAIN
GEOFFREY OF MONMOUTH

The next day being Sunday, there were some cowpokes who cleaned up and ventured across town to church. Some no doubt went out of a sense of religious devotion, others perhaps because they had struck a bargain with God during some recent stampede, and still others went in order to watch the pretty girls of North Platte.

Non-church cowboys lounged about in camp, smoking or playing cards or both, telling stories, exchanging bits of news from their particular corner of the great Western cattle range. There was a rumor in the air that the small herd of buffalo currently penned up not far from the arena was to be used in the bucking contests. Some had heard that Buffalo Bill himself was going to ride the wildest one. Other rumors had it he was planning a demonstration of how he used to chase them down on horseback. There were Texas longhorns in a pen next to the rough-stock corrals, massive ox-like beasts with muscles like steel and horns spanning five and six feet from point to point. Some said they were there just for show, others believed they were for sale.

"Nah," one waddie said. "Them are for the ridin' contest. Them horns are for y' to hang onto."

Nooning time came and went, then dinnertime, and then

all the talk of wild cattle and high-bucking buffalo brought out the inevitable suggestion.

"Well," said an anonymous cowboy in one of the camps, "generally speakin', back on th' ranch of a Sunday afternoon I just like take a little exercise by throwin' a leg over some darn' ol' outlaw bronc' and ridin' 'im to a standstill. Any of you boys happen to know where I can find me a real devil of a hoss to ride?"

"Well," bragged another, "looks to me like the wild stuff they brought in isn't all that wild. Why, wouldn't take but ten minutes to tame the lot of 'em."

"Shucks," one said, "my kid sister could ride them bronc's."

"I *do* wish m'own outfit had thought to bring along Old Sunfisher!" another one added. "Now *there's* an outlaw. Never has been rode to a stop. Say, listen here . . . one Sunday afternoon I figured to give him a try, you see? Well, son-of-a-gun arched himself and shot me so far up inta the sky the boys on the ground lost sight of me."

"Did it hurt much?" another asked, and chuckled. "When you come down, I mean?"

"Only in my wallet," the storyteller said. "Y'see, we was up there in the sky so long that we didn't come down till Monday noon, so the boss docked my wages for missin' a half day's work."

"Tell y'something," said another cowhand. "I'm grieved to have to tell you boys this, but I was countin' on ridin' them big longhorns and show y'how it's done. Can't do 'er, though."

"That 'cause your mommy told y'not to play with strange animals?" one said.

"She did, but that ain't it. No, what I just remembered is that when I'm ridin' wild longhorn, I always use me a six-foot rattlesnake for a quirt, and I ain't seen any rattlers no-where around here. I guess that ride's all off."

Link and Tory rode in from their host's place, bringing along the best of their remuda to put into the big enclosure north of the arena.

"Two bits a day per animal, boys," said the man in charge. "Includin' hay an' water."

Tory counted out money enough for three days. "We'll be back with these two," he said. "Goin' to ride around and look things over first."

They stayed at the fence a few more minutes to watch their horses mingle with the others. There was horseflesh of all descriptions, ranging from pintos and light draft animals to racers and cow ponies. Most of them were owned by men who, like themselves, were camped outside of town some-where and needed a place to leave a horse. Some, like those Tory and Link brought in, were at the Blowout to be sold or traded.

"Must be a hundred horses in there," Tory observed. "How'd you like to have the hay concession?"

"I'd rather have the two bits per each, per day." Link smiled.

They spent the next couple of hours just slowly riding around. They rode from camp to camp to see who was there, but avoided the Keystone wagons parked some ways off. Here and there they joined circles of horses and riders forming an impromptu arena around some young waddie who was showing off his skill as a bronc' buster. They stopped to watch another kid showing his friends how to lasso a steer. The boy's first loop went true, dropping nicely over the horns. But then he set himself up to do it again and the steer suddenly decided it was time to go home, which apparently lay somewhere over the farthest horizon. The kid's companions whooped encouragement to him until he was well out of earshot, riding after the runaway for all he was worth.

"Don't find this kind of Sunday fun back home," Tory said.

"You do if you work on the big ranches any more," Link said. "Back in the trail-drive days a man mostly tried to rest on Sundays. Nowadays 'most all cattle raisin' is done outta the bunkhouse. You find these kinds of shenanigans nearly every week."

"That so?" Tory asked.

"Yup. They just get restless. Remember that kid I pointed out to you, the one I said used to always cause accidents to happen?"

"Yeah?"

"He's one of 'em. Six days working from first light to dark, most of it in a saddle, and what does he want to do on a Sunday afternoon? Throw a saddle on some killer snake of a horse and try to ride it."

"To each his own, I guess," Tory said.

They sat quietly watching another bunch of cowboys showing off with ropes. After a time, Link suddenly spoke up again. "Women."

"How's that?" Tory asked.

"Women," Link repeated. "You find a ranch anywhere near town, and the women come out an' watch the cowboys on Sundays. Not that it's bad, no. But you oughta see what it makes those boys get up to. Why, they buy themselves fancy new shirts to ride rough stock in, and next thing you know they got a special Sunday Stetson and bright scarf and shiny spurs. I'm tellin' you, Tory, it's getting harder and harder to have respect for these flashy show-off types."

Monday found most all the men sticking to their respective camps to practice. One would ride the roughest horse the outfit happened to have with it, or would shake out a loop and chase after one of the outfit's beef cows as his friends shouted advice about his roping technique. Each man in camp had his own theory about roping, and each one knew exactly how a bronco should be ridden, but none of them had the least idea what to expect once the Blowout started. Some held that spurs were to be forbidden; others had read somewhere that saddles were to be slickfork only, and no rolled-up slickers tied to the cantle, either; one man was pretty sure that riders could hobble their stirrups, while another thought it was all going to be bareback.

As for the steer-roping event, many a nervous cowboy tried to look nonchalant as he strolled over to look at the shaggy buffalo with heads the size of cooking stoves or at the Texas longhorns with horns as thick as a man's leg. Three buckaroos straddled a top rail, studying a bunch of lean, tough-looking range steers. The steers looked bored, just standing around piles of hay with their heads down.

"I heard that if y'sign up for steer riding," one cowboy ventured, "they might bring out a longhorn or buffalo *or* a steer, an' they pick your name outta a hat to see what one y'get to ride."

"Jesus," one said.

"Count *me* out," said the other. He climbed down and walked away, adjusting the crotch of his Levi's as he went. Casting a backward glance, he thought those longhorns looked even meaner at a distance than they did up close.

A blast of gunfire caught the attention of Link and Tory as they did their tour of the pens and arena. Out of habit Link adjusted his Colt in its holster. Tory was also wearing a revolver, a Remington in the .44-40 caliber, and, following Link's example, he reached down and slipped the hammer loop free of the hammer.

The shots went off in batches, six shots, six more, then silence. Then the same pattern again. Over next to the railroad tracks a bunch of men had decided not to wait for the official shooting contest to begin and had started up their own brand of fun. Two of them were hastily shoving cartridges into their revolvers while the onlookers yelled encouragement. One of the shooters was the one Link had beaten. His face showed a fist-size purple bruise and one of his eyes was still swollen shut.

"Get 'im, Army!" A man laughed. "The train's gonna get 'im if you don't!"

"C'mon, Banks!" another chortled. "You can load faster'n that. Your supper's gonna get away from you!"

Sitting in their saddles overlooking the heads of the witnesses to this "contest", Link and Tory now saw the target. A small hen was tied by one foot to the railroad track. Her tether was about three feet long, allowing her to jump to the other rail, or to fly up in the air, or tumble squawking into the ballast. The distance was fair, about thirty yards, but the frantic fowl already showed blood and was dragging a wing. Two other chickens, both of them dead and mutilated with bullets, lay tied to the rails.

"That just don't look right to me," Tory observed with his teeth clenched.

"Gotta feel sorry for the birds," Link said.

"You going to do it?" Tory asked. "Stick your nose in, I mean?"

"Well, you're the one who wanted to join a turkey shoot."

"I think I've kinda lost my interest in it."

"I reckon I'll just join in for one or two shots," Link said.

Tory nodded. The two riders urged their horses nearer to the back of the group.

The one with the bruised face, the one who had been addressed as Army, finished loading and snapped his revolver closed. He took a stance like a French dueling master, holding the Smith & Wesson out at arm's length and placing his other hand on his hip.

"I thought so," Link said quietly. "That fellow learned to shoot in the Army. Or thought he did. They love to stand that way."

"Makes a man look like a sissy if you ask me," Tory said.

The one called Army carefully squinted with his undamaged eye down the barrel of his revolver and took his shot. The bullet blasted into the rock ballast next to the chicken, sending her into a screaming, squawking frenzy of leaping and flapping. The man raised his weapon to the vertical, pointing dramatically skyward, began to bring it down slowly onto the target.

"Horse manure," Link said quietly.

Army was hardly halfway through the theatrical process of taking aim when a pistol shot went off behind him.

Blam!

Link's shot was true, severing the cord that tethered the hen to the rail.

All heads turned to the dark-bearded horseman holding his Colt as casually as if it were just some tool in his hand. They looked back at the hen, now flopping her way across the tracks, dragging the remains of the cord. One of her legs was crippled and one wing was useless. She fell and struggled up and fell again.

"Ah, look at that," Tory said sadly.

Those who were looking at the two horsemen saw Tory's Remington slide up into his hand and saw the barrel come level without his elbow ever moving away from his side. They saw him thumb the hammer back and felt the concussion of the shot as the bullet whizzed over their heads to hit the unfortunate chicken dead center and send it spinning, dead, into the weeds on the other side of the track.

Link leaned one elbow on his saddle horn as he shucked the empty shell from his Colt and replaced it with one from his belt. He looked steadily into Army's mutilated face.

"You look to have something to say," he said.

"You started somethin' you can't finish," Army sneered. "You and me, we're gonna be quits before this shindig is all over. I got friends here."

Then the man they called Army made a mistake. He was still holding his Smith & Wesson, although he had nearly forgotten it in his rage, and now his hand began slowly to rise as if it had a will of its own and wanted to shoot the man on the horse.

Link saw the movement. He kicked Rico, and Rico took two steps toward Army, close enough to let Link slash downward with his Colt and fracture the wrist of the hand holding the revolver. It fell to the ground while Army howled in pain, holding his broken hand.

"Pick that up," Link said to a bystander.

The bystander very gingerly picked up the revolver. A quick wave of Link's Colt told him to hand it to Tory.

"Tory," Link said. He made a slight jerking signal upward with his head. Tory nodded. Gripping the gun by the barrel, he threw it as high as he could.

Link's own gun came up and paused while the flying Smith & Wesson reached apogee. Then the hammer fell.

Blam!

The onlookers saw the Smith & Wesson's cylinder flying off in one direction as its frame flew in another.

Blam!

The falling frame abruptly changed course in mid-air, tumbling over and over until it fell to earth across the railroad track.

"This Fourth of July is gettin' to be interesting," one witness remarked.

"That's the word for it," Tory said as he and Link turned their backs and rode away. "Getting more interesting by the minute."

The 4th finally came. Tory and Link rose early and rode for North Platte, and long before the town came into sight they heard the place cutting loose for Independence Day. It sounded like every buckaroo in every camp was emptying his revolver into the air. Men without guns or money for ammunition pounded on washtubs or blew into jugs or did anything else they could to make noise. Somewhere a steam locomotive whistle kept going and there was a periodic heavy *BOOM* from a small cannon. Close to the railroad tracks they saw a youngster of perhaps ten or twelve who was the envy of the little band of boys following him around, for his father had allowed him to take the family ten-gauge and a pocketful of shells with which to celebrate. One boy would pick a target — an old rusted-out bucket in a vacant lot, a tree trunk that seemed to have an insolent look to it — and the young shootist would hoist the heavy shotgun to his shoulder and blast away.

People were already lining the main street when they got into the town proper. Up at the end of the street, a band was either tuning up or conducting a cacophony contest among themselves. After a few minutes, they seemed to have arrived at some agreement concerning the key in which "Star Spangled Banner" should be played and the parade began. First the band, all male and mostly brass instruments, making up in volume what they lacked in actual musical ability. Close behind, forming an honor guard for Old Glory, came the G.A.R. assemblage complete with vintage uniforms and antique rifles. One of the oldest men Link had ever seen in a uniform led them as they marched, waving a ponderous cavalry saber in a manner that seemed to endanger not only himself but the onlookers.

Farther up the street, Art Pendragon, Moore, Garth, and the Pinto Kid perched on a hitching rail, watching the procession. Mac and Emil were not far away. It was the Pinto Kid, resplendent in his fancy vest and silver geegaws and silver hatband, who first caught sight of the parade's main attraction.

Buffalo Bill was coming.

"Lord Almighty! Would you *look* at that!" the Kid suddenly exclaimed.

Mr. Cody was a sight not soon forgotten. Here he was, a man only halfway into his thirties who had already ridden for the Pony Express, served in the 7th Kansas Volunteer Cavalry against the Confederates, worked as scout, guide, hunter, dispatch messenger, and Indian fighter. Here he was, parading himself between a gaggle of obsolete G.A.R. veterans and a giggling mass of marching schoolgirls waving red, white, and blue flags. A newspaper reporter later described him as **strikingly handsome, . . . resplendent in a suit of white corduroy pants and black velvet coat of military cut.**

To Art Pendragon he looked like everything that was going to hell in the cattle business. Most of the citizens standing and watching all this "tribute" to the "real Old

West" had never slept in the open or ridden through blizzard and cloudburst. Many of them, he suspected, hadn't even ridden horses since their childhood ponies. Yet to them it was all about fancy duds and prancing horses. All they knew about his way of life, or that of the Keystone riders, was what they read in those damned Buntline storybooks. To them the bronc' busting and steer roping was just a circus show, an entertainment with quaint cowboys. Buffalo Bill's theatrical get-up, his manner of waving a white gauntlet buckskin glove to the crowd, even his little mustache and goatee made Art want to challenge the man right then and there.

The Pinto Kid interrupted Art's thoughts. "That Buffalo Bill makes me feel downright shabby!" He smiled.

"Yeah," Art mused. "And here we all thought you were pretty much the last word in cowboy fashion. Why, shucks, he's got more silver on that one tapadero there than you got on your whole outfit, hatband included."

The Kid had to agree. He hooked his thumbs into his flashy *concha* belt and watched as Buffalo Bill went by. There rode a man who was headed into history, a legend. There was a man who had *been* someone and who looked it.

Art Pendragon also looked after the legend as it rode on down the street followed by the troop of children waving miniature flags. *If we aren't careful,* Art thought, *it'll only be a couple of years before we all start to look like dime-novel buckaroos.*

The Blowout committee in bunting-draped carriages came next in the parade after the children's flag squadron, the wives nodding to the spectators from beneath fancy parasols, the men doffing top hats and waving. Other carriages followed, dressed up for the occasion. Some were shiny new; others were lovingly preserved antiques. Three fine ladies riding side-saddle came behind the carriages, followed in turn by newly painted and polished heavy wagons drawn by four- and six-horse hitches.

There was one carriage that was not in the parade. It was more than a mile from the arena toward which the parade was headed, standing motionless on a low and sandy hill on the far side of the North Platte River. It was a dusty vehicle, long and black with weather-crusted windows all along its sides, and its mismatched team stood with heads drooped as if asleep.

The short, hunched driver began to unhitch them as a preliminary to making his camp. Far out in the distance he could see the entire panorama. There were the vast, empty grasslands, a seemingly endless and untamable paradise for cowboys and cattle. Nearer to him flowed the ribboned, meandering channels of the North Platte River. Next was the little town beside the thin, black scar of railroad track, then the street where tiny toy wagons followed one another to the music of brass horns and the careless popping of aimless gunfire.

By noon, North Platte's population was in a state of high excitement. A temporary lull came when the town's principal dignitary climbed onto the announcer's platform to make the mandatory patriotic speech, which was followed by one of the more ample ladies of the town rendering her vocal version of several patriotic songs. No one could quite figure out why she had chosen to include "Beautiful Dreamer" in the program, but most of the cowboys agreed she was a lady of considerable volume.

"That there lady could holler a hog outta a root cellar," was one 'puncher's way of putting it.

Mr. Parkton regained control of his booth and the events were on.

"And now, good people," he bellowed through his megaphone, "your committee and the Honorable William F. Cody have assembled a . . . well, an assemblage . . . of the finest cowboys from all over the Western range. These boys here by the gate are going to start off the occasion with a demonstration of riding and roping skill never before seen in these parts, or maybe anywhere. Boys, they're all yours!"

And with that the gate to the arena swept open and in ran five buffalo cows, wild-eyed and snorting long streams of snot. One had a calf with her. The cows began to run in thundering circles around the racetrack, keeping an eye on the cowboys while at the same time keeping the calf protected beside them.

The crowd gasped as four cowpokes stepped out with lariats, each man building his loop as he walked. One, rather taller than the others, had a calmness and self-assurance about him. The others simply looked tentative.

"Go on, Emil!" Moore yelled at the tall man.

"Pick a big one!" Garth cried through cupped hands.

The Pinto Kid looked at Art. "Reckon we'll have to take Emil home in a basket?" he said.

"Just so long as we don't have to take that damn' buffalo home," Art replied.

The Honorable W. F. Cody and his cronies had worked out a pretty spectacular opening act, it had to be said. These cowboys were to attempt to show, to demonstrate, how they "catch up" their horses in a corral, mount them, then "ride the green off" until the mounts were gentled down for the day's work ahead. And if they could do it with outlaw horses, why not buffalo?

Loops fell short. One loop went true, but, when the

193

plunging ton of buffalo muscle hit the end of the slack, the hundred-and-fifty pound man on the other end of the rope somehow lost his grip. Another cowboy got close enough to his animal to grab the woolly cape, but, when he tried to swing aboard, he either lacked inertia or conviction. Whichever it was, the next thing he was aware of was lying on sandy ground that seemed to be thrumming with hoof beats. He heard people cheering, but all he could see was sky.

Emil addressed the problem as he addressed every situation, namely head-on. While his companions yelled encouraging remarks, together with a few discouraging ones, he selected his target for her smooth gait and predictable movements. He chose his place to stand. He made a big loop and held it down by his side so as not to alarm her by swinging it. As she ran past, his arm shot out and, even before the loop went tightly around her enormous neck, he was running, closing in on her, hauling himself along the lariat.

He let the buffalo's muscles do the work, let the lariat tug him up against her, swung his right leg over the skinny hindquarters, and he was on. With his left hand, he got a good grip deep in the thick wool while his teeth and his right hand worked at the lariat until he had a second overhand loop in it. They went around the arena once that way, then started a second time around, and, seeing that his fellow contestants had given over the field to him, Emil figured it was time this show was over. He braced himself to dismount, then dropped his overhand loop down along the cow's flank to pick up her hind foot. There was little slack in the line. The animal took one helpless hop as she felt her head being pulled sidewise by her own hind foot. She fought for balance, felt the lightweight annoyance suddenly leave her back, and crashed, thrashing, into the sand. She was soon on her feet, savagely ripping the ground and foaming at the mouth.

Emil walked back to the rail where his *compadres* waited.

"Hope you didn't hurt her none," Moore said.

"I expect Emil's goin' to be swamped with job offers. Anybody as owns a buffalo herd'll sure see he's a top hand," the Pinto Kid said.

"I'll tell you wild buckaroos who *I* want to hire." Art smiled.

"Who's that?" Emil asked.

Art's smile became a grin. "The man who goes out there and gets your rope back."

The buffalo were herded out of the arena so that four local sports in checkered pants and celluloid collars could line up their sulkies for a trotting race around the track. Art had little interest in watching skinny horses towing fragile carts, so he strolled off to find a beer. He walked past Link, who was standing with a foot on a corral rail watching the collection of outlaw horses as they milled around. Each man gave the other a slight nod, the way strangers do who pass on the street. Art went on over to the beer booth and came back with two foaming mugs, handing one to Link.

The man in the silver-belly hat and yellow neck scarf accepted the mug. Art raised his mug in a toast to his old friend.

"Link," Art said simply.

"Art," Link replied. "How you been?"

"Tolerable," Art said.

"That's good." Link took a swallow of beer and wiped foam from his mustache.

"Working around here somewhere?" Art asked.

"Nope. Place called H-Bar-C Ranch, down on the Colorado border a ways. Horse outfit. Good men. Just the two of them, but they know their business."

"A three-man outfit," Art said, sipping his beer. "Must seem kinda lonely after the Keystone."

"Well, there's an old man. Mostly he stays at the house and builds stone walls and such. He's the boys' father. There's a girl there, too. I guess callin' her a woman would be more like it. Nice. Quiet, but nice. She made me this here bandanna . . . see, there's the ranch brand on it. H-Bar-C."

Art raised an eyebrow at this. For a cowboy to wear a girl's favor, he generally had some kind of serious understanding with her.

The two of them stood at the rail watching the outlaw horses, neither one speaking except to point out some unusual feature to the other, such as the Roman-nosed dun with slightly deformed hoof.

After a time, Art spoke again. "I guess you'll be in the contests later on," he said. "I hear there's even more tomorrow."

"Plannin' on it," Link said.

"Real cowboy work, riding snakes like these here," Art said. "I see they got us some pretty rangy ol' steers for the roping contest. But I was looking around some of the camps, an' I don't see much competition. Lot of youngsters. Saw a few old-timers, real cowpokes, but I don't think they'll be in the bronc' ridin'."

"Yeah?" Link said.

"Things are changing, Link. These kids, they just want to work anywhere they can and save up to buy their own places. Word comes around about a spread payin' more money, and off they go. They don't want to be cowpokes all

196

their lives. Mostly they like to dress up and ride around, lookin' to impress people. I don't see where they've got the grit it takes to make it out here."

"You seem to be circlin' around some kind of point there," Link observed.

"Aw, I'm just bothered, I guess. Buffalo Bill, for instance. Would you want to ride with a dandy rigged out like that, if you were goin' up against a gang of horse thieves or trying to stop a stampede?"

"Maybe. Maybe not. He does seem more like a show horse these days."

"Link," Art said, draining the last of his beer, "I don't want the Keystone to get like that. I want it known as a place that hires only the toughest men, men you can count on when trouble starts. Men who don't step aside, not for any man, men who stand up for women, and men who make other men prove up on whatever braggin' they do."

"I thought we did all that," Link said.

Art took a step back and looked at his young friend. It was hard to tell it was Link, with the light-colored Stetson pulled low in front, the heavy, black beard, the yellow shirt, and fancy vest.

"I'm the only one so far has figured out who you are. Know that?"

"Well . . . to tell the truth, Art, I kind of had a plan for that. . . ."

He was thinking he'd tell Art all about his idea of pitting himself against the Keystone riders who came to this Blowout. And now that he had gone around the various camps, like Art had done, and had sized up the competition, the more certain he was that the only worthwhile opponents in strength and skill were going to be the Keystone men.

"Here's what I'm thinking," Art interrupted. "You and your partner look like you could make this whole shebang into a real horse race. This committee of townfolk and Buffalo Bill put all this together as entertainment. They're just out to flog their little town to the newspapers and bring in more people. What if we could show 'em how real cowmen work for a living? We could turn their little party into a real shivaree, one they wouldn't soon forget."

"What do you have in mind?"

"What about if I talk to the committee? Or to that Parkton character? They seem to do whatever he recommends. Change these events around a little. I'll take care of that. What I'd like *you* to do is really give my boys a hazing. Push 'em hard . . . get 'em mad. Be a big favor to me if you could give 'em a chance to show what they're made of."

Link liked hearing that word "favor". If Art's scheme did work out, he'd get Art to return the favor by giving his backing to Tory and Lavaine. With the Keystone brand behind them, the brothers could write their own ticket.

"I could use the exercise," Link said. "But once it starts, I won't pull any punches."

"Wouldn't want you to," Art said. "Now, I need to find that Parkton fellow."

Parkton knew the reputation of Art Pendragon, of the Keystone Ranch reputation, and was flattered when the man sought him out. Pendragon's suggestions made sense, too. Given the unexpectedly large numbers of cowboy entrants and the limited space, plus the fact that the 4th of July celebrations couldn't go on for more than two or three days, it made sense. Following the three-hundred-yard race, he made his announcement.

"The winner, as you all know, is our own druggist,

Mister Tobias Brooks on his fine mount Worthington! Second place goes to Joe Andersen of Andersen's Haberdashery, and third is Calvin Knowles. Pretty exciting race all around, and thanks to all the racers for a fair, clean contest!

"Now for a little change in program. Some of you have expressed concern that we could be here all night long if we give every single entrant his chance to ride his bronco. So we had a quick meeting a minute ago and decided on a kind of battle royal sort of bronc'-busting demonstration. The committee will act as judges, and we'll sure pick who's the best bronc' riders. Later on, we hope to do the same with the steer roping. More of a free-for-all. So if any of you cowboys want your entry fee back, you can see my assistant at the announcing booth. Otherwise, get your gear and get your helpers and we'll get on with the bronco busting!!"

The crowd cheered good-naturedly, although they didn't have much of an idea what was about to happen, and cowboys who had plunked down three dollars apiece to have a chance to show off on a wild horse went and found their sidekicks. The men in charge of the outlaw horses mounted up and rode among them, using rope ends and quirts to stir them up.

Link and Tory joined six other cowboys in the arena, including Garth and Mac from the Keystone. Each rider was allowed to have one helper. Each man had two lariats. Chaps were permitted, but spurs were forbidden. Their saddles rested on the ground beside each pair.

"First go-'round!" Parkton announced with a flourish.

In came the frightened horses, bunched up and plunging right and left, twelve or fifteen of them going full speed around the board walls of the arena. Dust and clods flew. A smell of horse sweat and a sense of panic spread across the ground. Pairs of men swinging loops ran at the racing mass of horseflesh, swinging wild and swinging calmly, until each team had its horse caught. The arena was a confused whirl of twisting horses with cowboys hanging from their necks and circling them with saddle at the ready. One by one each outlaw was saddled, and one by one they found men on their backs where some had never felt weight before.

Loose cinches slipped and saddles turned and men fell under hoofs. The horse was caught again, the saddle put in place again, and again the cowboy swung aboard to see how long he could withstand the punishment of a wild bronco plunging and kicking.

Tory got hold of their horse's head and had the halter in place in no time. Thanks to his strength and his perfect calm, the horse only stood and glared with wide eyes as Link tossed the saddle on its back and cinched it. It danced sidewise and kicked out in protest as Link stepped into the stirrup and up into the leather seat. Tory let go and retrieved his rope. He intended to lasso another bronc', just in case they needed it.

Link's horse kicked out with both hind hoofs. It arched its back and jumped, coming down with both front legs stiff. Again and again and again the hind legs lashed out, and he felt the powerful haunch muscles jolting the cantle, nearly knocking him over the horse's shoulder. Whenever he could, Link used the halter rope to aim the beast at one of the other teams of men struggling with horses. Just as Garth and Mac had theirs in position for the saddle, Link crashed into its hindquarters and they had to begin again.

The outlaw lashed out, plunged, arched, and finally settled into a teeth-jolting run around the arena, following the loose horses. He was through; all he would do now was run. Link yelled to Tory, and Tory was there to grab the halter and help get the saddle off. According to the hastily made rules, a cowboy could ride as many mounts as he could catch, and the contest would keep going until the horses stopped bucking.

The second horse was a twister, snapping its neck back like it wanted to bite the leg of the man on board. Over and over, Link was heaved to one side until he nearly toppled out of the saddle. But over and over, he recovered his balance and rode on. After he'd had enough of the hammering punishment, Link began to reward each plunge and twist with a kick to the horse's ribs. Eventually the animal got the idea and, like the first one, settled into a hard, pounding run punctuated by outbursts of twisting fury.

Link spotted Mac getting a good ride out of his outlaw and dragged his own horse's head over so it would go in that direction. Mac cussed when Link got close and started to spoil the show he was giving the judges.

"Get away, you bushy son-of-a-bitch! Get away!" he yelled.

Link grinned under his beard and pulled the horse's head over again, crashing it into Mac's.

Tory had a third snake roped and ready the next time Link came by, and, by the time the dozen outlaws were worn down to where they stood wearily in the arena with defeated looks in their eyes, he had ridden four of them, the last two to a standstill. Link felt better than he had felt in as long as he could remember; this was the old way, riding the green off a string of ponies as a start to the day's work. You had to be a real man to do it, a genuine article. City dudes might ride race horses around on a track or prance around in little sulkies behind Thoroughbreds, but it took a working cowboy to control a horse with spirit.

He rode the last one back into the holding pen. He and

Tory were walking toward the beer stand when he spotted Mac and Garth limping along, glaring in their direction. He also saw Art, and Art looked pretty damned pleased with himself.

Chapter Twelve

Men should be what they seem
Othello
Act III, Scene iii, Line 126
WILLIAM SHAKESPEARE

"And now, folks," Mister Parkton shouted into his megaphone, "we're going to let those bucking broncos rest up a bit, but there's another go-round later on."

He put his hand over the mouthpiece and belched. It seems the beer vendor was giving it away free to the committee members.

"Meanwhile," he went on, "a bunch of boys have signed up to show you folks how they rope steers at roundup time out there on the open range. Me and the other judges are going to keep a tally" — there was another muffled belch — "and, according to the rules, a cowboy has to rope his steer *from* horseback, bring it to a stop, and throw it. Just like they do for branding or dehorning. Then they let it go again. The cowboy roping the most steers, in the time allotted, is goin' to be our winner. Provided the judges agree he did it with good form, of course!"

Two dozen hopeful rope-throwers lined up on their horses against one side of the arena as an equal number of steers were let in through the gate, rangy-looking animals with short horns or no horns at all, long-legged and slab-sided. Moore and the Pinto Kid looked at the steers and at each other and laughed, and so did Mac. Back at the Keystone such poor-looking animals wouldn't even be gathered in at roundup time, but left for the wolves and coyotes.

At the other end of the line, two big men, one with a heavy, dark beard, also appraised the cattle.

"Reckon you can manage to rope one of those?" Link asked.

"Oh, I s'pose maybe ·I can snag that sickly-looking yellow one, if I really put my mind to it."

"Use you a big enough loop and you could catch up three or four at one toss," Link said.

"Wonder what they use such cattle for?" Tory pondered.

"Leather, I reckon," said Link. "That and bones. There's sure no meat to bother with."

The starter's gun went off and the whole half-mile length of the arena suddenly turned into a circus of running cattle and whooping riders. Six or seven cowboys were eliminated almost immediately. One busted a cinch and stood there dusting himself off as his saddle went bouncing away, still tied to the spooked steer. Another would-be buckaroo didn't see any point in using a tight dally. He soon learned. When his steer yanked him out of the saddle, his horse didn't wait around for him, either. A couple of town boys had borrowed horses and ropes on the presumption that this business of lassoing cows couldn't require *very* much skill. Their ropes were too soft, their loops too small, and they'd tied their hondas too snug. So, instead of impressing their girlfriends the way they had planned, they ended up mostly trying to avoid being trampled.

Link and Tory worked separately in the mêlée, each one plunging into the pile-up of cattle, roping one at random, dragging it out of the herd to throw it and release the lariat. Lavaine had trained his Rico horse for just this sort of business, and Rico made Link's job ten times easier by keeping his eye on the steer and keeping the rope taut. To Tory, steer catching was just child's play. He made a game of it by deliberately not catching the same steer twice.

Link spotted Mac urging his horse to cut one particular steer from the bunch. With a malicious grin under his mustache, he turned Rico to cut in front of the Keystone man and shot a loop over the steer's head. In less time than it takes to tell, he had jumped down, thrown the steer on its side, retrieved his lariat, and remounted.

"Your turn now," he said to the other cowboy. It was a dirty trick, but if the kid couldn't cut it. . . .

Link wheeled Rico around and saw Moore building a loop for a catch. Link quickly spun his own loop out bigger, and, as Moore's rope sailed toward the steer, Link's rope hit it in mid-air and knocked it to the ground.

Moore turned with eyes glaring and an oath on his lips for the bearded stranger in the tan Stetson, but Link's back was turned on him as he gathered in his rope and rode to find his next target.

Tory was busy, too; in the general plunging and clouds of dust, he had singled out the Pinto Kid and managed to make him miss a couple of easy throws, once crashing him and his horse into the board fence. Long before the judge's whistle blew, the battle lines were drawn. Everyone in the arena could see that it was Link and Tory, the two tall men on the two big horses pitted against Mac, Moore, and the Pinto Kid. Some men who knew the Wyoming range wondered at this; those three cowhands carried the Keystone brand on their saddles and it seemed like some kind of insanity to challenge the whole outfit that way. Yet here were these two strangers on big horses, out to make trouble. And enjoying it.

Link leaned on his saddle horn and turned to Tory. "Now *that* was fun," he said. "Just like the old days. You ever been on roundup, Tory? Remember those first couple of days when everybody's ridin' around, ropin' calves out of the herd, maybe two boys chasin' the same calf? One boy bustin' a cinch and everybody laughin' at him. Just a bunch of beeves, a good bunch of men, horses all eager to chase calves."

"Sounds entertaining," Tory said. "Never had the pleasure myself. Of a real big roundup, I mean. But entertaining would be the word for it."

"One day out in Kansas, Moore and me . . . he's the older one there, the gloomy-lookin' *hombre* in the torn shirt . . . we chased the same calf together all the way out of sight of the herd. That little dogie dodged and ducked, went under my horse once, and we took after him all the way to hell and gone, both of us laughin' like maniacs all the time. Good days."

The announcer picked up his megaphone and consulted the paper in his hand. "Have your attention, folks! Winner in this event, without question, is a roper name of Tory from the H-Bar-C Ranch in Colorado. Six clean catches. He'll get a new shirt of his own choosing from Henderson's Haberdashery, along with two free steak dinners at Barnes's Manhattan Restaurant here in town. Now, in a little bit we're going to see the second go-'round of the bronco busting, and we got a surprise for you. In addition to the finalists you saw riding in the opening event, you're going to see a rider who's already a legend, a late entrant in the bronc' busting. None other than Mister Samuel T. Privett himself, fresh out of Texas! Meanwhile, Mister Cody has arranged a little demonstration of how to chase buffalo. . . ."

The crowd cheered with gusto. Not many knew who the hell Samuel Privett was.

Fewer knew what a buffalo chase might look like.

But it was Independence Day! Nothing could spoil such a day, although some people noticed how the clouds were rising on the horizon far to the north. It was just a thin line of gray haze, at first, with some wispy streaks very gradually becoming darker. The breeze shifted direction, and it had a strangely different feel to it.

"Might get rain tomorrow," one farmer said to the man seated beside him.

That man squinted knowingly at the skies. "Might," he said. "Sure could use it."

"If y'ask me," said another, "there might be more rain comin' than we can use."

Many miles south and many miles west, in a green valley between two mesas, there had been no sign of rain in weeks. Each day, the skies became the color of turquoise as soon as the sun was up, and stretched in unbroken blue monotony from horizon to horizon all the day long.

In the afternoon, the sun slanted in at the narrow window of the tower and found the woman at her rituals. Following dinner and the cleaning up, after her father sought his napping chair in the shade of the back porch, she took the kettle from the stove and the basin from its nail and went upstairs to her tower room. She undressed. With a sponge she washed herself, then dried herself, standing in the narrow rectangle of sunlight, wary for unexpected observers.

She did this twice each week.

Without dressing and without so much as a towel about her spare nude body, she crossed the room to the trunk. She drew aside the embroidered cover she had sewn for the saddle that rested on the trunk. She took a cloth and stroked it through a clay bowl of neatsfoot oil blended with beeswax and rubbed the saddle with it, first the stirrups which she held in her hand as if holding the hand of an invalid while tenderly applying the oil, then the broad, smooth fenders over which she ran the cloth as if caressing a lover, and finally the seat and cantle and the saddle horn.

When she was finished, she wiped the saddle with another cloth and replaced the embroidered cover. She dressed and went to her seat next to the window, picked up her sewing, and watched the road from the south.

"Booger Red," said one of the men standing at the rail next to Art.

"Booger Red?" Art said.

"That's who Samuel T. Privett is. Booger Red. You never heard of him?"

"Nope. How come they call him Booger Red?"

"He's red-headed. Seems like everybody always called him Red. The way I heard it, when he was a kid, he tried makin' his own fireworks. Somethin' happened and they burned up on him, damned near killed him. Anyhow, some buddy of his said somethin' like 'ain't Red some booger, though' and the name stuck. Booger Red."

"He's only about the best damn' all-around bronc' rider you ever saw, that's all he is," one of the men said.

"Cowboy?" Art asked.

"Hell, man, he's a damn' showman. Cowboy! Why, he's been toppin' bronc's since he could walk. Talkin' to him, he told me he don't see a future in cowboyin' any more. Bill Cody, now, he's got the right idea . . . you get yourself a show together, an' you go around lettin' town people pay to watch you ride."

"Damned if *I'd* ever do that," Art snorted.

"You mark my words. Cody's already plannin' a travelin' show, kind of a circus. He's fed up with the theater business. And Booger Red told some newspaper the same, too. No more cows for him except just the ones he has in his show."

A veteran cowboy, standing alongside Art, put in his only contribution to the conversation.

"First barbed wire. Then damn' dirt farmers. Now we got people payin' to watch horses tryin' to kill cowboys. God-damn' cowpunchin' is goin' to the god-damn' dogs, if y'ask me."

The second go-around of bronco busting was more structured, with the finalists taking turns on well-rested outlaw horses. As the beer got Mr. Parkton more and more wound up, he took to describing each rider's background, telling stories about him, and exaggerating the bronco's viciousness. When he got to Link, however, Parkton realized he couldn't read the signature the big bearded rider left in the registration book. So he mumbled through that part, said the entrant was "out of a horse ranch in Colorado", and let it go at that.

Tory and Link walked into the arena with ropes and saddle to catch the outlaw Link had drawn for his ride. The two men and the spooky horse went around and around in a spinning, whirling dusty dance until Tory got control of the head and Link could throw the saddle up and get it cinched in place. Then came the issue of bridling the wild horse without losing a finger or thumb to its slashing teeth.

As Art was standing with others at one of the pole gates, his foot up on the bottom rail, Moore came sidling up beside him and spoke low so others wouldn't overhear.

"I think I recognize that *hombre* out there," Moore said.

"Look at how he handles that horse. His steer ropin', now, that seems different somehow. He's a deal heavier, too, and sportin' a full face mattress, but if that ain't my old trail partner, Link, I'll eat my hat."

"You can save yourself the indigestion." Art smiled. "That's him. I already talked to him."

"What's the deal?"

"I'm not sure. He came to the Blowout so's he could go against you Keystone boys, that's all he told me."

"Go *against* us? Hell! Between him and his partner and the five of us, we pretty much run this whole Blowout thing. I mean there don't seem to be any cowboys here can hold a candle to us."

"Hope it stays that way. Meanwhile, let's kind of hold back and see if Garth and the others figure out who he is. On their own, I mean. Don't tell 'em."

"Gotcha."

Out in the arena, Link clutched the saddle horn and cantle and got his foot into the stirrup. In the next whirl-around, he swung the other leg over and was as ready as he could ever be.

"Let 'im go," he said.

Tory removed the jacket from the horse's head, released his grip on the bridle, and then stepped back. At first, the bronc' stood stockstill. Then it lowered its neck and took several steps backward into a crouch like a jack rabbit ready to leap. And the leap came, sudden and explosive, both hind hoofs lashing out at once, the haunches jolting up-ward. Link felt his head snap back, then forward, like a rag doll's. He gripped with his legs and heels, tried to come down centered in the saddle each time the horse arched its back and sunfished into the air, tried to keep one hand free like the rules said. This bronco had a trick of going up straight and heaving to the right, throwing its heavy head around so that the landing was a jolt with a mean twist in it. Link would feel the twist throwing him off balance just before feeling the hard slam of the hoofs coming down stiff-legged.

Men whistled, women cheered, and boys lining the rails yelled encouragement to man and horse alike. To Link it was all a single roaring noise. Over the roar, all he heard was the steady *whumph!* of air exploding from the outlaw's nostrils with each jump, making a sound like a blacksmith's bellows being pumped by a maniac. He heard the protesting groans of twisting saddle leather, together with the wheeze of his own breath being forced out of him every time the hoofs hit the dirt.

After what seemed like a hundred trips around and around the arena, the outlaw began to tire. The twisting jump ceased. He stopped throwing his head down and merely lashed out with the hind legs. Then even the hind legs settled down to a walk. Link rode him back to the gate where Tory waited to help him strip off the saddle and bridle.

"Nice ride," Tory said.

"Was it?" Link said. "Funny. I don't seem to remember much about it."

"I liked the part when he tried to put both hind hoofs into the stirrups at one time."

"Yeah," Link said. "I liked that, too."

The next pair of cowboys, together with the next wild bronco, entered the arena with caution. It was their turn. Out on the range or back at the ranch, getting ready to ride the green off of a horse, they would have been feeling careful and apprehensive. Doing it here, with hundreds of strangers watching them, they were downright nervous.

Down at the farther gate, Art and Moore ignored the new contestants and resumed their conversation. They'd seen bucking horses before. Art took out his clasp knife to trim a rough end off the old belt of his chaps. Moore picked up a stick to clean manure off the instep of one of his beat-up boots.

"Speaking of all these whangdoodle cowboys and other terrors of the range," Art said, "whatever happened to our three renegades?"

"Which would that be?" Moore said, concentrating on the manure.

"The ones Link crossed swords with, first thing. I guess there was somethin' about a boy swingin' on a gate, and then a quarrel over shootin' a chicken."

"Yeah, I heard about that chicken. Say, here's a man could tell us, I'll bet. Hey there, mister! Got a minute?"

Mr. Parkton's assistant happened to be passing just when Moore called to him.

"Howdy, boys," he said. "Fine Blowout, eh?"

"Mighty fine," Moore said. "Best I ever been to."

The assistant's chest swelled with pride, not realizing this was probably the only such gathering Moore had been to.

"What can I do for you boys?" the assistant asked.

"We were wondering, Mister Pendragon and me, what some acquaintances of ours were entered in. Thought you might know. You seem to see everything."

"Oh, the boy with all the silver and the black chaps you mean . . . ?"

"No, that's the Pinto Kid. No, we meant that mean-looking one that got his wrist broke earlier on. They call him Army, I think. He's got two buddies, one of 'em wears a bright blue scarf."

"Oh, *now* I know the ones you mean. They got the contract to bring in the bucking horses and the steers. One of them told me they were also here to look for fresh breeding stock. Horses, mostly. He *is* called Army, now I think of it. Other one is named Banks. I don't know the name of the one with the blue scarf, but I know who you mean. They didn't enter any contests. In fact, I think they spend most of their time over at the horse pen. A lot of these boys brought extra horses they hope to sell. They're all down there in the pen. Say, I got to run now. Good luck to the both of you!"

"*Hmm,*" Art said.

"Kind of strange," Moore agreed.

"You know what's *really* strange about those three?" Art said. "They show up with a batch of scabby mustangs and skinny steers, stuff nobody'd want, right? Then they say they're interested in buyin' some of the bred stock other people brought. They don't look to me like they've got twenty dollars between them. It's like bone-pickers lookin' at purebreds."

"*And* now," the announcer's voice rang out through the megaphone, "a *real* treat, originally from Erath County Texas, a *premier* bronco buster in the territory and *probably* in the whole U.S. *of* A., Mister Samuel Privett aboard the man-killer outlaw, Tornado!"

Moore and Art rested their arms on the rail and watched.

A resounding cheer went up again from the Independence Day enthusiasts. The red-headed young man with the boyish face didn't care whether they knew his name. He was there to ride wild horses, his way, and nothing more. And ride he did, staying in full control of one of the wildest, heaving, leaping, sunfishing stallions anyone had ever seen. Despite Tornado's fierce frenzy, Booger Red easily made the horse go anywhere he wanted it to. Tornado's high jumps ended in back-breaking landings as he tried every trick in the book to unseat his rider. Yet the lightweight redhead kept guiding the bronc' around and around the arena like he had the animal up for auction and wanted everyone to get a good look. Other bronc' riders, Art noticed, kept their eyes on the bronco's neck, watching nothing but the horse. But Booger Red was different.

Booger Red watched the audience. While Tornado tried to kick him into the next county, he seemed indifferent to the punishment he was getting and just smiled a little-boy grin at the pretty girls. He waved to the men, even bowed to the ladies as he jolted by. After passing them, he looked over his shoulder and laughed.

"I'll be right back!" he called.

"Lovely hat!" he shot over his shoulder to a lady, as Tornado took him three feet into the air and came down poised like a tiger for the next leap.

"Mind gettin' me one of those?" he said to an onlooker who was holding a glass of beer.

Art frowned. *Mr. Booger Red puts on a good show,* Art thought. *But he sure makes working cowhands look dull and ordinary.*

"I wonder how he'd do on a real outlaw, out on the open range without an arena?" Art mused aloud.

"Pretty good I'd imagine," Moore replied.

Garth and the Pinto Kid came up to the two older men and joined them in leaning on the rails.

"Hear about the big race?" the Kid asked.

"Nope."

"The committee decided they'd have two horse races all at once, or pretty close together."

"That right?" Moore said.

214

"It's because of there being so many entrants," Garth explained. "They figure they'll have a short race around the inside of the arena, mostly for these farmers and feather merchants to show off their skinny race horses. Then there's gonna be a long race across country outside of the whole grounds, startin' and endin' back at the corrals."

"That's the one to get in on," the Kid said. "Might be a hundred riders in it. First prize is twenty-five dollars and a new suit of clothes!"

The committee billed it as a "steeplechase contest, just like the ones in England and Ireland."

The riders were to start from the rough-stock corral outside the arena. Then they would ride toward the silo that could be seen standing on a hill about a mile in the distance. Once there, they would turn and race to the river. They could cross it on the old bridge or they could elect to go through the water, the Platte being a braided collection of channels no deeper than a horse's belly. Once across the river they'd head up a road toward a twin pair of windmills on white, wooden towers, then west around Frauson's Hill, south on a main road to the new bridge, and finally back to the saddle-mount paddock.

"Twenty-five dollars doesn't seem like much of a prize for all that ridin'," Art said.

"They said they didn't have but the one sponsor yet, but it mightn't matter since none of the racers was expected to make the whole course. There's a passel of ditches and fences and plowed fields and what-not. Long way to go at a full run, too."

"That bushy bearded bastard in the fancy vest, him and his big partner, I saw them sign up," the Kid said. "That's why I'm goin' to be in it, too. Those heavy horses of theirs can't hold a candle to a real cow pony. After what they did to me in the ropin', I'm going to show them a thing or two about rough ridin'."

"Me, too," Garth said. "These little races where y'trot around in a circle just ain't my style at all. This long race, across rough country and all, why, it'll be like chasing after a stampede, only without the cattle."

The organizers announced that more prizes had been put up, including a nearly new Menea saddle donated by the livery and a pair of fancy coal-oil lamps for the parlor courtesy of the General Mercantile. One of the judges called the interested entrants together so he could describe the course and the rules. Another judge rounded up a handful of volunteers to ride out and act as markers on the route at places where a rider might get confused and go the wrong way. Hopeful racers jockeyed and jostled their horses into position in a ragged line outside the rough-stock corral, tugging cinches tight, re-buckling breech straps and headstalls, testing their reins, and setting and re-setting their hats so as not to blow off.

Chin straps, known as "stampede strings", were pulled up tightly. Guns were left with friends, along with lariats, scabbards, slickers, and saddlebags. Some checked their horses' hoofs, picking out small stones and packed clay. Others were in the saddle, shoving forward and back and twisting right and left to check for loose latigos. More than one young horseman, keyed up with the excitement of his first steeplechase, looked toward the bearded man calmly sitting on the big *palomilla*, waiting for the starter's gun. Some of the veterans of horsemanship figured the race would come down to a matter of power and experience against agility and eagerness. After the morning's events, that one single bearded cowboy among all the others had come to represent something to the younger buckaroos.

They secretly aspired to be like him. At the same time, each one of them wanted to be the one to show him up.

They wondered who he was. And they wondered, with a feeling like apprehension in the seldom-explored parts of their souls, whether they really wanted to know.

For his own part, Link sat, relaxed and ready, and scowled out from under his hat brim. He didn't care much about prizes and all that. What he cared about, he realized, was the testing of the men from the Keystone. That little touch of concern in Art's voice haunted him. If those boys weren't men enough, weren't cowboy enough to keep the real kind of life alive, then a big part of the West was going to vanish like the buffalo herds.

The judge called for the riders to form a straight line for the start. He raised his pistol and cocked it.

The clouds far off to the north had swollen a mile into the air. The tops heaved skyward like massive, puffy mushrooms in glaring mounds streaked with soot. All over the western horizon the sky looked gray as old bullet lead. To some, the horizon clouds looked like feathers. To others, they resembled plowed fields or lines of combed wool. But whether feathers, fields, or wool, they went relentlessly on, growing ever higher and arching ominously over the land.

On Frauson's Hill, north of town and the river, the small, bent figure untied the picket ropes of his two mismatched horses and walked them into the shelter of the elm trees where he had already stretched the tarp over the hearse.

Many miles west, the storm had already passed over Keystone Ranch, leaving flooded gullies and deep, standing pools along with glistening roofs and the pervasive smell of wet earth everywhere. Gwen sat at Art's large roll-top desk writing a letter. She paused, tapping the end of the pen against her straight white teeth, thinking. She was aware of herself, dressed in a form-fitting, lovely afternoon dress, conscious of her erect, proper, careful posture.

She was poised as if to receive guests. Yet — and this is the thought which had brought on her sudden pensive mood — she knew no one would come. The tall stranger in town working for John Peters turned out to be just a stranger. Leaving Will at the hotel, she had said she would drive herself to her friend's house. Then, on the pretext of thinking one of the horses had a loose shoe, she drove to the smith to have Mr. Peters look at it. The new man was polite and friendly. He was looking around for a place to buy so he could bring his wife out from somewhere back East.

Gwen smoothed her skirt and picked up the pen again to resume writing her letter. All dressed up, just to write some letters. Art and the others wouldn't return for days. And with this storm and all the mud on the roads, no one else was likely to come visiting, no one at all. Even a lone rider would stay wherever he found shelter. She may as well be wearing old coveralls, for all anyone would care.

With a sigh she dipped the nib into the inkwell.

Chapter Thirteen

Into the Storm

The red, white, and blue banners around the saddle-mount corral popped in the freshening wind. At the arena the band enthusiastically played again its repertoire of four patriotic songs. Women visited and laughed together in circles of parasols and bonnets while the men lounged at the grandstand or leaned against the arena wall, sharing chewing tobacco, cigars, and politics. Cowboys in wide, flapping chaps and broad-brimmed hats made an informal but persistent promenade past the animal pens and then past the seats of the young and presumably eligible young ladies from town. Many a lad was torn by indecision: should he hang around where he might be noticed by the ladies, or stay with his friends and discuss livestock?

The storm clouds by now were near enough to make the racers squint up into the sky, so close that townfolk began to think they might pack up and head for home pretty soon. But the opinion of the farmers in the crowd, and many of the cowmen, was that it could just as easily pass them by. It could veer north a little and miss them. No point worrying about rain, they said, until it was overflowing out of your boot tops. Not in this country. Why leave all this fun until you have to?

Two shots were heard in succession and two horse races began simultaneously. Inside the arena, the long-legged, slender mounts stretched out side-by-side, urged along by lightweight town sports wielding riding crops bought from

Eastern mail-order catalogues. Women in long summer dresses cheered and men in three-button, striped coats yelled. Outside the arena, a crowd wearing homespun and leather gave the racers a quieter send-off, one that was more of a running low murmur of approval for horses and men. Hoofs churned the dirt. Short, thick rawhide quirts rose and fell in the mass of horseflesh. Legs pounded away from the spectators leaving the ground trembling underfoot. The dust roiled up until spectators could only identify their favorite rider by his hat until the pack spread out and the leaders gained ground and once again the individuals could be made out.

Someone said the hill where the silo sat would make a good vantage point to see almost the entire race, and the crowd began to drift in that direction. It was nearly a mile, if you wanted to be right on the very top of the hill, but people walked along cheerfully, more to be in the crowd than to see the race. Those at the front of the pack, several of them carrying field glasses, kept the others apprised of the race's progress.

"They made the silo," one said. "Yep, looks like that flashy kid with the pinto horse is leading. And there's a little black pulling up on the lead now, don't know who he is. Oh, yeah, and there comes that fella that won the roping. What a horse *he's* got under him!"

Half walking, half running, panting people hurried to find any vantage point from which to see the racers cross the river. One onlooker, looking through his field glasses, was of the opinion that all the racers should be required to use the bridge even if it was so narrow and all. Another said that *he* would choose an upstream crossing because he knew a place where it would be firm footing and shallow channels. Still another, pointing out that the windmills were eastward from the crossing, said that he would cross downstream and thus save distance. Under his breath Art whispered to Moore that he wondered why these armchair experts hadn't entered the race themselves.

"As soon as they get across the river," Art continued, "why don't we hike back to the starting line and pick up our horses and ride out to the new bridge? Get a good look at the finish from there."

"I'm with you," Moore said. "Looks like we could use our slickers, too."

There were three riders who were not in the cross-country race. Nor were they in the arena. They weren't on the hill with the spectators, or in the grandstands, or at the beer and food booths. They were on their horses beside the saddle-mount paddock, these three. One had a bruised face. One had an empty holster. The third wore a bright blue neck scarf. The horses, on which they sat, shivered nervously at the approaching storm, feeling the cool wind ahead of the rain and hearing the distant thunder.

"That's luck for us," the bruised face said. "Won't need to wait till dark. I say we do 'er while they're all off chasin' around. Do 'er now."

Blue scarf agreed. They could haze everything straight into the storm and there'd be total confusion. Nobody would know what the hell was going on or what to do about it.

"Banks," he growled, "get in there an' throw th' connectin' gate open. Army, you git over to the rough-stock pens and git ready to let 'em loose. Soon as they're outta the pen, you haze 'em this direction."

Next to the saddle-mount corral and adjoining livestock pen was a haystack, just far enough from the corral fence to be out of reach of the horses and within a stone's throw of the river.

On the racecourse the riders were rounding the silo, hoofs thundering and men shouting, horses lunging into each other as they fought for position. Link had already cut Emil off, using the size of the heavy *palomilla* to shove Emil's lighter mount into a pack of other horses. Then going for the inside track, Link swung around Mac and made him swerve to miss him. Up ahead he could see Tory in second place, and grinned. Good for Tory; nobody would catch that black of his once they were off the road and into rough terrain.

Also ahead of him, he saw trouble in the making. There was a young cowpoke in the race, a kid barely old enough to be away from home, but riding well up to now. As Link leaned over Rico's neck, urging the big horse on, he got close enough to see the kid's saddle starting to slip sidewise. In another minute he could go down under the pack of horses coming up behind them.

Atop the haystack next to the saddle-mount corral, there was another boy, the same boy who earlier had incurred the wrath of the one called Army. He had ridden his pony to the haystack, stood on the saddle, and clawed his way up the slippery hay so he could get a good view of the horse race as it went across the distant horizon and came back toward the arena. It was a good spot; he could see Frauson's Hill and the new bridge and most of the road the riders would come down on the last leg of the race.

He could also hear the conversation going on below and wondered what he should do about it. 'Most everybody in town had a horse in that corral, and these men were fixing to steal them all.

The boy looked around. The sheriff, he knew, was one of those who had volunteered to be stationed along the course to keep riders from going the wrong direction. There were adults at the arena, he could warn some of them about the crooks. But two of the crooks were right in his way.

He looked toward the river and the old bridge downstream. Mr. Cody was there on his flashy horse, the figure in the white pants and black jacket and big hat. Buffalo Bill, he'd know what to do! When the boy heard the one called Army ride away toward the rough-stock pens, he bellied feet first down the back of the haystack to his pony, gathered up the reins, and rode for all he was worth.

Buffalo Bill would know what to do.

Moore looked around at the thickly packed group of spectators.

"Haven't seen those three nasty-looking types lately," he said. "I kinda thought they'd get into this race and try to pull somethin' on Link. Trip him up or something. Or get him into a fight, at least. Funny they never did anything about it, after what he did."

"I know what you mean," Art said. "They're keeping their own counsel, that's for sure. They're playin' somethin' close to the chest. But it's not any of our business, I guess."

"Guess not," Moore said. "Hey, look! The first one's at the river. Looks from here like that little black horse. He's goin' to take the bridge. Link's partner, he's next! And there's the Kid right behind him."

"There!" Art pointed. "There's Link! About ten places behind. You can spot that big, pale horse a mile away."

"Mister Cody! Mister Cody!"

They heard the cries at a distance, and turned. A kid on

223

a pony was galloping toward Buffalo Bill, waving excitedly.

"Wonder what's goin' on there?" Art said.

They saw Buffalo Bill bending down to listen to the lad, then saw him wheel his horse this way and that like he was agitated about something and looking for someone. With a shout and a slap of his hat across the horse's flank, he turned and came full speed toward the spectators.

"Damn!" Moore said. "That Buffalo Bill is a helluva rider, isn't he?"

"Look at him come," Art agreed. "Damn' fine rider."

Buffalo Bill drew rein hard when he reached the edge of the crowd, setting the horse on its haunches. He waved his hat to get attention. Art saw the boy on the pony coming along behind.

"Trouble!" Cody shouted. "Trouble back at the arena! My young friend here just now heard three men planning to rustle the horses! We need help down there!"

A man with field glasses trained them on the arena.

"He's right!" he yelled. "Somebody's let all the rough stock loose! Buffalo and longhorns and all! They're running toward the saddle-mount pens. Oh, no! Somebody's letting the saddle mounts go! I can see somebody down there driving them away! Here! *My* horse is in that bunch!"

Cody assumed command. "Young man," he said to the boy, "you and I have to be the cavalry here. You take your pony and ride like the dickens for Frauson's Hill. I'm charging you to intercept the racers there and give them the word."

The boy put his heels to his pony and went.

Cody turned to the crowd. "You, men! Get on down there and gather up whatever mounts you can! Go into town for horses if you have to. And get your guns. I'm going after the racers! We'll all meet near the new bridge . . . !"

And the legend of the plains was gone in a whirl of dust, leaning low over his horse's neck and riding full out just as he had done as a Pony Express messenger, determined to catch up with the racers and bring them back to aid in stopping the stampede.

Moore and Art ran for the hitching rail at the starting line.

"Got a plan?" Moore asked.

"Not much of one," Art panted. "But somebody'd better keep that cavvy in sight while Buffalo Bill gets his cavalry together. Why don't you do this . . ." — they reached their horses and swung up into the leather. — "you see if you can cross the river and head up there after the riders. But don't follow them, the way Cody's doing. Just head to the left of those windmills, straight across country. That kid has plenty of sand, but he isn't goin' to make it in time."

The bridge loomed in sight. The leaders were already over it. Some cowboys had chosen to take to the water instead, but most of the pack elected to crowd and jostle their way across the narrow bridge.

Link knew the kid ahead of him was in trouble. The young buckaroo desperately leaned his weight to the side, what little weight he had, standing on the stirrup to shift the saddle back into place. But it was hopeless. Link pushed Rico hard to come up alongside, forcing the kid's horse toward the outside of the bunch. Harder and harder he pushed, reaching out and grabbing the kid's sleeve to keep him on top of the horse. They slowed down together, finally coming to a halt, with Rico making a shield between the unfortunate young cowhand and the rushing mass of horse-

225

flesh going by. Link let go and the kid let the saddle slide with him off the left side of the horse.

"Thanks," he said breathlessly, setting his saddle back in place and tightening the girth. "Sure appreciate it. Could 'a' been tromped."

"Tromped is the word," Link said.

The last of the racers pounded past them on the way to the bridge, and Link heard the planks thundering. Behind him, the thunder seemed to echo the sound. A lightning bolt gleamed, slashing a stark rip through the clouds to the west. Another boom of thunder rolled.

Link saw something else, a lone rider going like hell toward the river upstream as if he was trying to take a short cut to get into the race. Even at a full run the man rode heavy and business-like, like a tall sack of oats sitting in the saddle, and Link knew it was his old partner. It was Moore.

"You better get goin'," he said to the kid.

He turned Rico and put him into a fast run up along the river. He didn't know quite why he was choosing to leave the race and intercept Moore, no more than he knew why the little rise of ground they called Frauson's Hill seemed ominous to him. He only knew that it seemed to be the right direction to go.

"Moore! Hey, you, Moore!" he yelled.

Moore turned. He recognized the big, pale horse, the rider with the black beard.

"Link! We got trouble!"

Panting, Moore rapidly explained the situation.

"Where's Art?"

"The crazy bastard went after them all on his own. Cody sent the men on foot to find horses, and he's over there tryin' to catch up with the tail end of the race. But all these cowpokes in the race are gonna have their horses winded before long. On top of everything, we got us a damn' dangerous-lookin' storm brewing."

"You think we could catch the others at the hill?" Link asked.

"Sure, easy," Moore said. "We could cut 'em off, even if we don't push our horses."

Thus as they had done in past years, the two rode together. They rode upright in the saddle with their horses side-by-side moving in a ground-eating, steady lope. When they came to the river, they took to the water without the slightest break in their stride and plunged across the shallow channels with spray flying. Lightning flashed to the west and thunder boomed across the river. They rode on in a straight line through the willow thickets on the far side of the river and went, together, up the hill.

Art was alone in the stampeding bunch of horses and steers, using his spurs and quirt to force his horse through the rough stock. The bunch ran in a panic, but Art's horse gradually gained on it, passing one wild-eyed steer and one plunging bronco at a time. The whole teeming mass crossed the last road and headed for the river. Beyond the river lay the sandhills, a maze of hillocks and bluffs and brush-choked arroyos and draws. Once the horses and cattle got into that tangled terrain, it would take weeks to round them up again.

Quirting another steer out of his way, Art was pretty sure he knew what the rustlers had in mind. It was the same as the Indians used to do, and the cattle thieves in Kansas. Stampede a herd into rough country, then round up what animals you can and get away. One of the Texas longhorns wheeled to face him, annoyed at having this cowboy so close to his backside. Art drew his Colt. But he didn't dare fire it, not in this mêlée. Instead, he swerved his horse to put another steer between himself and the longhorn.

It meant more lost time.

Drops of rain began to patter down, making dark freckles on his horse's neck and on his chaps. Even in the bawling, whinnying surge of animals he could hear the drops hitting his hat brim. *Big drops*, he thought. *Damn.* Thunder rolled over the din of hammering hoofs. It was getting too dark to see the front of the herd clearly.

Link and Moore together reached the crest of the saddle between Frauson's Hill and the windmills just as the first riders came pounding past, the Pinto Kid among them.

"Hey! Kid!" Moore yelled out.

At first the Kid didn't hear him over the din of the race.

"Hey, KID!"

Now he heard Moore yelling at him to stop. Had it been anyone else, he'd think it was some town cowboy just foolin' around. But it was Moore. The Kid pulled out of the pack and slowed to a trot.

"I'm winnin'," he said, nearly out of breath.

"No doubt about it," Moore said. "Where's the others?"

"I dunno. Oh, there comes Emil! And Mac!"

These two were also hailed, and they pulled out of the race to join Moore and Link and the Pinto Kid. Mac volunteered to ride back along the racecourse and find Garth.

"We got trouble," Moore said. He explained what had happened. "Art's down there alone somewhere in that stampede, tryin' to keep track of the rustlers. We think they're the same ones Garth and Link here chased into Dakota a couple years back."

"Link?" Garth's eyes went wide.

Link nodded. "It's me."

"Son-of-a-bitch," Garth said.

"No kiddin'," Emil echoed.

"Tell you about it later," Link said. "Look here . . . we got some prime horses in that bunch, and I want 'em back. And I want that slab-sided motherless son-of-a-bitch called Army behind bars. You boys with me?"

Five Keystone riders peered into the distance. All they could see, under the low, leaden sky, was lots of rough country being lit up by frequent flashes of lightning. The storm was cocked to go off and send half of Noah's flood down all around them. Their horses were sweating and panting. The only gun among them was Moore's. They had no slickers, no canteens, no food, not even jackets.

Without hesitation and without speaking, they fell in line beside Link.

Link started Rico at a lope, and the others rode with him six abreast, these Keystone men, headed straight into the storm, aiming themselves as they had always done, straight to where the trouble was.

They rode on around the hill with rain beginning to splat down into the grass and sagebrush. Off to the left, atop the hill, Link thought for a moment he saw a wagon parked under the trees. But the darkness was thick and the rain made everything look distant and strange. Still riding six abreast, they crossed the last road and labored up the steep rise on the other side. From there they saw the stampede, the stragglers just crossing the river. A lone cowboy rode the flank near the head of the bunch and he was hazing them hard. Two more riders were on the far side, somewhat farther back, keeping the animals at a run.

Now, running their horses at top speed, the Keystone men charged toward the nearest rustler, the one working alone.

Garth yelled — "There! See that?" — as a flash of light blinked from the middle of the stampede. In a moment they heard the *pop!* and saw another flash. Art was in that swarm of animals somewhere, firing at the rustlers.

"Get Art outta there!" Link ordered. "Now!"

And four Keystone riders swerved and charged headlong into the stampede, quirting steers and broncos out of their way, forcing their horses forward. Link's Colt was in his saddlebag, but his lariat was at his knee; as he and Moore closed in on the rustler, the rustler looked back to see the dark-bearded man on the pale horse swinging a big loop. He dropped his own coil of rope and went for his gun, but too late. The loop dropped over him, went tight, pulled his hand holding the reins tightly to his side, made the horse lunge sidewise, then dragged him out of the saddle. In a flash, Moore was on the ground, running down the rope to hog-tie him.

"Record time, I'd say," Link panted when Moore came back to the horses.

They saw more men on horses coming. Cody must have broken speed records himself, bringing two dozen men with him. Moore looked down at the hog-tied rustler.

"Leave him?" he said. "I got his gun."

"Leave him. Let's go after Art!"

The stampede was slowing but was no less dangerous. With each peal of thunder and lightning strike, there were steers climbing others in panic, horses rearing up to lash out at everything around them. Art went more cautiously, edging past each animal. He saw and heard his Keystone boys coming through, coming to him, and waved them on. Rain slashed down in torrents, then moved on and left breathing room before the next wind-driven wall of water came along.

Art had his horse's chest up against a small steer, pushing it, using it as a living shield to block a wild-eyed bronco from getting to him with its slashing forehoofs. He looked at the riders coming toward him through the slanting, driving, cold rain. Suddenly, so suddenly he blinked to see if he had imagined it, Art saw the horns of the steers in a blaze. Each animal had blue fire tipping its horns, ghostly glares that danced up from poll to point, then stood on the points like elongated, bluish candle flames. When one of the heaving brutes pushed into another one, the flames shook and sparked from one to the other, always coming back to shimmer at the horn tips.

The sky was a deep, solid gray; the rain in curtains, wavering, coming and going. The mass of animals was so thick you couldn't distinguish one from the other. Under the sodden sky and above the glistening herd, Art saw four riders coming, then two more, but he saw them through blue flames. Each rain-soaked hat was black, each shirt black as well in the dark. It looked like a procession of monks in mourning, moving with ghostly slowness through the gloom of a monastery lit only by sputtering candles.

Almost as quickly as it had come, the eerie flames stopped.

"You boys see that?" Art said as the men drew rein.

"Yeah," said Mac.

"Seen it before," Emil said. "Ghost fire, some call it. Like scuffling your feet on a carpet and touching the doorknob."

The Keystone riders formed a wedge around Art and his tired horse and worked their way toward safety at the far edge of the herd, where the other two rustlers had last been seen. Moore gave the confiscated gun to Emil. Link reached back and wrestled his Colt out of his saddlebag. Art reloaded as they jammed and shuffled through the slowing herd.

"You boys can handle those other two *hombres?*" Link shouted above the bawling and whinnying and thunder. "I think I see three, maybe four of Tory's horses over there. Like to cut 'em out before they get up in these hills."

"Go on and get 'em," Art shouted. "You want help?"

"I'll manage," Link replied. He turned Rico, and began forcing his way through more cattle, watching for another glimpse of the H-Bar-C horses.

"So that's Link!" the Pinto Kid shouted. "Never would 'a' known!"

"Bein' soaked and covered in mud like you are," Art responded, "I can't even tell *you* five range bums apart! C'mon, let's get after those two wahoos and leave it to the town boys to collect the herd. This way!"

The rustlers, seeing the hopelessness of the situation, gave up trying to drive the stampede into the badlands and slashed their horses into a run through the thickening mud and up the nearest gulch. Opportunists turned rustlers, they were now common fugitives, fugitives with six Keystone riders on their heels, pounding through the sodden earth and driving rain.

Chapter Fourteen

Cowboy Down

The rain lessened and daylight came creeping back under the clouds. It spread tentatively through the sandhills, gradually showing itself as if afraid the lightning was still out there, waiting. Link recognized three of Tory's horses near the edge of the milling chaos of steers and broncos and reined Rico toward them.

"Hah!" he shouted. "Rico! Get 'em!"

The *palomilla* was never bred to be a cutting horse, but Tory had taught him the trade anyway. With ears pointed forward and eyes wide and watchful, he bent toward the three chestnuts. To Rico's instincts, there now was one job and only one job, and it was to get to those three horses and keep them together.

In his enthusiasm for the task at hand, Rico made a sudden, quick turn that brought his shoulder slamming into the flank of a frothy-mouth longhorn. There was no giving way, no yielding; this was no glancing blow between a small cow pony and a lightweight steer, but a full force collision of two brutes. Down went the longhorn, thrown off balance on the slope and sliding in the mud. Down went Rico over him, pawing his forelegs frantically to stay on his feet but finding no foothold except on the longhorn underneath him. Horse, man, longhorn, and all went down in one mud-slick tangle of legs and leather.

The longhorn thrashed violently, trying to get up,

throwing his head this way and that in panic until one of the horn tips slashed Rico's side just behind the saddle. Rico screamed out in a shrill whinny and lunged and lunged to gain his legs, but could not extricate himself from the longhorn. Link used a hand to push down on the saddle horn so he could pull his leg up out of the way, but he lost his grip and then the saddle. He slid off, grasping wildly for any kind of handhold, and went down and felt Rico's hoof catch him in the ribs.

Link's foot was caught in the stirrup. As Rico got to his legs, the longhorn felt its head free of the weight. It jerked its head up, the point of its horn catching Link as if someone had shoved a red-hot running iron into him just above his gun belt, a little to one side of the buckle.

His foot fell free. Rico left his rider lying there and clawed his way up the muddy slope to flatter ground where he ran fifty yards before stopping to breathe. The steer's horns kept on slashing from side to side like cavalry sabers and inflicted another slashing wound on Link's thigh before the brute realized it was free and ran, stumbling, after the other cattle. Link lay alone, chest down across a clump of sagebrush. The smell of crushed sage was the last thing he sensed before passing out.

Blood trickled from his side and his leg and mingled with the sodden earth.

Buffalo Bill's impromptu posse came along in the wake of the herd, their main goal being to keep the bunch together until they could get it stopped. Tory and one of the townsmen spotted Link off to one side and broke off from the posse to go to him.

"Looks bad," the man from town said.

"Yes," Tory said. "See what you can do for him. I'll

catch up his horse. We're gonna need it to get him back to town."

Rico came to Tory willingly and was content to stand ground-reined with Tory's own horse while the two men examined Link's wounds. Link's shirt was torn and soaked in blood. His chaps were slick with it. His scarf and hat were gone.

"Better get him to town," the man said. "We oughta be able to find the doc somewhere."

For one brief moment, Link's eyes flickered and his lips moved in a low, hoarse whisper. Tory leaned in to try to make out what he was saying. "Keystone . . . ," came the croaking voice.

"We'll find them. Don't worry," Tory said.

"No," the croaking said again. "*Not* them. Don't . . . can't let them . . . take me back like this. . . ."

The eyes closed, and Link's mind slid back into bottomless shadows of shock and pain.

Rather than heave Link across his saddle face down like a sack of oats, Tory got the other man to help get him into the saddle in front of him while he sat behind to hold him up. Rico trailed along behind them, his head hanging down like a guilty dog's. With careful haste they made their way back to the flat terrain along the river, then along the river toward the new bridge.

"What the hell . . . ?" the man exclaimed.

A long, black vehicle was stopped on the approach to the bridge, waiting for them. The design was very, very old. Even the freight wagon running gear looked ancient.

The driver was a short, ageless figure with crooked back, and he did not speak. He got down and opened the back doors at their approach, then helped the other two men load Link into the hearse. He resumed his high seat, tapped the two horses with his whip, and drove across the bridge. He bypassed the arena and stock pens and drove all the way to Front Street, Tory and the man from town following.

"You might as well go back and help them finish rounding up the strays," Tory told the stranger. "We can find the doc on our own. Appreciate your help."

"Sure," the man said. "I think I will go back and help. Just keep on down the street, and past the barbershop you'll see his sign pointing down an alleyway."

"All right," Tory said. "And thanks again."

"Right," the man said. "Maybe we'll see y' when all this is over with."

"Might be," Tory said. "Y'never know."

Tory and Old Tim found the town doctor in a surgery behind Front Street. As soon as he had seen the chaos and commotion at the arena, the doctor had gone straight into town to get ready, because, with all that shooting and stampeding, he knew for certain there would be people injured. Link was the first.

He found several ribs broken, how many he couldn't say, together with a deep puncture wound that might have hit a kidney, certainly the bowels if not the kidneys, and another deep puncture and slash along one leg. About all he could do was douse the open wounds with sulfa powder and bandage them up and hope for the best. He wrapped the ribs tightly and helped Tory load him back into the hearse.

"Shouldn't really move him around too much," the doctor advised. "You say your place isn't far?"

"We won't go far," Tory said.

"Well, I don't know. One good bump and there might be a busted rib go into his lungs, and it's all over. I think he might have a concussion, too."

"We'll take it easy," Tory said.

"You watch him real careful." The doctor frowned. "Keep him warm. Just watch him, that's all."

"Watch him for what?"

"Bleeding, for one thing. If he complains about blurry vision, or can't seem to say anything that makes sense, he's probably got a concussion."

"Then what do we do?"

"Nothing to do but keep him quiet, keep him warm. I'll give you something to help him sleep."

Old Tim snapped the lines, and his team stepped out with the hearse.

"You go ahead," Tory told him. "Take it real easy. I'm goin' back for the horses. You know which way to head."

Late afternoon gingerly eased itself down into the narrow band of light between horizon and cloud banks. Six Keystone riders drew up abreast atop a hill to let their winded horses breathe. Their quarry, on fresher horses, kept moving. They could see them far in the distance. For the time being, Art was satisfied to let them go. The runaway livestock was pretty much still in one bunch, and Buffalo Bill's boys were getting them turned and headed back toward North Platte. As for himself, he was as tired and wet as his riders.

"Let's break it off," he said. The other five looked at him, then at the two tiny dots almost to the horizon in the late afternoon light. He was Art. They would keep on after the rustlers if he asked them to, even if they didn't have food or jackets or guns. Or they would go back with him, rest, equip themselves, and take the trail with him tomorrow. He was the boss and it was up to him. They looked at each other and each man knew that the others understood this. This was what it meant when they signed up to ride for the brand.

"We'll get ourselves dried out and get some sleep, get organized tomorrow and start the wagons for home," he said as they turned back. "Moore and me and maybe one more, we'll swing north on our way back and pick up their tracks if we're lucky."

"It'll be good to be back at the Keystone," the Pinto Kid said, "even if it ain't always as excitin' as town is. Too many people, though. I never feel too much at ease in town."

Three miles later, leading Rico and the three chestnuts tied head to tail in a string, Tory reached the ranch where they were staying. He put the horses in the corral, took care of the saddles and bridles, then went toward the barn. The hearse was standing outside.

Inside the barn, he saw a tall, dark figure bending over Link lying on blankets on a bed of hay. He wore a long, black oilskin with a hood on it, which he pushed back when Tory came in.

"Tory," he said.

"Father Nicholas," said Tory.

"I think he can travel," the priest said. "When we get back, he should stay with me at Old Tim's hut for a while, instead of your place. It seems best that Elaine not see him like this. Do you agree?"

"Yes," Tory said. "In fact, I'd been kind of worrying about that. But he didn't want to go back to the Keystone Ranch, so. . . ."

"Yes," the priest said. "I know the story."

"I *don't* understand, Art, I don't understand it at *all!*"

"Can't help that, I guess," Art said. "It's just like I told you. Link was there, he rode against us, we think he got hurt bad in the stampede, and then he was gone. One of these days we're goin' to catch up with those horse thieves. They caused it all. They deserve to hang."

"And you really looked for him?" Gwen said, her face taut with frustration. "You and Emil and Moore and the rest, you couldn't find any sign of him at all?"

"Like I said, just that scarf there. In the mud, and what looked like blood on the ground. Could've been anybody's blood. Horse blood, for all we could tell. That scarf, though. . . ." — Gwen was holding it. Art had given it to Mary to wash, along with other clothes, but there was a bloodstain on it she hadn't been able to get out. It was also ripped and stretched at two corners, as if it had been knotted around someone's neck and torn loose. Gwen looked at the hand-sewn edges and the H-Bar-C embroidered on it. — ". . . that scarf is Link's, there's no doubt about that. He wore it the whole time we were there. Told me it was made by a woman at the ranch where he worked. Sewed the ranch brand on it."

Gwen was no longer interested in the brand, and dropped the scarf onto the table. She turned to Art with her fists clenched and her eyes hard. "And you didn't even ask where this ranch is? How are we ever going to find out if he is alive or dead? Didn't you even think to *ask?*"

"It just never came up in our talk, that's all," Art said. "Where the place is, I mean. You don't understand how it is with men, sweetheart. Men don't spend a lot of time asking each other . . . I mean you might ask a man how the grub is, or what the horses are like, but. . . ."

"One of your best friends?" she interrupted. "Certainly the best man you ever hired? First, he rides out of here without an explanation, *and* injured. Then you find him at that . . . that . . ." — she looked for a word — ". . . that *exhibition* in North Platte, wearing strange clothes and some woman's needlework around his neck, and it *never* came up? Art, have you no curiosity at *all?* At least some sense of concern?"

"All I know is Tory came back for the horses, and said Link told him he wanted 'em to take him back to the H-Bar-C. I said fine, take care of him, let us know if we can do anything. They'll send word soon. I'm pretty sure of it."

Gwen's eyes held a barely veiled coolness. They gave Art the feeling she found him annoying and thick-headed and disappointing.

"I'll tell Mary we're ready for supper," she said after a long and silent space.

As she swept out of the room in a rustle of skirts, she paused briefly to look back over her shoulder at him. She pointed to the yellow bandanna on the table.

"You may as well take *that* and put it somewhere to keep. I'm sure he'll want it if he ever comes back here again." And she found it impossible to withhold the final cut: "*If* he's even still alive. For all *you* know."

Elaine heard the news in her room. She stood with downcast eyes and her neck bowed, one hand resting on the covered saddle as her brother told her what had happened.

"Will he . . . ?" she ventured.

"Live?" Tory answered. "Father Nicholas thinks so. We just can't tell what the damage is, inside, I mean. He might get gangrene or something. We just don't know."

"I'll go to him," she said. "I can at least take him something to eat. And blankets, a soft pillow."

"I'd better take it," Tory said. "You don't want to see him the way he is. We have to remember your own health, you know. We'll get him awake, and we'll get him on his feet. You just leave it to us, all right?"

She went to the window and looked out in the direction of the hills. Somewhere behind the hills — although she had never been there — strange Old Tim had a hut and a shed for his hearse. Sometimes she had seen him digging his graves, but she had never seen where he lived. But now, wherever it was and whatever it looked like, the hermit's place would be the focus and center of her thoughts and her prayers. She would obey her brothers and remain in her tower as a prisoner of her affliction, keeping her heart pure and strong until the day the Keystone rider once again appeared beneath her window.

Meanwhile, Link lay in a room scarcely large enough for the narrow bed made of poles and rawhide webbing. In a niche in the adobe wall a candle sputtered and flickered. The stool next to the bed held a small jug of water and a bowl of thin soup gone cold and scummy. He twisted and groaned in his blankets, sometimes muttering the words to some dream begotten by the fever. His face was deathly pale, yellow in the candle's light, and his beard was matted and streaked with his own spittle.

For the most part he was alone. Lavaine, still a stumbling weakling from his tick fever, had to let Tory do the nursing. Tory was also trying to regroup the livestock, patrol the various bunches on range, and keep the whole operation going. Old Tim rose each morning and cooked himself porridge that he ate in the gloom with tea, hunched over his small table, talking to himself. Each morning he scraped the remains from the pan into the bowl when he had finished with it, took the leftover tea in his mug, and went to the doorway to peer in at the figure in the darkness.

Hearing no sound and seeing no movement, Old Tim

was satisfied that the patient did not want to eat and so he left bowl and mug on the table and went out on his day's rounds. Old Tim was perplexed by this man in his bedroom. He did not know what to feed him, or how to do it, or whether to keep replacing the candle, or whether more blankets or fewer blankets were needed.

More than Link's unresponsive condition, what perplexed Old Tim was the matter of a grave. Several times, he hitched up the team and loaded his shovel and pick and pry bar and drove most of the day on the high seat of his hearse, meandering in long loops and circles, unsure where a grave for a man should be located. Graves for women were a simpler matter. A woman could lie at the edge of a flowered meadow, for instance, or at the foot of a rock outcropping facing west. She might like her deep and final resting place overlooking the forest or beneath the guardian branches of a giant pine. Tim understood such things about women.

But where to put a man's grave. High up under the overhang of the bluffs where no one could come at it from behind? Or hidden in a narrow gorge along running water where thick, tall grass and bending ferns would soon obliterate all trace of it? Old Tim drove far out of the valley and into the sand-drifted places, desert places where there would be nothing between a grave and the stars turning in their never-changing tracks.

Should it be a deep grave, for safety and quiet, or a shallower grave where a man might hear the footfalls of his horses and friends as he slept? Obscure and quickly forgotten, the way some men seem to want to be, or in some prominent spot marked with some kind of enduring stone?

He had to take care, too, not to begin digging over that one certain sort of stone. If he did, then Bernard would come with his old cart and his vague, hangdog expression to take slabs of it for his walls. Old Tim was not certain, not at *all* certain, whether it was proper for stone from a man's grave to be used in a wall around a woman. Knowing what he did about women, he finally puzzled it out — a woman would not mind walls quarried from a woman's grave, but she would not want to live behind those taken from a man's.

The only person who seemed unconcerned with these issues of death was the tall priest, Father Nicholas. It was he who came once a day with the thin soup and a new candle. He changed the dressings and laundered the bloody ones far away from the house in order that Elaine not see. Sometimes he sat on the stool next to the bed and read aloud from the Bible, and from time to time he drew from his pouch two green leaves which he crushed in his fingers and applied to the unconscious cowboy's lips.

Over and over the cowboy dreamed of long, gleaming horns slashing like sabers through driving rain, of the screams of injured horses, and of muzzle flashes in the gloom. The dream would rage and thunder over him and all around him and then would subside and fade into an older dream, one of long, green pastures where peaceful horses grazed. In this dream there was a house and a woman. Her hair was golden and the house was somewhere far, far away from any house he had ever known, and it was his and so was she.

He would lose the dream when that big hand came behind his head to lift his mouth to the warm broth, but afterward the quiet would return, and then the deadly horns again and the horse screaming in the rain.

And one morning, in the deep purple darkness that comes between the inquiries of night owls and the monotonous matins song of the robins, he realized he no longer dreamed of the tower. Not since Christmas.

The Keystone came alive again following the return of the six men from the North Platte Blowout. In the bunkhouse there was once again talk of being a special kind of outfit, an outfit of men the likes of whom would never be found among mere merchants and grouchy farmers and one-horse cowboys. People in town sometimes treated them like they thought cowboys were illiterate, trouble-making, hard-drinking, uncivilized bums. But it wasn't true. They were independent, sure. And had a lot of pride. Pride and independence were what kept a good cow outfit together. You wanted men to be proud of turning out good herds, and proud because they rode for a straight-up good outfit. People in town might trust their neighbors to borrow tools and such, but a man who rode for a good brand was a man you would trust with your life.

As the six returning riders sat with their comrades after supper, sharing Durham and the packets of cigarette papers they called their "bibles" or showing off a new pocket knife bought in town, the stories they told were like new wine poured into old bottles. The special feeling of being chosen to ride for the Keystone surged back.

Some remembered they had not been to visit their friend Kyle and his wife Fontana in months, and came riding and shouting to his front gate. Mac and the Pinto Kid talked about the squatters up on the Lucy Creek range and wondered how it had been ignored for so long, and rode out to deal with it. A friend came from town complaining about a gambler who had not only cheated him at cards but had kissed his wife. Art and Moore rode back with him, stirrup to stirrup, and backed him with their hands resting on their gun butts while he escorted the gambling man to the eastbound stage.

Once again the Keystone riders swept the range. Women whose drunken husbands needed warning could call upon them. Small landholders would hear pounding hoofs in the dawn and come out to discover their strayed milk cow or plow horse was back in the pen. Cattle were herded up and moved away from overgrazed pastures or away from hay-fields. Children picking berries, who once would hide from the sound of approaching horses, now scrambled to the roadside to wave at men riding straight and proud in saddles marked with the familiar Keystone symbol.

It was a pure blue-sky summer, with only a single dark cloud hovering.

"Hey, Boss?" Moore called to Art, who was walking past the bunkhouse.

"What's up, Moore?"

"Mind if I walk along with you a minute?"

"Nope. What's on your mind?"

"I hate to be the one to bring it up. But since I was Link's partner before we even got into this country, I guess I'm the one who's. . . ." He was stuck for a word.

"Responsible?" Art said.

"Yeah, responsible. I guess we shouldn't have come home without finding where Link was. The boys, they've kinda noticed how Missus Pendragon is kinda upset about it. Me, too, for that matter. And I guess what I gotta tell you is that she kind of . . . well . . . she kinda asked me the other day when I was goin' to look for Link."

"You?"

"Well, it figures," Moore said. "And I oughta do it, too. So, I was thinking, now that things are more or less gettin' back on track around here, maybe you could spare me and I'd go have a look for him. Probably have to start out at North Platte and work my way south. I'm pretty sure he said that place was south and west, just inside Colorado."

Truth to tell Art, also, had deep worries about Link. And Gwen. But he'd shoved them into a place where he wouldn't have to think about them, the way he shoved certain kinds of mail into pigeonholes of his desk. Link probably was out there somewhere, probably still down and needing friends. On the other hand, Gwen seemed to be starting to get over it. Still strangely moody at times, still staring off into space once in a while, but less likely to snap and snarl at him. No, that wasn't fair. She didn't snap at him. She just looked at him as if she'd like to. And maybe he was just imagining it, anyway.

"You were puttin' in some head gates, weren't you?"

"Yeah. Almost done with that job. Mac and Garth can handle it."

"Kyle's stud finished with that mare of yours?"

"Yeah. I'll drop him back by Kyle's place on my way to Nebraska. That's if it's all right if I go."

"Sure," Art said, although he was really not sure at all. "Sure. Draw yourself whatever food and bedding you need. Stop off at the house later on and I'll give you some travelin' money. Your month's pay, too."

Two days later, as the sun was beginning to show a bright, brass curve over the eastern horizon, Moore rode out to go in search of the missing Keystone rider. Gwen stood at her window, watching him go, then turned and walked back to the bed, her nightgown flowing down off her shoulders to make a lavender mound on the floor in the morning light.

Chapter Fifteen

Valley and Grave

Moore figured there was time to swing by Kyle's place, drop off the stud he'd borrowed, and still make another twenty miles before nightfall. But he hadn't figured on Fontana; she never let a visitor refuse a meal, and she certainly was not going to begin with Noah Moore. She was setting another place at the dinner table even while he was standing there telling Kyle he needed to be going on.

"Not until we hear all about what happened at North Platte," Fontana said, taking his hat and firmly pushing him toward a chair.

It was getting toward three o'clock before Moore was finished answering questions about the great Independence Day Blowout. He recounted each event, described the town and the shops, told Fontana what hats the ladies were wearing, and described the horses to Kyle. Kyle finally rose and stretched and consulted his pocket watch.

"No point in you starting out this late," he said.

"Certainly not," Fontana agreed. "The spare room is all made up, and I've already got a ham in the oven for supper. So that's settled."

"Ever notice the way women can settle things so easy?" Kyle said.

"I have," Moore said. "Generally speaking, they don't seem to give a man a chance to argue."

"True enough."

The two went out to put up Moore's horses. Kyle was proud of his improvements to the place, especially the new house he built to replace the one that had burned. He gave Moore the grand tour from gate post to backhouse, ending up on the porch in comfortable chairs, enjoying Fontana's coffee.

"You've been over all the country south and east of here," Moore said.

"Pretty much," Kyle agreed.

"Where do you figure Link would head for, anyway?"

"I've been giving that some thought," Kyle said. He pulled out his bandanna and used a corner of it to wipe the inside of his black eye patch, the way he always did when he was thinking how to figure out things. "You said you might go to North Platte and try to pick up his trail there. But I'm thinking . . . from what you said . . . that you might save some time by just heading straight south."

"Why's that?"

"Well . . . and you know him longer than I do . . . seems to me he'd have a place in mind to head to. Don't figure him to be the kind who's comfortable straying from one ranch to another, at least not without he knew he was going *to* somewhere. Link strikes me as the sort who'd always be traveling toward people he knew."

"I guess so, maybe."

"He didn't come here," Kyle pointed out. "You said he'd been workin' on a place south and far enough west to be in Colorado country, down in the dry part. So, my hunch is he was thinkin' to end up at Pasque's place down on the Purgatory. When he started out from the Keystone, I mean. All things considered, Pasque's would make a good place for a man to hole up."

"Might be," Moore said.

"If I was you, I think I'd drift that way and forget about North Platte. Along the way I'd ask about horse outfits. Somebody's bound to know it if there's a ranch breedin' good horse stock anywhere within fifty or a hundred miles of 'em."

"Well, you oughta know . . . ," Moore began.

Fontana came out to get the empty cups.

"If you two aren't doing anything, but talk horses" — she smiled — "you may as well come inside and shell some peas for me."

"Kinda late in the season to still be pickin' pod peas, isn't it?" Moore said as he and Kyle got up and started for the door after her.

"You don't know Fontana." Kyle grinned. "If she wants something to grow, it grows."

At Burr Creek no one remembered a tall rider with a big, black mustache who carried his arm in a sling and was traveling south. After all that time, Moore wasn't surprised. If Link had crossed the Platte at Jack's Ferry, no one at the crossing recalled it. No memory of such a man at Julesburg or at the store and saloon where the Arikara River ran into the Republican. On the Arapaho reservation Moore stopped to talk to a man who spoke broken English and who said he had seen a tall *wasichu* on a big horse with the mark on the saddle — he pointed to the Keystone brand on the fender of Moore's — the same. He put two fingers under his nose, crossways: the white man had a mustache.

"Any more *wasichus* around here, breeding other big horses?"

The Arapaho pointed west toward where a low line of horizon clouds showed the invisible and distant Rocky Mountains. "There," he said. He made the sign for bad men, many of them, men who take horses. After making the sign for white men, the finger drawn across the forehead, he threw his hand toward the ground as if it was a handful of horseshit. *Very bad men,* Moore thought. *Evil beings.*

"A good man, my friend," Moore said. "One horse only. One and a pack mule." He had nearly forgotten about the mule.

Instantly the Arapaho turned to point southeast. Same man. Tall horse and a long-ear carrying pack saddle. He thought a moment, then made the sign for two days of riding.

"What then?" Moore said. "Ride two days. What's there?"

Again the finger drawn across the forehead, but this time followed with the palm up. A white man, a good *wasichu.* The Arapaho signed again. The white has a woman and young boy this tall. Good horses, too.

One day's ride took Moore across Sand Creek and off the reservation. By the evening of the next day he came to a road and soon he saw in the distance the small, neat house and the solid, strong corrals of the Dunlap farm. A gangly boy in outgrown coveralls was in the yard, tossing grain to a flock of clucking chickens.

"Howdy," Moore said.

The boy left the chickens and walked over to Moore. "Howdy," he said, solemnly reaching up with a handshake.

"Wonder if I might water my horse?" Moore said.

"Sure thing," Davy Dunlap said, staring at the brand on the saddle fender.

"Is your father around?" Moore asked.

"I'll fetch 'im," Davy said, still looking from the brand to the rider. "Why'n't you light down and water your horse, and I'll be right back?" The boy tossed the rest of the grain at the chickens and hurried toward the barn to inform his father they had company. Then he ran back, ahead of the older man, and made himself useful by pumping more water into the trough. He watched the two men with great interest.

It was the second Keystone rider to appear at their doorstep and shake hands with his father. Davy could hardly believe in such a thing. Two Keystone men. At their place. He looked at his father with new respect, thinking there must be something more to this farm, and to his father, than he knew.

Dunlap told Moore the same story as the Arapaho had, but in more detail. There was a band of outlaws, horse thieves. Rumor said they had a huge layout somewhere far up in the mountains, a vast complex of scattered ranches. Their favorite method of rustling was to sneak into a range and gather up pregnant mares, keep them until the foals were weaned, then turn them loose. Often a rancher thought his mare had strayed for six or eight months, and then strayed back again, their hoofs crippled and their mouths raw. These were rustlers who preferred not to rob at gunpoint, preferred to stay unseen and unnoticed, if possible.

"They say there's even a hell town up there, and they own it. One of those busted-down mining towns. An old grubstake miner told a whiskey drummer, I guess, and he told 'most everybody else. Now it's a town full of renegades and men with a price on their heads, and whores of every description. Ugly place, ugly as sin, they say."

"I'd doubt if my friend went there," Moore said. "You say he delivered a couple of horses for you?"

"Yep. I can draw you a map how to get there. But you'll

stay to supper? Got a nice bunk out at the barn you're more than welcome to."

" 'Preciate it." Moore smiled.

"Just one thing. . . ." Carl hesitated. "Wonder if you'd mind letting the boy unsaddle your horses and take care of your gear for you? He's just awful proud to meet a Keystone rider, y'see."

Moore set out early the next morning and rode patiently now that he could be sure he was on Link's trail. Another day or two and he'd find others who had seen him. Moore was getting into sand country, long, flat stretches of sage and yucca and piñon with only a few lone buttes for landmarks. *It wouldn't take long for a man to get over into Pasque's territory*, he thought. *Maybe Link* did *go there after delivering the horses.*

The two buttes finally came into view, the twin mesas drawn on the farmer's map, and in a couple of hours he came to the crossroads. The main road curved and dipped down into a valley out of sight, then emerged in the distance and curved around the buttes. But Carl Dunlap's directions were to take the narrower track, the one leading into the buttes. Moore's instinct told him the farmer was right. He didn't know how, but he felt that Link had been here, and that he had gone that way.

Still, he hesitated. He sat looking a long time toward the remote Rockies to the west, letting the horse crop dry grass. Moore was curious. Somebody ought to go over toward the mountains and have a look at this hell town so he could maybe get started doing something about it when he got home. Kind of like being out on the range and coming across a big, old nest of rattlers and warning other riders about it. He hesitated, considered, then pulled the horse's head up and turned him to ride down the narrower road.

Link has to come first, he thought.

He hadn't gone more than a few yards when he suddenly turned in the saddle and looked back. He could have sworn he had caught a whiff of smoke. It wasn't like wood smoke. Not like a campfire. It had more of the odor of smoldering coal, like you might smell if you were downwind of a coal furnace or a forge.

Moore sniffed again, shrugged, and rode on.

The odor of burning coal was coming from that place where the main road dropped out of sight into the creek bottom. If Moore had gone another hundred yards down that road, far enough to see the creek, he also would have seen Evan Thompson's camp. At his forge between his two wagons, the blacksmith was heating a steel rod to plunge into his evening cup of spiced wine. Except for the rod the forge was empty and the coals were cooling off. He would not be forging a link for the chain today. The Keystone man had chosen the track leading south and east, the narrow track. Had he elected to follow the western way into the mountains, the way toward the hell town and the hidden outlaw lair — he would have found the blacksmith blocking his way.

The blacksmith's boy came to him with a slab of bread.

"Is the cowboy going to come tonight?" he asked.

"No," Thompson told him. "One day, the Keystone men will come down this road. But not one man alone. And not now."

The hot steel sizzled into the wine and the giant blacksmith drank.

Just inside the throat of the valley, Moore made his

camp at twilight. He slept uneasily, turning and twisting in his blankets to the sounds of phantom horses running in the dark and old wagon wheels creaking among the piñon and cedar trees.

In the morning, everything was muffled by an opaque mist. A cloud had wandered into the valley and was sitting right on the ground, turning even the nearest trees into dim, dark shapes. He heard the horses grazing like spooks in the fog. Moore heated coffee and bread and beans, and ate breakfast, shivering, then struck camp, packed up his damp bedroll and his wet pot and plate. He put the saddles on the horses and finally stepped to the stirrup and settled his butt down on the mist-slippery leather.

He and the horses plodded along, following the road. Occasionally, from the woods, he heard the sound of running hoofs, and from time to time he thought he saw low mounds of earth, like prospecting holes left by gold miners. But he paid these things little attention as he concentrated on following what he could see of the road.

It looked as though the sun might just break through the fog when he saw the figure in the road ahead of him. The cloud filling the valley was starting to take on a spreading luminescence so bright it made him squint to look into it. The figure he saw was nearly seven feet tall from the bottom of its black oilskin cape to the point on the top of its black hood. One hand was raised in greeting, or perhaps in warning, and Moore looked twice to see if it held a scythe, for the reaping hook was all it would have needed to look like the figure of Death himself.

"Noah Moore," the phantasm said.

Riding closer, Moore now saw the face beneath the cloak.

"Padre," he said. "Seein' you standing in this fog like that, black cape an' all, I thought you were the Grim Reaper waiting for me."

"Not today, Noah. Not today. You've come to find your friend?"

"That's right."

"This way. Follow me."

The cloaked priest turned and strode up through the trees. Moore reined the horse off the road and followed, tugging the other animals with him. There was no trail or track, and, although they passed several of the strange mounds, he saw nothing to show that humans lived anywhere near here. The priest led the way across two low hills, across a well-used trail, and then a wagon track and they came to an adobe hut. On one side of the earthen building was a large *ramada* sheltering an antique hearse, and on the other side two equally antique horses stood asleep on their feet in a *jacal* where they were out of the drenching mist.

Inside the hut a small iron stove kept the cold fog at bay while the sickly flame of a coal-oil lamp struggled against the darkness. An old man sat on a crude leather chair in one corner, sharpening his shovel with a hand-held stone.

Stooping so as not to strike his head on the *vigas,* the priest took two candles from a shelf above the stove and handed one to Moore. He lit his from the chimney of the lamp, and then lit Moore's before leading the way into the next room.

The man on the bed was pale, thin, bandaged, and looked near death. The black beard reaching to his bare chest was incongruously large for the white, starved body, so that he looked more like an effigy than a man.

"Here's Noah," the priest said in a voice too large for the room.

The effigy turned its head and the two eyelids fell open, exposing the red rims and yellowed eyeballs to the candle glare.

"Why, it's Moore," the bearded skeleton whispered in a creaking voice.

"How y'been?" Moore said calmly, despite his initial shock at seeing Link's emaciated form.

"Tolerable," Link wheezed. "I been better."

"I've seen y'looking better," Moore agreed.

Father Nicholas helped Link raise his head to the cup of water he was holding for him. Link sipped, and fell back again.

"What's that smell?" Moore asked, sniffing the air.

"Azafrán," the *padre* replied. "Not really saffron, as the name implies, but that's what the Spaniards called it. Does much the same thing, draws pus from wounds, stimulates the heart, takes the fever down."

Moore asked Link what had happened to him after the stampede, but Link only managed to speak a few words before falling asleep.

"Better leave him," Father Nicholas said. "You'll camp with me, just a stone's throw from here. Tomorrow we'll ride over and meet the family."

A week passed, and then another. Moore made himself useful by helping Tory and Lavaine when they needed it. He cut and stacked firewood at Old Tim's hut, cleaned out a spring, and improved the fence that kept cattle from fouling it. Although it was early in the season for hunting, he went out twice and brought back venison to hang in the shade of the *ramada*. Old Tim jerked much of the meat, and the rest he cut up and put into the pot of green chili that forever simmered on the iron stove.

One day, Link sat up. A few days after that he was able to sit outside up against the adobe wall in the warm sun. Father Nicholas unwrapped the bandages and announced that fresh ones were not going to be needed, for the awful seeping wound in Link's side had closed into a glaring, long, red scar. Likewise, the gash in his leg had finally scabbed over, although it was swollen and painful to the touch.

Moore volunteered to ride fence for the brothers, and, when he returned in the afternoon two days later, he found his friend again sitting in the leather chair against the adobe wall in the sun. But his friend was much altered, much changed. Tory had brought Elaine to see him. Not only that, but her brother had suggested she bring her comb and scissors to clean him up and make him look more human. In addition to now having a closely trimmed beard and clipped mustache, Link was wearing a clean shirt.

Moore made an exaggerated show of standing there with his arms crossed to examine this freshly shorn apparition.

"I see you're struck dumb by all this handsomeness," Link said. "Miss Elaine is of the opinion that I'm the purtiest gent around. Said so herself."

"Well," Moore said slowly, "she's entitled to her opinion. You remember a long time ago out in Kansas when we saw that Indian powwow, those skinny characters dancin' around a fire, wearin' buffalo heads?"

"Yeah. So what?"

"I was kinda gettin' used to you lookin' just like that."

Link's first few walks encouraged him. Better yet, they gave him back his appetite. Moore had to go in search of another fat deer for the pot, while Old Tim clattered away atop his hearse and returned the following evening with a half dozen gunny sacks of chiles. And then the day came when he wanted to ride. Moore had been asked to supper at the house, and Link said he'd mount up and go along, too. Knowing the futility of arguing with him, Moore caught up Messenger. But he did insist on riding the big horse first, just to make sure it wouldn't mind being a saddle mount again.

The two men kept the horses at a walk through the piñons and over the two long hills. Once, at some distance, they glimpsed Old Tim's hearse. They made out the hunched figure digging on an open slope not too far from the trees, a spot where the morning sun would warm the earth no matter what the season.

The ride over to the house convinced Link he wasn't up to a long trip, and he said so over supper. Tory and Lavaine agreed, and so did Moore.

Elaine said very little, as usual, but at the word "trip" she seemed to blanch a little. "He's just getting well. Why would he think about a trip?"

"What I'm goin' to do," Moore told Link, "is ride back to the Keystone and tell 'em you're all right. There's nothin' much you need me for around here, and Art's probably worried back there."

"Do you still want that horse?" Lavaine asked. Moore had had his eye on one of their big horses, a black gelding they called Licorice.

"You bet I do. If you'll take a down payment now an' trust me for the rest," Moore said, "I can get back before the leaves turn, probably."

"Done," Tory said. "That'll be good for business, people seeing you leading Licorice all the way back to Wyoming."

"All right, then," Moore said. "Day after tomorrow, I reckon I'll just start back north."

Chapter Sixteen

Wherein lies happiness? In that which becks
Our ready minds to fellowship divine,
A fellowship with essence; till we shine,
Full alchemiz'd, and free of space.
"Endymion"
JOHN KEATS

In two wedges of black wings against the endless open sky, the first geese of autumn flew over the Keystone valley as old Lou went out on the porch to bang the gong for dinner-time. They were high and pointed south. The leaders looked down at the hayfields and pastures, at the chessboard of fence lines, at the ditches and thicketed gulches. A few ponds could be seen, silver in the sun, but no fields of grain or corn. Hours of daylight remained. The outriders, those geese at the far ends of the wedge, honked the question. Leaders honked the reply, and a hundred pairs of strong wings beat on against the invisible air. They passed over the fields and lakes that lay beneath them and within their reach and went on, trusting the strength of their bodies and the beneficence of their Creator to carry them to a resting place before nightfall.

Art Pendragon was hurrying in his long-legged stride toward the house, not wanting to be late for dinner, but he stopped at the sound of sky-borne trumpeting and looked up. That, too, seemed right, the coming and going of the migrating geese to mark the end of summer and the onset of fall. Ever since July, there had been a renewed sense of order and purpose at the Keystone. Like a V of geese, there was again one figure in the lead and two comrades of equal strength flanking him. And more behind those. Like the geese, one at the head and one on each wingtip, one at the wing of each of those, and one more and one more until the whole thing was more like a single living creature with a single purpose.

Art watched the geese until they were nearly out of sight. Then his thoughts returned to earth, and he went quickly through the kitchen door. He washed his hands at the sink and entered the dining room.

There they were, the riders. Each Monday, at dinner, ever since July, he had ordered — no, they all had agreed — that this noonday meal would be an informal gathering to give reports and air concerns. Sometimes Gwen would join them and offer her opinions; sometimes she would not. On this particular occasion, she opted to have a simple meal in her room, instead. Plates of sliced beef and bowls of mashed potatoes already stood on the table and some of the eighteen men had already poured themselves glasses of buttermilk from the earthenware pitchers. But none would begin to eat until Art had said grace.

That being done, they pitched in with a will, joking and talking between mouthfuls. Art chatted with Bob Riley on his right and Will Jensen on his left. In a voice loud enough for Noah Moore to hear across the table, Riley ventured the opinion that they'd need to put up a few extra tons of hay to feed that worthless show horse Moore had brought home with him. Art grinned from behind a thick slice of buttered bread.

"That so," Moore countered, while cratering his mashed potatoes to receive a small lake of brown gravy, "well, you just wait till those snowdrifts get butt-deep to a bowlegged bull this winter, and *then* we'll see whose horse is worthless. Speakin' of feedin' the livestock, though, I noticed, when I rode in on Friday, your ol' roan was lookin' kind of swayback. And now I see you had to let your belt out a coupla notches."

"The leather shrunk up." Riley smiled. "It'll do that."

"Yeah," Will Jensen added. "Same thing happened to the girth on his saddle. Shrunk right up and left that roan swayback and outta breath."

"You might as well know, Noah," the Pinto Kid said, "our ol' bachelor friend here has been doin' a little extra grazing down the valley where that widow lady and her purty daughter moved in. Riley's broke down, what? Ten horses now? Just hurryin' from her dinner table to get back here in time for supper."

Riley blushed deep red. Moore chuckled and pushed his plate back, happy to be home.

Art wiped his mouth, folded his napkin beside his plate, and called for the reports to begin.

"Garth, what's up with the wood gang now?"

The boy pushed his chair back a little.

"The new system's working out real well," he said. "Got three men camped up in Munch's Gulch haulin' logs down off the mountain, and two wagons goin' back and forth for 'em. I'm putting the best ones in one pile for timbers if we need 'em, and got two boys buckin' the rest for firewood. It sure works out better, lettin' the cuttin' gang stay there, instead of havin' to stop and haul the wood clear back to the Keystone every week."

Art nodded as Garth sat down. "Dick?" he said.

Dick Elliot unfolded his long legs from where he had wrapped them around the rungs of his chair and leaned forward. "Not much to report. We got all the Lucy Creek herd rounded up and moved onto the flats there by Clay Creek. Figure to keep 'em there till first snowfall, at least. Had to doctor a couple, but they're in good shape. One of the boys thought he caught sight of one of those longhorns."

"That so?" Art said. "Might have to send ol' Garth out to kill it for you." The reference was to the new kid's first run-in with a remnant of Art's scheme to raise Texas longhorns. Garth had gotten a little too enthusiastic about roping a longhorn bull and ended up breaking its neck. The boys chuckled at the mention of it, and Art, grinning at Garth, said: "Emil?"

The big, quiet man got to his feet. Even standing in a dining room hatless and without his gun belt, Emil was a figure men looked at with careful respect.

"Glad to be back," he began. "Mac and I trailed those horse bandits almost down to the South Platte where it meets the Poudre River, and then lost their sign. Word is, down around there, there's a small army of no-goods and thieves livin' up in the mountains somewhere. We figured they rode in the river, headed west, but whether the Poudre or the Platte, there's no way to know." Emil sat down again.

"Come spring," Art said, "I think you and a few of the boys oughta scout that situation. Moore here, he heard a rumor about the same outfit. More than that, the man he talked to was thinking *he* heard they were planning to move their operation north, maybe into Brown's Hole or somewhere on the Green River. Gettin' crowded down in Colorado, what with all the mining. All right. Moore, let's hear about your trip."

Moore put the tale in simple terms, how he had located his old saddle partner on a slick, little, family horse-breeding place nearly to New Mexico.

"Kind of like Riley, here" — he grinned mischievously — "Link has a lady lookin' after his care and feeding, and he's coming along real good. When I left him, he was already sittin' up and eatin' regular and even tryin' to ride a little. They're real nice folks. . . ."

Moore continued to describe the two brothers, Tory and Lavaine, and stumbled around, explaining the Hacienda Chalana or H-Bar-C name. Being a horseman first and foremost, his talk was mostly about the various mounts he had seen there and the possibilities he envisioned for the breed of big, black horses the brothers were working with.

When he had finished, Art stood up.

"Some of you are wondering where we stand in this Link business," he began. "So I'll tell you. First off, he's been a Keystone man ever since he came out of Kansas with Moore here, and probably one of the best men ever rode for our brand. What I'm saying . . . and I think every man here agrees with me . . . is that he's got a job here whenever he wants it, and, if he's sickly, well, we're here to look after him. Do the same for any one of you."

The cowboys murmured agreement. They knew that. They all knew that.

" 'Course, he may just want to stay down there. But if this horse-thief operation comes into our territory, then I'd sure like to have his gun with us, if we have to go against 'em. Right, Emil?"

"Yes, sir," Emil said. Emil's accuracy with a long gun was legendary, and it was known that even *he* would hesitate to wager he could beat Link at any kind of shooting.

"What I mean to do is kill a couple of birds with one rock here. I'm sending Moore back down there, maybe with one other man if we can spare one. First of all I want him to find out what Link's feelin's are about coming back. Secondly, maybe along the way he could ask around about this bunch of outlaws stealin' horses. Finally, I'm askin' him to dicker with those two brothers for a pair of breeding horses so we can start a line of our own. Riley's right in sayin' they eat a lot of hay, but I'm picturing how they'd look hitched up to a light cart or a fancy buggy. Some of those town cowboys down in Cheyenne would pay a pretty penny for horses like that to show off. Anybody got anything else we need to hear about?"

The Pinto Kid remarked that the windmill on Crow Creek needed attention.

"All right," Art said. "Why don't you take some tools and see to it." Then he added, looking at the Kid's fine shirt and flashy vest with a twinkle in his eye, "maybe you could borrow some work clothes from one of the other boys."

The eighteen filed out, still laughing. And when the laughing died, one of them would repeat Art's jibe and it would begin all over again. The idea of the Pinto Kid's climbing a sixty-foot windmill tower, carrying a bag of tools and a can of grease, was vastly amusing. Just the fact that the Kid had brought it up and then got saddled with the job himself tickled them no end because, like all cowboys everywhere, they'd almost rather do anything than have to climb up a tower and grease a damned windmill.

There were very few smiles and no laughter at all at the stone tower surrounded by water, far to the south. Sitting at her embroidery, Elaine also heard the passing of the autumn geese, their faraway honking barely audible through the window. To her, they were an echo of finality, a note of mournful sadness carried on the wind. If she felt anything for them at all, it was pity. Season after season, year after year, the poor birds had to obey the call of some unyielding inner voice and blindly follow the migration route, never knowing when storms or darkness would drive them down into barren fields where predators lurked.

She did not plan to be sitting there as the geese went over. She was supposed to be downstairs at the farewell party for Link and Moore. But while she was getting dressed, she found herself looking at the picture she was embroidering. It was large and complicated. It required her largest embroidery frame. Looking at it, almost casually admiring it, she happened to notice there was a broken thread in the pattern. She paused in front of the frame. She picked up her needle to fix the flaw.

From force of habit, she sat down on the stool and made another stitch, then another. Soon she was absorbed in the design again, even allowing the top of her unfastened dress to hang off her bare shoulders unnoticed. It had been her mother's dress; in fact, it was in this very dress of dark-red velvet that her mother had been married.

Elaine was half conscious of the mumble and murmur of voices coming from downstairs until they began to become distinct and recognizable. Pausing in her needlework to listen, she made out the low, unhurried conversation of her brothers, the higher voice of young Wen Nordanger, who had come with his father and mother to wish the Keystone riders a safe journey. The riders themselves spoke in strong, firm voices so much alike that she could not distinguish between that of Link and that of his friend, Noah Moore.

"That's the word for it!" she heard a voice exclaim. Tory had said it.

Elaine thrust the needle into the embroidery and left it there, turning toward her mirror to finish getting ready to go down. It was a very old mirror that time had clouded, but still it showed her a red blur of dress, a white splash of shoulder and neck, a pale face, and dark hair. As she fastened the dress and began to brush her hair, she saw the window reflected in the mirror, a dim and wavy image of the last, dying colors of the sunset sky, streaks of dull bronze against gray.

Downstairs, old Bernard's whiskey punch was enlivening the conversation even though he himself preferred to sit in his favorite chair and just listen to the chatter of the guests clustered at the fireplace.

"With all these railroads we've been promised," Mrs. Nordanger was saying, "I just don't know if folks will be wanting carriage horses in the future. I wonder if it might not be wiser for you boys to work on breeding cow ponies, instead."

"Not sure I can agree," Moore said. "With people traveling back East more, and more Easterners coming out here to open up stores and such, why, they're bound to want fancy carriages and good teams. Just to show off, you know, but, of course, also because an ol' buckboard and work team is an awful uncomfortable way to get around."

"I'd agree with Mister Moore," Lavaine added. "I mean, *we* raise our horses for strength and endurance, but there's many a banker and shop owner who'd like to have 'em just to be one up on his neighbor."

"How about us?" Mr. Nordanger asked. "Small places, farms mostly, we need a horse you can put a saddle on, or you can use to drag a cultivator, or pull a muck wagon with, then hitch up to go to town on Sunday. Your cow pony won't do, and your heavy team is just too much horse for some jobs."

"Well," Mrs. Nordanger said, "I do hope you're right, if only because I would hate to see any of you boys go broke trying to raise animals nobody wants. When we . . . oh, here's Elaine! Would you excuse me . . . ?"

The pale girl in red appeared in the doorway, and Mrs. Nordanger was there in an instant, relieved to have another female in the room.

"How *are* you, dear?" she said. "It was so nice of you to ask us, even if it's so sad that your Mister Link has to be leaving. Never mind, though, he's sure to be back soon. Now, I want you to try this gingerbread cake I brought over. Made it just for the occasion, but you'll have to tell me if I have too much spice in it. I think so, but Mister Nordanger says not. What a pretty dress! You are so lucky to have that talent for needlework, my dear, I just can't seem to so much as sew a patch on."

The two women went to the kitchen. When they returned, Mrs. Nordanger carried a plate of sliced gingerbread cake in one hand and a plate of sugared doughnuts in the other. Elaine followed, carefully bearing a silver tray. On the tray was a set of delicate china.

"Just *look* what Elaine has brought out in honor of our guests!" Mrs. Nordanger exclaimed. "Her mother's best! Isn't it *lovely!*"

Elaine set the tray on the table and arranged the small cups on their tiny saucers. With shy pride drawing up the corners of her thin lips, she lifted the tall, slender vessel and poured hot chocolate into the cups.

"It's Limoges ware," she said, handing out the full cups on their translucent saucers. "It was given to my grandmother as a wedding present."

The men's hard hands, strong and callused, cradled the china uneasily. Returning to their place near the fire, they walked as if they were carrying eggs through a dark room full of strange furniture.

Like the others, Link accepted a second cup of the sweet chocolate and a third helping of cake. It was when he was returning the cup and saucer to the table that tragedy struck. He later wondered if he had stumbled over something on the floor, or if the lamplight had flickered for a second, or if his muscles had twitched with some spasm from all the injuries, but nothing really explained the fact that he sent the saucer crashing into the edge of the table. To the floor it went, the thin cup and the saucer already snapped in half, bursting on impact into a dozen pieces.

He had no words. No one in the room could find what to say. Elaine gasped and visibly stiffened, standing as rigid as one of those steel-wire mannequins in the mercantile. She went to the fireplace for the coal shovel and hearth broom, and silently swept up the remnants, throwing them into the fire.

"I'm sorry," Link finally said, breaking the interminable silence. "I don't know how that happened or what. . . ."

She raised her eyes from the floor, and he could see the tears rolling down her cheeks. Everyone saw the vague, lost, dazed look in those eyes.

"It's all ruined," she said. Her voice frightened him, although it was soft and even. "A chocolate set needs eight settings. Things never last, do they? Never, never, never last."

She turned from them and walked through the dark doorway toward her tower. As she went, she seemed to grow smaller with each step she took.

"What can I do?" Link asked the others. "It was an accident, God knows."

Mrs. Nordanger looked toward the doorway as if debating with herself whether to follow Elaine and offer womanly comfort. Instead, she gathered the remaining Limoges cups and saucers on the tray and carried it to the kitchen. The washing up would need a light touch. She was the one who should do it.

Oddly it was old Bernard who broke the terrible silence. Not with words, but with action. He rose from his chair, gathered up the neglected cups and mugs, refilled them with his punch, and handed them around. The men lifted their drinks in a silent salute to their host as he returned to his chair.

Conversation gradually returned to fill the hollow place Elaine's departure had left in the room, and Bernard's punch helped to make the hours fly by, and soon the last log in the fireplace broke and fell into the coals and no one moved to add a fresh one. All that remained of the ginger-bread and the sugared doughnuts and the plate of cold meat and bread were some crumbs, and all that was left of the punch was a thimble's worth in a puddle at the bottom of the bowl. The guests retired to the spare room. Tory lit a lantern, and led Moore and Link through the dark to his cabin where they would spend the night. Come morning, they would rope up the four horses they had bought from the brothers, load their packs on two of them, and start the ride north to the Keystone.

Come morning, Link would look back and see the tower for the last time.

To Davy Dunlap, this fifth visit of Keystone riders to his father's farm seemed a sure and certain confirmation of his own destiny. The first time he had met Link, when he was bringing that cavvy of horses home, his reaction had been boyish awe. Then Moore had come through their place and confirmed the reality for him; there really was a place like the Keystone, and there really were cowboys there. Moore

269

had stopped again, on his way back north, and repeated the invitation for the family to "drop in" when they got to Wyoming. On his next visit, Moore had been more like an old family friend. Without realizing it or even thinking about it, Davy began living with the certainty that he could visit the Keystone someday. Not only visit — maybe work there. Now Moore was back again, and the other one, Link, with him.

While the cowboys stripped packs and saddles and halters from the big black horses Davy lingered as close as he could without looking like a nosy britches, studying the cut of their chaps, the tilt of their Stetsons, the easy way the big Colt's revolvers hung in the dark holsters ready to hand. He eagerly pumped water into the trough for them to wash away the trail dust. He gave each of them a flour sack towel and filled the dipper for them to drink.

Davy marveled to see Moore tilt his chin skyward and swallow down a whole dipper of water in one long flow. He would have to practice that, he thought. And he'd practice doing it left-handed like that, keeping his gun hand free while he drank, just in case. And not closing his eyes when he tilted the dipper up, either, but staying watchful. He'd practice that.

"I been figurin' on those horse thieves," he ventured to say during supper, glancing at his father to see whether he'd overstepped his bounds. His father often lectured him on overstepping his bounds.

"And what did you figure?" Link asked.

"Well . . . ," — this time young Davy's quick sideways look was toward his mother, who he wished would suddenly need to leave the room — "well . . . I figure maybe they stole enough horses for a while, 'cause nobody we've talked to even seen 'em since the start of summer, did they, Dad?"

"Haven't heard a word in a long while," Carl Dunlap agreed.

"So I'm figurin'," Davy went on. This was it. What he said next was either going to get him sent to his room, or his mother was going to be upset, or they'd all laugh at him.

"Yes?" Moore said, opening another biscuit to receive a slap of butter.

"Figurin'," Davy said, "come next spring, those outlaws'll be showin' up again, up to their old tricks." He thought that sounded pretty grown up — *up to their old tricks.* "So what I'm thinkin' is that, come spring, maybe you and some more of the riders from the Keystone, they might like to come here. Our place could be a kinda headquarters. So you could ride out after those outlaws, you know. And. . . ."

"And what?" Link asked.

"And I could go along." There. He had said it. Davy braced himself for the storm of laughter that was sure to follow.

"Kind of like a guide," Moore said solemnly. "We'd sure need a horse guard, too."

"I dunno," Link said. "Davy's never gone up against guns before. If you were to ride with us, Davy, you'd pretty much have to stay to the rear. You understand?"

The boy's eyes widened. Up against guns? It suddenly sounded a little *too* grown up. "Yeah. Oh, sure. No, I can't shoot good enough yet," he stammered. "I mean, just go part way maybe, to show you the trail."

Two days later, the Keystone riders were gone. At the Dunlap farm there seemed to be an emptiness where they had been, and at the same time a certain sort of new importance, a fresh significance to everything from the water trough and the open corral gate to the long road curving up over the hill.

She went over and over his last moments as she sat on the porch next to her father's chair. She absent-mindedly stroked the yellow silk scarf lying over her knees.

"I'm really sorry about your china," Link had told her on the day he left. "And I'm sure sorry I lost your bandanna. It must've got torn off in the stampede." He handed her the other scarf, the long narrow one. "You really oughta keep this one," he said. "You said you made it out of your mother's dress, after all. Someday, a good man's gonna come along here and just want to carry you away, and you oughta keep this for him."

Afterward, he went to Tory's cabin, leaving her standing on the porch, then he and Moore returned with the horses to take their farewell. Tory and Lavaine met them at the far side of the bridge. Link and Moore both waved to her father, who merely looked up and nodded. Another wave to her, which she acknowledged only by lifting her chin. Leaning down from their saddles, the two riders took a last handshake from each of the brothers.

"Come back," Lavaine said.

"We sure will," Moore said. "And you come up to the Keystone. Stay as long as you want."

"Door's always open," Link said.

"Good luck," Tory said.

"Same to you," Link replied. "Keep an eye on that high pasture."

"We will. And you watch your backs, mind."

"*Adiós.*"

"So long."

She watched the Keystone riders turn and go, driving the

band of horses ahead of them. The two men rode stirrup to stirrup, both with their broad hats at the same angle, their backs straight, their right hands resting easily at their sides. Everything they needed in the world was packed on two horses, and they could, if they chose, leave even those by the wayside and ride ahead with nothing more than saddlebags and slickers. *Like the migrating geese,* she thought, *they could keep going so long as they had enough just to carry them to the next horizon, to the next nightfall.*

Where she had felt pity for the geese, so seemingly without any one place they could call their own, she now felt a kind of mournful envy. Suddenly her tower seemed too solid, too immovable, too safe.

She watched the two riders growing smaller and smaller as they went away down the road. She had not been on that road herself for two years or more, and then she had gone no farther than the gate marking the edge of her brothers' land. It had been even longer since she had been as far as the crossroads.

She went inside and up to her room where the first thing she saw was the immigrant trunk, with its humped lid, where Link's saddle had rested for so long. The saddle had been part of her room, and now it was gone. Somewhere in her soul she knew it would never be there again. She touched the peg on the wall where his bridle had hung. She sat down before her embroidery frame and looked at the mirror, but the mirror was dim and dull and lightless.

That night, and the night after, and for many nights to come, she dreamed of dark, rectangular graves. As each night's dream faded into the next day's dawn, it always ended with a silhouette of the gravedigger. She knew it was the gravedigger from the shadow outline of his shovel, the blade resting on the ground behind him, and the long handle protruding in front.

After a week of troubled dreams, she lost her appetite for food and merely went through the motions of preparing meals for her father and brothers. After two weeks, the chilling winds of late autumn whispered coldly around the tower walls, slipping inside through invisible cracks and crevices to make icy drafts across the floor. A week of hard frost followed, and there came a morning when her father left early with his funny little rock cart and her brothers took food with them to visit a far corner of their range. She had known this day would come, this day when father and brothers would be far away from the house. For more than a week she had known which day it would be. So did her father and her brothers.

She took out her mother's two best quilts and unfolded them before rolling them up and strapping them with rope. She wore her best dress and packed her extra clothing and her brush and comb in a carpetbag. She wrapped her warm woolen cape about her shoulders and went outside where she walked across the narrow bridge. On the other side, she sat down on the rolled-up quilts to wait. It was not long until he came, as if in answer to a summons, pulling the team to a stop in front of her.

She made a sign to him, pointing at her mouth with two fingers. Did he bring food for himself, enough for many days?

In reply, he leaned off the side of the high seat and tapped his whip against a long, black box fastened beneath the hearse. Everything he needed, he carried with him.

Elaine opened the glass doors, entered, closed them. She unbound her mother's quilts and arranged them, then lay down on them. As the driver snapped his whip and the hearse moved off, she remembered the scarf. She sat up and opened the carpetbag and found it, then she lay down again, her hands crossed on her breast with the yellow scarf draped over them.

Old Bernard and the two brothers returned in the late afternoon to find Father Nicholas sitting on the porch, wrapped in his great, black, oilskin slicker, writing in a leather-bound journal. The book was soiled and worn smooth by time and very much handling. The giant priest looked up from his writing, and the men knew why he had come. They knew what he had come to tell them.

Chapter Seventeen

A fine and private place
"To His Coy Mistress"
ANDREW MARVELL

"Listen to this," Art said. "It's a letter from William Cody. Buffalo Bill?"

Gwen Pendragon looked up from her own letter. "Oh, yes," she said. "What does he have to say? Don't tell me he wants you to go on stage with him in one of his theatrical productions!"

"Say, don't you go gettin' *too* smart, young lady." Art scowled his best scowl, but his eyes were smiling at her, anyway. "No," he went on, "Cody wrote to say he's recruiting top hands and prize livestock for a new kind of show he has in mind. It seems to be some kind of outdoor entertainment. Listen to this . . . 'Hard upon the success of the Old Glory Blowout, I conceived the idea of organizing a large company of Indians, cowboys, Mexican *vaqueros*, famous riders, and expert lasso-throwers, with accessories of stagecoach, emigrant wagons, bucking horses, and a herd of buffaloes, with which to give a realistic entertainment of wild life on the plains.' Sounds like quite a scheme, doesn't it? He goes on to call it a 'Wild West' show. I guess he means it's supposed to be a sort of a circus."

"I wonder," Gwen said, "whether people would really be interested in paying money to look at Indians and ranch hands riding around in an arena, chasing tame cattle."

"Wouldn't surprise me," Art said. "Lots of folks these

days seem to talk about an 'Old West' like it's some kind of fairy tale. They hunker down in their little houses in their big towns and forget there's real men out here, men who spend every blessed day in the saddle making sure people like them have beef to eat."

"Not to mention the way you have to watch out for the welfare of the territory."

Art looked to see if she was saying it in jest, but her face reflected a lovely seriousness.

"That's right," he said. "Town people, they've got their police force and law courts and church charity. Hell, even down in Cheyenne, there's public institutions to take care of the insane and the cripples and the down-and-outers. Up here, if a man's broke or crazy or crippled, we're the ones that end up watching out for him. If he asks, that is."

"I've never seen you turn anyone away," she said proudly.

"Well, we just can't. Just wouldn't be right to have all this and not be willing to take in somebody who's down on his luck. Just like it wouldn't be right to have this whole bunch of top hands that're crack shots and not let 'em root out that bunch of horse thieves."

Gwen smiled. Ever since summer, Art never missed a chance to make a "subtle" announcement of his intention to mount a posse against the mysterious band of rustlers. It was the sort of thing he lived for, and she was proud of him for it.

"It's an obligation," she suggested.

"Right. An obligation."

"So, will you send your top hands to be in Mister Cody's Wild West show? You *did* say the North Platte Blowout had done wonders for their spirits. You said that."

"Well, it did. No denyin' it. But to go troopin' around

after Buffalo Bill and a bunch of reservation Indians, shootin' blanks and wearin' fancy clothes? No, I don't think we need it. But I'll share his letter with the boys. They can make up their own minds if they want to go work for him. Nobody need feel obliged to stay here if they don't want to."

"I'm going to remember you said that," Gwen said. "You'd just better watch out, Mister Art Pendragon! I may just take it in my head to run off! Perhaps Mister Cody could find a place for a woman in his Western extravaganza."

He smiled at her. She was smiling, too.

"Well, just *you* remember," Art said, "I still know how to . . . how did Buffalo Bill say it? . . . 'throw a lasso'." I'd just come after you and drop my loop over those pretty shoulders, and, in no time flat, you'd find yourself hog-tied and back here where you belong."

"Oh, really?" She laughed. "I think you'd better go share all your big-man talk with the bunkhouse while I decide whether to feed you supper or not."

"Hah!" Art said. "*You're* the little lady who might find herself goin' to bed without supper!"

"You're so tough!" She laughed again. "I think we need to find a terrifying name for you, like 'Buffalo Bill'. Let me think . . . shall we call you 'Antelope Arthur'? Or, no! I know! Isn't one of Mister Cody's acquaintances known as 'Pawnee Bill'? We can call you 'Arapaho Pendragon, the Fury of the Short Grass Prairie'!"

She was still giggling at him as he stooped over her chair to kiss her gently on the mouth. Like a gentleman taking leave of a lady, he raised one of her hands to his lips.

"It's gonna be a real pity," he said, "to see these soft, little hands of yours out there digging post holes and stringing barb wire tomorrow. With a workin' ranch, everybody's got to work."

"Get thee to the bunkhouse," she said, laughing and pulling back her hand. "You have just three hours until supper."

Art mounted his day horse, the one he kept saddled in the small corral just behind the house. It wasn't a long walk down to the bunkhouse, but like most men born to the saddle, he would rather ride than walk. It was said that some of them would spend an hour walking down a horse just to ride to the barn.

Link and Bob Riley were likewise mounted when he rode up to the hitching rail, and Mac was leading his horse to the rail as well.

"What's up?" Art asked. As late in the day as it was, and cold as it was, he was surprised to see three men ready to ride out somewhere.

"Got a visitor. Just leavin' to go check on it," Bob replied, handing Art his field glasses and pointing into the distance. "Over there across the creek. 'Bout a hundred yards this side of the trees."

Through the glasses Art saw the shape of an old hearse with a team pulling it. The driver seemed to be lost, aimlessly driving here and there, back and forth, all around the slope of the hill.

"Is that a hearse I'm lookin' at?" he said, handing the glasses over to Link.

"It is. He's got a wagon sheet over it, that's why it looks that way. Like an Army ambulance."

"Reckon who it is?" Art said.

"I was about to say it's some peddler lookin' for a place to camp," Mac said.

"No," Link said. "I know who it is. Know him by his rig. He's an old mute that lives down there near the H-Bar-C where I was. He's the same one that took me outta North Platte after the stampede. I stayed at his hut while I was gettin' well again."

"He's a mute?" Mac said. "I guess I don't recall you tellin' that part."

"Yeah. Strange ol' guy. I can't figure what he's doin' this far from home, though."

"I remember your tellin' us about him," Art said. "Well, let's ride on up there and say howdy, an' maybe he's got some way of tellin' us why he's here," Art said. "We'll find room for him in the other bunkhouse and a place at table in the cook shack."

As they started out to greet the old hermit, Art had another thought.

"Say, you don't suppose there's trouble down at the H-Bar-C, do you? Maybe that bunch of horse thieves did somethin' to your friends!"

Link peered ahead at the hearse. "Don't think so," he said. "For one thing, he's actin' awful calm. He'd've come straight in to the house, if he was lookin' for help, don't you think?"

"Guess so," Art replied.

The four men rode slowly and stayed close together, and, as they drew nearer, they saw that the mute had halted his team and climbed down from the high seat. He was using a spade to mark out a section of ground.

"Now what's he doin'?" Mac asked.

Art raised his hand, and the four riders reined in their horses.

"Link?" Art said. "You know him. What's he up to?"

"Just what it looks like he's doin'," Link said. "I told y'

he had graves dug all over the place down there. That's what he's doin' right now, layin' out a grave."

"A grave?" Riley said. "Who for?"

"Doesn't have to be for anybody," Link said. "Down to the H-Bar-C, there's empty holes all over hell and gone. He just digs 'em. Sometimes he gets that priest . . . Father Nicholas . . . to bless 'em after he gets 'em dug."

"Well, what the hell for? If there's nobody to put in 'em, I mean."

"Couldn't say," Link continued. "He just does it. But I sure don't know why he drove all the way up here to do it. I know he's peculiar, but I didn't think he was *that* damn' peculiar."

Somewhere in Link's mind was a memory trying to tell him there was more to it, something particular about all those graves, but he couldn't recall what it was. Maybe it was how they went unmarked even after they were filled in. No, that wasn't it. He couldn't remember.

"One of the brothers told me he drives around or walks around for days at a time, lookin' for the right place to dig. But what the hell brings him here, I just couldn't say."

Art was quiet. The gravedigger had chosen well. It was a spot where a young pine grew alone at some distance from the edge of the forest on a gentle slope where the morning sun would warm the earth early. It was where the wildflowers would bloom first in spring, overlooking the little creek where willows and rushes made a winding strip of dark green in summer.

"Nice spot," Art said. "Never really thought about it as a place for a grave, but it's a nice spot. Let's go see if he needs anything."

They rode on up to the place where Old Tim was methodically laying squares of thin sod to one side of the grave. At their approach he stuck his shovel into the newly bared ground and went to stand by the hearse.

" 'Afternoon!" Art greeted him. "Just rode up to see how you're doin'. If you need anything."

There was no reply.

"Like to have you to the cook shack for supper, later on," Art continued. "When you're finished here, I mean. You could put your team up in our main corral. Mac here can show you where."

There was no reply. Old Tim looked up, but only at Link.

"Tim," Link said. "Good to see you."

There was not so much as a smile or a gesture in response.

"Everything all right?" Link asked.

The gravedigger turned away and began untying the ropes holding the wagon sheet. Going around to the other side of the hearse, he pulled the canvas off. The four horsemen leaned forward to peer through the time-pocked glass and saw the figure of a woman lying inside, her hands crossed on her breast and a long, yellow scarf draped over them.

Link looked more closely.

"Elaine," Link said very quietly. "Elaine."

Art straightened up and looked at each of his riders in turn as if searching in their faces for an answer, for something to say. But he saw no answers there. Link had told them about the odd hearse and the odd little man who drove it, but they never expected to see it really carrying a corpse.

The gravedigger folded up the wagon sheet, and, from the long box under the hearse, he took a steel bar, returning with it to the grave where he commenced to chip at the frozen dirt.

Art felt he needed to say something, even if the mute

couldn't reply, but, as he started to speak, he felt Link's hand grip his arm.

"He don't want help," Link said quietly. "I don't even think we oughta ask."

The four horsemen sat looking reverently at the black coach. Except for the *thud* of the digging bar against the earth, there was long, wide silence lying over the sloping meadow.

It was Link who finally spoke. "She'd like it here," he said. "I think she'd be happy with it. It's a real pretty spot."

"Yeah. Well," Art said in a louder voice, so the grave-digger could hear, "I guess we'll be gettin' on back now. If you need any help . . . well, whenever you're ready, you just come on down to the house and one of the boys can show you where to put up your team."

Old Tim looked up from his digging. He went around to the back of the hearse and opened one of the glass doors, reached inside to take something from a carpet bag, and signaled for Link to come closer.

What he handed him was a small piece of paper, folded and sealed with a few drops of red wax. He closed the door and returned to his grave.

Whatever was in the note no one ever learned. The tall rider with the dark mustache sat on Messenger alone, apart from his companions, reading it to himself. Mac, with his young and romantic notions about worldly goods and women, thought it might be a note in which the dead lady bequeathed her fortune and lands to Link in return for some kindness he had done her. Bob Riley, whose view of life tended toward practicality and reason, figured it might be some kind of instructions for a funeral and the upkeep of her grave, or something like that.

Art Pendragon had heard Link's account of the time he had spent near the stone tower and near the pale, slender woman, and, being married himself, he could read between the lines of that simple story. Pendragon knew better than any of them that there is a maze of bewildering trails leading to the center of a woman's heart; there can be many a wrong path and no forgiveness, ever, for the man who wanders into one of them no matter how innocently and no matter how ignorantly. Art Pendragon watched his friend's face carefully and saw guilt stamped on it, guilt as clear to read as a brand burned into a plank.

Link folded the paper and tucked it into a pocket of his sheepskin.

"Later, then," Art said to the gravedigger, and turned his horse to lead the men away.

"You go ahead," Link said. "Seems to me like I ought to stay here a while."

"Sure," Art said. "Sure."

The three rode back toward the house and barns and bunkhouse, leaving a tall, lonely figure sitting motionless on his horse, watching the gravedigger at his work. A light wind from the mountain tugged at the tall man's neckerchief, ruffled the mane of his horse, then flowed southward. As it went, it bent the tips of the dry grass. Evergreen branches bowed to it as it went by.

When they arrived at the bunkhouse hitching rail, Art looked back up the hillside where the pines made long shadows across the earth. Horseman and hearse made a single dark outline.

"Bob," Art said, "next time we've got a couple of hands with nothing much to do, let's see if we can't build a proper fence up there around that grave. Maybe I'll send off for one of those nice, iron fences they use in cemeteries. Or

John Peters might be able to make us one. Come to that, let's mark out a bigger place, maybe an acre. That grave he's digging up there could be one corner of it. Big as the Keystone is, we oughta have a graveyard of our own. That's sure enough a good place for it, don't you think?"

"I'll start workin' on that right away," Riley promised. "Well, as soon as our visitor is gone again, that is."

Over supper, Art told Gwen about the mute gravedigger and about the dead woman they had seen laid out in the old hearse. Gwen was strangely quiet, almost as if disinterested. Afterward, she went up to her room somewhat earlier than usual and sat in her dressing gown before her mirror, brushing her hair until it shone in the lamplight. *Link,* she thought. *Link* could *have shown the poor woman more kindness,* she thought. *So many come and go whenever the mood strikes them and never give a second thought to whomever they might be hurting. Sometimes all a woman wants is a just a little kindness, nothing more. Just a little recognition, even a little compliment now and then. Men like that should learn to be more like Art,* she thought. *But,* she supposed, *they really can't change. Not really.*

As the darkness deepened, it found Link standing on the porch of the bunkhouse, hunched into his sheepskin with his hands thrust deeply into the pockets. He was not looking at the dark hillside where he had watched Old Tim mound up the fresh earth over the grave. He was not looking at the strange hearse now parked next to the corral. Instead, he was looking at all the stars speckled across the black sky, seeming to come on one by one as the blackness grew. At the main house of the Keystone, the lights were extinguished one by one, until there was only the one remaining in the upstairs window.

Acknowledgments

Once again I am indebted to dozens of fellow scribblers whose books breathe life into the facts and legends of the American cowboy and his lifestyle. From works such as Ike Blasingame's *Dakota Cowboy: My Life in the Old Days* and "Teddy Blue" Abbott's *We Pointed Them North: Recollections of a Cowpuncher*, I drew many a first-hand detail. Books like Lillian Schlissel's *Women's Diaries of the Westward Journey* and Kenneth L. Holmes's *Covered Wagon Women* provided authentic accounts as well as deep insights. And I shamelessly gleaned facts from Robert A. Carter's fine biography, *Buffalo Bill Cody: The Man Behind the Legend*, as well as Gail Hughbanks Woerner's good rodeo book, *Belly Full of Bedsprings: The History of Bronc' Riding*.

The hospitality of North Platte, Nebraska and its remarkable efforts to preserve Scout's Rest Ranch certainly needs mentioning, as do the various artifact collections such as Warp's Pioneer Village in Minden, Nebraska and the Douglas Museum in Douglas, Wyoming, where a novelist can confirm that steel singletrees existed in 1880 and that Limoges porcelain might be found in Western dining rooms.

I'm also grateful to Queen Victoria's Poet, Alfred Lord Tennyson. It was his poems about the court of King Arthur that breathed life into those legends for me. In one of those poems, "The Lady of Shalott", I found the mythical foundation I needed for this story.

James C. Work

RIDE TO BANSHEE CAÑON

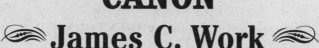 James C. Work

Kyle Owen, a one-eyed cowboy working for the great Keystone Ranch, has finally been restored to physical and mental health following a harrowing ordeal. He knows that he was sent to a hidden valley in the mountains, and he knows what happened there almost killed him, but other than that, the journey is a large blank spot in his past. Kyle feels duty-bound to search for answers and uncover the hidden truth. Against everyone's objections, he sets out on a quest that will reveal the meaning of all that has happened to him, and begins the greatest adventure of his life.